Readers an
raving abou
Eclaire mystery series!

Behind Eclaire's Doors

"A bright and breezy excursion through the elegant town houses and sleazy back alleys of the Big Easy. Sophie Dunbar has pulled off a smashing debut."
—*Clarion-Ledger* Jackson, Mississippi

"Makes the pulse pound—for several reasons. May there be many of these ribald, racy romps."
—*Washington Times*

"Delightfully irreverent, slightly wacky, and sizzlingly sexy." —*Sunday Magazine*, Baton Rouge

"A sassy, stylish, slightly trashy debut I hugely enjoyed." —*Booknews* from the Poisoned Pen

"A fast-paced and racey read, with deliciously colorful characters, spicey patois, steamy sex and New Orleans' own peculiar social distinctions." —*The New Mexican*

"Cleverly plotted with quirky characters and a good sense of New Orleans." —*Sun-Sentinel*, Ft. Lauderdale

A Bad Hair Day

. . . and watch for the fourth in this series, coming next spring from Intrigue Press

Redneck Riviera

Sophie Dunbar

Intrigue Press

For information, please contact Intrigue Press, P.O. Box 456, Angel Fire, NM 87710, 505-377-3474.

ISBN 1-890768-06-5

First Printing 1998

This book is a work of fiction. Names, characters, places and incidents either are the product of the author's imagination or are used fictitiously. Any resemblance to actual events or persons living or dead is entirely coincidental. Although the author and publisher have made every effort to ensure the accuracy and completeness of information contained in this book, we assume no responsibility for errors, inaccuracies, omissions, or any inconsistency herein. Any slights of people, places or organizations are unintentional.

Psalm 118:22,23

In loving memory of my precious mother, Irene, who sang hymns and read detective stories to me when I was a little girl. Thanks, Mamma. This one's for you.

Author's note: at the time of this writing, neither the Miss Gulf Coast Beauty Pageant, nor any other contest title mentioned herein, the city of Crestview Cove, Mississippi, nor the Bell Sands Resort Hotel existed anywhere but in my (notoriously fevered) imagination.

—S.D.

The courteous assistance of Chief Investigator Kevin Ladnier, Police Department, City of Biloxi, and Chuck Patton, Executive Director of the Mississippi State Gaming Commission, is very much appreciated. As always, bouquets to the talented Barbara Hutnick. And extra special gratitude to that "detecting woman" Willetta Heising, who turned up evidence of things not yet seen and is therefore greatly responsible for the manifestation of this book.

CHAPTER I

CHAPTER 1

Lee may have handed over his sword to Grant at Appomattox, but no Southern woman ever surrendered her treasured tiara. Whether this crown symbolizes status, wealth or beauty, there is distinct protocol regarding its display. For example, while entirely permissible for a lady to wear a tiara with her bathing suit, only some tacky bubba-belle would be caught dead wearing one with her birthday suit, when it wasn't even her birthday. And if she hadn't already been dead by the time I caught her, I just might've killed her myself. . .

CHAPTER 2

"Claire!" Dan bellowed. "You downstairs anywhere, darlin'?"

It was a sticky-hot, New Orleans September Tuesday afternoon, and I had decided to christen my new peach satin bikini in the swimming pool.

"Out here!" I called back, and Dan came through the kitchen door, which opened onto the flagstone terrace. As always, the sight of him made my pulse quicken, even today when his tie had wilted at half-mast, and the seersucker suit, summer uniform of all Southern lawyers, clung damply to his burly contours. I propped my elbows on the pool ledge and arched backward to give him a good view. "Come on in, honey, the water's fine."

Dan smiled and set his briefcase on the green wrought iron table. "The water ain't the only thing that's fine," he observed, and proceeded to do a slow striptease until he was down to those tantalizing, button-fly Italian silk boxer shorts he wears in hot weather, When he stepped casually out of them, delicious shivers rippled through me despite the heat.

My husband is just over six feet, broad, powerful and furry. Because I'm small and blonde, my friend Charlotte calls me Fay Wray.

Dan plunged in and swam underwater beneath me, grabbing my bathing suit top in his teeth like a hungry shark. He slung it out of the pool and before I could escape, became an octopus, laughing as he trapped me between mighty thighs.

"Well, thank you for that lovely Sea World encounter," I told him. "But I'm real disappointed. I guess the big old whale's not going to jump out of the water this time."

Dan's strong legs tightened around me. "Guess again," he invited. And sure enough, there was Shamu . . .

🐗 🐗 🐗

Later, when he'd poured us each a tall Meyers's Dark on the rocks with lime, we sat outside and talked. Dan told me the reason he'd come home early was that his big trial, involving a patent on some kind of pulp processor at a paper mill, had been continued until the end of October, so he'd immediately jumped at the unexpected chance to take a few days off.

"And, Lord!" He rattled the ice cubes in his glass emphatically. "I am ready for it!"

I knew exactly how he felt. Life had been *trés* intense of late. We had been married, divorced, and remarried, with a few murders sandwiched in between.

"Only thing is, Claire," Dan drained his rum. "Will I get in your way if I just hang around here and catch up on my reading and generally make myself useless?"

After our second wedding, Dan had sold the big house on Octavia Street. Not so much because of the bad memories, but because it didn't hold enough good ones to pick up and start over with. Presently, we lived in the upstairs portion of an authentically restored townhouse off St. Charles Avenue in the Garden District of New Orleans. The ground floor contains my beauty shop, Eclaire, filled with tapestries, terra cotta and pine, allowing clients to bask in an ambience more French country cottage than hair salon.

Eclaire's E comes from my first name, Evangeline, which my Danish *au pair* mother got from Mr. Longfellow's poem. So caught up in that Acadian fantasy was she that she lived it, marrying a Cajun fisherman named, yes, Gabriel, and dying with him on his shrimp boat in a storm out on the Gulf of Mexico when I was a baby.

On Eclaire's apricot-washed, rough plaster walls hang large oil portraits by local artist Ambrose Xavier, the subjects of which are all clients of mine wearing hairstyles created by *moi*. When Ambrose replaces the paintings quarterly, the previous models get a chance to purchase their own portraits at a substantial discount.

An eight-foot stone wall encloses the backyard, where herbs and roses planted around the pool mingle their luxuriant fragrances to create a dry, subtle perfume—Eau d'Eclaire, as I'd come to think of it.

Occasionally, I toyed with the idea of trying to capture and bottle that elusive, mossy essence. It would be quite a coup, to have a salon with its own signature perfume. But then I'd recall my recent confrontation with the dark, dangerous side of the billion-dollar fragrance industry—which, let me tell you, does not smell pretty at all—and decide Eau d'Eclaire could wait.

When Dan returned from a trip to the kitchen for more ice and slices of lime, I assured him his concern about getting in my way was totally unfounded. "As a matter of fact, baby, your timing is perfect!" I announced, as he topped off my drink. "I have just finished doing all my regulars, so they won't be needing me for at least two weeks. Plus, Renee left for Houma today. Her sister Yvonne's getting married and she's bridesmaid, remember? Then after that, she's scheduled to take her State Boards in Baton Rouge."

I was very selfishly relieved when Renee's boyfriend Beaudine Guidry, a second-string linebacker for the Saints, got his contract picked up by the New York Giants, and she'd decided not to get married and go with him. My invaluable assistant possessed all the makings of a true artiste, and once she had her license, she could start building her own following.

Rather, she could soon as we got a new manicurist. Right now, in addition to assisting me, Renee Vermilion was also temporarily doing nails since Angie, our original manicurist, had been one of the recent murderees.

When I told Dan I was taking a small vacation of my own, his blue eyes gleamed in the gathering dusk. "Now, that is good news. Maybe I'll get to catch up on something else besides reading?"

Although our second wedding ceremony and reception had been nothing less than a mega *fais-do do*, we'd only managed a forty-eight hour honeymoon in the Pontchartrain Hotel penthouse after several months of celibacy. Since then, both of us had been working six days a week, which left a whole lot to be desired. Dan was right. It was definitely time for a nonstop ride on the love train.

"Shall we take a little excursion somewhere?" he went on. "Or just unplug the phone and—" At that very moment, the instrument under discussion buzzed like the serpent in the Garden of Eden. Dan grimaced and picked up the receiver. "Hello," he spoke reluctantly, and listened. "Yes, she's right here," he continued, surprise in his voice. Covering the mouthpiece he hissed, "Claire, it's Mrs. Shelby Bell."

Puzzled, I took the receiver from him. What on earth could "Hell's Bell," as Renee and I had nicknamed her, be wanting? On her last visit to the shop, she'd made her next appointment for October 1, since she and Mr. Shelby Bell would be away at the Mississippi Gulf Coast hotel they owned, the Bell Sands Resort.

Too bad I never thought to ask why she'd be there all that time after the tourist season was pretty much over.

"Claire, honey!" trilled Mrs. Bell, at her Suzanne Sugarbakeriest. "You know what? Mr. Bell and I were just sitting here on our *divine* balcony overlooking the waves, and we got to talking about you and Dan. And I said to Shelby, 'Shelby, why don't we invite those two *precious* people to come stay with us? As our guests, of course. *Bless* their little hearts, they've been through so much lately, and just getting married again, and all. Why, the Bell Sands would be just what the doctor ordered!' "

"And what did Shelby say?" I asked, when I recovered my voice. Mrs. Bell is a totally self-centered, smart-mouthed, big-haired brunette, who's filthy rich and tighter than the bark on a tree. Since Eclaire's opening, I had spent many hours on that big brunette hair, and she'd always kicked up a fuss about the bill. Now, here she was offering us an all expenses paid holiday? *Quelle fishy!*

"Why, my big old Shelby was all *for* it. Of *course.*" She purred like a cream-sated Persian cat.

Big old *pussywhipped* Shelby, I thought, and stifled a giggle as Mrs. Bell continued.

"In fact, it was his very own idea it might be a whole lot of fun if we just sent our whirlybird over for y'all." She paused. "Say, tomorrow afternoon?"

"Why that's extremely. . . generous of you both," I hedged. It was also extremely short notice. "I'll . . . just mention this to Dan and . . . and let you know."

"Well, *honey*, why don't you just go ahead and mention it to him right *now*?" she suggested in a steely coo. "I'll hold on."

Dan had lit a big citronella candle while I was talking to Mrs. Bell. By its glow I could see him smile when I covered the receiver and explained.

He arched a thick eyebrow at me. "Now, Claire, we both know this sounds too good to be true. But on the other hand, it also sounds too good to pass up. Don't you agree, baby?"

"Well, I'm definitely curious to find out what's really going on. And it would be a change of scene," I conceded.

Dan took the phone . "Good evening, Mrs . Bell? It' s Dan Claiborne. Claire was just telling me—" he listened. "Well that's real kind of you folks, and we do accept. With pleasure, I might add . . . no, don't bother to send your um, whirlybird . . . it's a nice drive up the 90, take our time . . . that's right. Early afternoon." He listened some more, and frowned. "Bring what? Uh-huh . . . I'll tell her . . . you, too."

Clicking off the phone he looked across at me and chuckled. "For better or worse, the deed is done. What about we pack first, then go get some barbecued shrimp at Manale's? I'm starving."

My chair bumped upon the stones as I pushed away from the table. "Suddenly, I got a real bad feeling this is going to be even worse than we think," I said.

"Oh. Incidentally, honey." Dan pressed his lips together, trying to hide a smile. "She wants you to bring your 'adorable little tool kit with all the scissors and things' as she put it."

I couldn't help but laugh. Trust Hell's Bell to concoct the perfect scheme to get a free touchup out of me! Probably I should take it as a high compliment since the Bell Sands' Bella Salon was run by Ricky Gomez, a pretty big name in these parts. Quite flattering, really, that she'd grown so dependent on Claire Claiborne she was willing to import her. Oh, well, I thought, a little smugly. Some big hair maintenance was a small price to pay for our much-needed second honeymoon.

And so it would have been, if a shampoo and blowdry or two—or even three or four—had been all Mrs. Shelby Bell wanted.

CHAPTER 3

Dan reached to grab a lock of my hair and twisted it around his thick forefinger. "Hey, darlin'? You want to stop off at Captain Ezra's for some oysters, or just keep on rolling until we get to Crestview Cove?" He took his eyes off the highway for a moment and zoomed a quick look at me over the rims of sexy retro sunglasses with flesh-colored frames that matched my own. His strong teeth clamped onto his cigar while he grinned.

I grinned back. If anyone ever in his life didn't need oysters, it was Dan, despite the fact he was nearly twelve years older than my twenty-nine. None of that nonsense about decadent New Orleans blueblood growing thin and pale, or pitiful declining sperm count in *his* family!

Dave Louis, Dan's father, had explained that ever since the first of their particular branch of Clabornes—Delesseps Louis, son of a French mother and English father—made his pile from sugarcane and moved to the city, none of his descendants had ever been caught in the trap of marrying into a society so closed that by now, with all the inbreeding and adultery, you could be wedding your own half-brother or sister and not even know it.

"Delesseps set us the right example," Dave Louis chuckled, "by courting whom he damn well pleased, which turned out to be the pretty mam'selle French governess of the younger sister of the girl folks were pressuring him to hook up with!"

The governess, of course, had said, "*Oui, oui!*" So, there was never any danger of accidental incest, especially since the Claiborne progeny ran almost exclusively to males.

Only one or two per family, but oh, my! The size and quality more than compensated for the lack of quantity.

Dave Louis got his wife, Rae Ellen Blaine, from some Kentucky horse people, but Dan had broken tradition by trying it once the New Orleans way, with a local debutante.

When they'd parted, Melissa Bonnie married her maid-of-honor's ex, while Dan, returning to his Delesseps roots, had wed an outsider. And he'd have been hard pressed to find more of an outsider than me.

When my parents set off on that fateful shrimping expedition, they'd left me in the care of Gabriel's much older brother, Hebert, and his wife Jeanette. Permanently, as it turned out.

N'oncle Hebert and *Tante* Jeanette had long before wearied of swamps, alligators, water moccasins and *pirogues*. Happily leaving the Jennerette family fishing business to Gabriel, they decamped to the Bayou St. John area of New Orleans where they became city Cajuns and ran a successful appliance store.

Hebert died when I was still quite small, so I had been raised by *Tante* Jeanette, who must have felt like she'd hatched the proverbial cuckoo's chick. All my grownup cousins were darkhaired, darkeyed, and indisputable Cajuns. I, on the other hand, had turned out petite, golden blonde, and completely Danish.

According to *Tante* J, my mother had divulged very little about her background. But, unless she'd been an impoverished aristocrat or something before migrating to America, there was no logical explanation as to why, at age five, I should demand that I be served *real* tea in a *china* cup from a *silver* pot when invited to childhood tea parties. And more than one rouged and lipsticked little creature had tearfully wobbled away from me on tacky high heels, because I was sharply critical of their mommies' taste in clothes.

Ironically, though the rest of the kids on our block attended a nearby neighborhood school, I was the only one who lived on my side of the street, and the vagaries of the zoning system saw me bussed Uptown where I looked, spoke and dressed exactly like all the other girls. I thought I fit right in, but they, with unerring instinct, knew I wasn't really one of them, and treated me accordingly. Then I would be the one to rush home in tears.

As a bluecollar child with expensive tastes and educated beyond my geographical and social position, I had no true friends in either world, Unsurprisingly, much of my time was spent immersed in fashion magazines and hacking off my dolls' hair. Once in awhile I was able to coerce a real person into letting me experiment, and poor *Tante* J was the only woman among her acquaintances to sport a Jane Fonda shag, à la *Klute*.

Eventually, I had grown up to become a hairstylist and was introduced to Dan by the man whose wife wound up murdering two people, one of them right in my beauty shop.

Uptown lady till the end, she had personally apologized to me for the latter, not twenty minutes before she'd blown first her husband's, then her own brains out in my rose garden.

No doubt she intended for the apology to cover both breaches of etiquette.

Dan let go of my hair and turned his attention to the stretch of Highway 90 that ran along the sugar-white sandy beach. You needed to be extra careful driving around here. Those Mississippi State Troopers had a way of coming out of nowhere and they'd nail you in a minute.

I, however, was entirely free to watch Dan. He was looking particularly luscious this morning in a pale green silk T-shirt and khaki shorts. The muscles in his big thigh flexed as he eased on and off the gas pedal, and I lightly stroked the movement with my fingers.

A shower of sparks danced across the dashboard as the sun caught facets from the enormous heartshaped canary diamond on my wide gold wedding band.

At my touch, Dan slid a little lower in his seat and inquired, "Hmmm?"

We have this thing we do sometimes in the car, which Dan calls "a drivethrough." I shook my head regretfully. "Better not, Dan Louis. What if one of those mean old State Troopers spots us? For all I know, it's against the law in

Mississippi!" But I continued to caress the inside of his thigh.

"Oh, little lady. You are playing with fire," he growled.

Just then, we flashed by a green sign that informed us Crestview Cove was another 58 miles. And almost immediately, the tall Captain Ezra's sign loomed ahead.

Abruptly, Dan swerved the BMW into the seafood restaurant's large parking lot. He brought the car to a stop, and got out without another word. Amused and excited, I waited to see what he was planning to do. I could hear him rummaging around in the trunk, where he carries everything but the kitchen sink. Then Dan came to my door and jerked it open.

"Get out !" he ordered, and strode across the parking lot toward the beach with a huge blue and yellow umbrella and a blanket jammed under his arms, leaving me to follow.

There were already people scattered around on the sand, maybe the tail end of the tourists trying to squeeze in a little more tanning time before heading home, but there were still some good spots available. Dan found one between a tall dune and the water, stabbed the umbrella into the ground, then yanked me down beside him. It was very private, almost like being in a tent.

"Now, Claire." Dan warned. "I don't want to hear one word about the gritty old sand on your delicate skin. You brought this on yourself, darlin'."

I slid my hands beneath his silk T-shirt, and grabbed bunches of the thick, soft fur on his chest. "You have every right to be angry," I murmured. "I know I deserve whatever—"

"Oh, you most certainly do," Dan agreed. "You think you can just tantalize me, then concoct some State Trooper story, and expect me to drive 58 more miles till I can get you into a hotel room? Well, you have just lived to learn different!"

However, once we were lying prone, the late night spent packing for this trip, combined with an early rising, took their toll. Desire faded into languor as the warm, white sand beneath the blanket adjusted to the contours of our bodies like a customized orthopedic mattress.

Drowsily, I suggested to Dan that beach-sand beds could revolutionize the sleep business. Different sands, collected from beaches of the world, each with their own unique properties, some more exotic than others. Combine several for your individual needs. All very now and holistic.

Before we realized it, the rhythm of crashing waves rocked us to sleep and we didn't wake up until the first raindrops spattered onto the umbrella.

Dan yawned and untangled himself from me, squinting at his watch in disbelief. "Two o'clock already? This is all your fault, Claire!"

I raised up on an elbow. "I'm sorry. Shall I promise never to do it again?"

"Don't you dare!" Dan laughed, then peered around the edge of the umbrella to see what was happening. It had stopped raining momentarily, but the sky had turned that nasty color it does when the weather's getting ready to pitch a fit. The rest of the beach was deserted (Captain Ezra's always makes out great in a storm) and the only people we could see in either direction were a few surfers much farther up. A couple of those strange little black water birds bobbled atop heaving breakers a hundred feet or so out.

Dan wrinkled his brow. "I'm not that much of a sailor, but those waves are looking mighty high to me, Claire."

We'd played tapes ever since leaving New Orleans, and hadn't heard a weather report all day. "Uh-oh. You don't think there's a big storm brewing?"

"I sure hope not, sugar. The only tropical disturbance I want to know anything about for the next few days is our own personal private one."

We hastily rearranged our clothing and dashed across Captain Ezra's back pavilion, just as the rain started pelting down in earnest.

A blast of country music from the jukebox greeted us, the incomparable Brenda Lee wailing "Sweet Nothin's," as Dan and I pushed through the crowd of locals and refugee tourists jammed around the big mahogany bar amid the odors of beer, fish, and tobacco. With amazing good luck, we wound up standing behind a couple getting ready to leave, and we nabbed their stools before anybody else realized what was happening.

"Afternoon, Mr. Claiborne, Miz Claiborne," Captain Ezra greeted us, continuing to open oysters from a big washtub filled with ice. Two other men were doing the same at strategic spots farther down the bar, while an inaudible *Magnum* rerun flickered on a large TV screen behind them. "Ain't seen you folks around here in a long while," he commented, arranging a dozen of the shellfish on a metal platter of finely crushed ice, which was immediately snapped up by waitress in a mini-sailor suit. She added a lemon wedge and parsley garnish before delivering it to her table.

Ezra was right. Though during our first brief marriage, Dan and I were fairly regular customers, the last occasion we'd been here was almost a year back—not long before that awful night that led to our divorce. Dan had found a big black pearl which I'd intended to match and have a set of cufflinks made for him, but never did.

"What'll it be?" asked Ezra, eyeing the big umbrella propped against the bar with a knowing expression. From floor-to-ceiling plate glass windows providing a panoramic view of the ocean, that blue and yellow umbrella must've stood out like a sore thumb. Several of the grinning honky-tonkers had also noticed it. Somebody muttered , just loud enough, "Sheeyut! Thought they'd gone and opened one up of them farr'n Ikea places out there!"

"Couple of dozen r'awsters as usual, sir?" Ezra inquired blandly.

Dan nodded. "I'll take a Dixie beer." He knew better than to order Oranjeboom in here. "And one extra-hot Bloody Mary. Right, Claire?"

"What else!" Even New Orleans couldn't top Captain Ezra's Bloody Marys.

Ezra removed his thick oystering glove. "Pedro! Come take over my tub!" he yelled to a handsome Tex-Mex seated at one end of the bar, interrupting a promising flirtation with the sassy waitress.

Dan lit a fresh cigar, and I excused myself to visit the restroom designated "Mermaids," to freshen up before our drinks arrived.

There was a line, but once I acquired a stall, I took advantage of the privacy to strip and shake astonishing amounts of sand from my baggy linen shorts and shirt, the inevitable consequence of playing Beach Blanket.

Afterward, I had to compete for a spot at the long wall mirror with a cluster of bathing beauties—whose micro-bikinis had never touched water until they'd gotten caught in the rain—frantically trying to resurrect soggy bouffant hairdos. It's a certain kind of Southern thing, and probably always will be, God bless America.

They cast condescending, yet envious, glances at my relatively flat tresses. Marcel, the genius who'd trained me in the beauty business, had designed a new style for me a couple of months ago, and it was still holding up. Just a few passes with a comb and dab of Aveda's "Brilliant," and I was out of there.

The bouffants quickly closed ranks behind me, and I didn't give much for anybody else's chances at that mirror for quite some time.

Threading my way back through the increasingly boisterous crowd to the bar, I saw the sky had darkened. Streaks of lightning cracked on the horizon. I shuddered. Somewhere out there, on that very Gulf, my mother and father had met their fate. Was this the way it looked when the storm caught them? At least they'd been able to cling to each other. Which is more than some people can say, not even managing to live together, much less die together.

What had it been like for them? Who was first to be snatched from the desperate embrace of the other and swept away by the roaring wind into the tossing waves?

But when I tried to visualize their faces from the only snapshot of the two of them *Tante* J had been able to find among their things, the picture blurred, and the faces somehow became those of Dan and me. I thought well, if I have to go Lord, please let it be with him. And with a sudden sense of peace, I knew that's exactly how my parents had felt.

When I came back, Dan pulled my stool close to his, out of grabbing range of the cowboy/fisherman type who'd started to hit on me. Idly glancing at the television set behind the bar, I noticed that the ancient *Magnum* had been replaced by a supremely tailored and coiffed young man ("Just hired outta L.A.," one barfly said laconically.) pointing to a knotty whorl on a weather map. Ezra, glancing over his shoulder, saw it, and touched a hidden button somewhere, causing Michelle Wright to dwindle away as the TV volume rose.

". . . and that's good news for all of us here on the Gulf Coast!" chortled the weatherman. "Tropical Disturbance Babe appears to be heading east, toward Jamaica, and—" Loud whoops and applause drowned out something about storm warnings still being in effect. An irrelevant detail, as far as anybody under *this* roof was concerned. Hell, there wasn't gonna be no hurricane, and too bad for Jamaica if Babe decided to drop in for a visit. Michelle picked up her song from where she'd left off, and at least half the people in the place ordered another round of drinks to celebrate.

"Sorry your Bloody Mary took so long, Miz Claiborne," Ezra said, sliding a double oldfashioned glass mercifully free of protruding celery foliage toward me. As always, he waited until I'd taken the first sip, savoring the perfect mix of tomato, Worcestershire, Tabasco, cayenne, lime, black pepper and whatever other magical ingredients he put in. I let myself surrender to the delicious shock.

"Whoo!" I gasped, feeling the tears well up. "Is smoke coming out of my ears yet?"

"Your *ears* ain't where the smoke's coming from, darlin'!" Dan teased, wrapping a possessive arm around my waist and drawing me even farther away from the cowboy/fisherman type, who was showing signs of persistence.

Ezra smiled and nodded before he turned back to his oyster shucking, barely blue eyes twinkling in the tan face framed by curly silver hair beneath a generic captain's hat. He could've been any age from forty-six to sixty-four. Rumor had it that he was a Navy helicopter pilot in Vietnam, but nobody really knew anything about him, including whether or not his name was actually Ezra.

Apparently, he had plenty of money, and lived in a big, plantation-style house on the far northeast shore of Bay St. Louis, where he grew his famous oysters. There'd been vague stories about security that was strangely tight for a mere oyster ranch, and something about a private landing strip in a cow pasture, which gave rise to speculations that he was involved in everything from drug running to paramilitary training.

But as to his personal life—whether he was married, divorced, had kids, or even dated anybody—we'd never heard a word. However, Dan and I were convinced of one thing: Captain Ezra was certainly not the character he'd spun, for whatever reasons, from equal parts of New England codger and good ol' Southern boy.

Ezra plunked two tin trays of oysters in front of us, and

I set about the ritual of preparing the sauce, my sacred duty since I'm the Cajun part of the family. Catsup, lemon juice, Tabasco, horseradish, and, an exclusive feature of Captain Ezra's, a touch of finely minced jalapeños.

As we worked our way through the succulent oysters, contentment stole over me despite the black and angry sky. The jukebox was playing nonstop country oldies, and I was with the love of my life who loved me right back, and we were going to have days and nights filled with love, love and more love. A storm might only make it better.

Ezra came over to see if we wanted anything else before he rang up the bill. Dan looked at me inquiringly, but I shook my head. I had two oysters left to go, and they would hold me until we had dinner with the Shelby Bells.

"Y'all drivin' on back to N'awlins, now?" Ezra drawled, as he counted out Dan's change.

"No, Ezra. We just stopped off on our way over to the Bell Sands," Dan answered. "Taking a little vacation."

Ezra's pale eyes narrowed in mild surprise. "Big hotel over to Crestview Cove? I'da never figgered you for the type," he added cryptically.

Dan, absorbed with dispensing tips replied absently, "Yes, it's our first time. Sure hope that's not a real hurricane blowing up out there after all." He indicated the TV screen where the weatherman still prattled soundlessly. Maybe it was just my imagination, but that small churning knot on the satellite picture seemed to have expanded slightly.

"Naw! That ain't no hurricane, bubba!" The cowboy/fisherman type was determined to assert himself. "Babe's just a lil' ole squall, makin' a lot of noise. Like all babes do!" He winked at me. "Can't take none of 'em serious!"

He never knew how fortunate he was that I bit down on something hard. Another black pearl! Dan was going to get his surprise cufflinks after all. Everybody cheered and demanded to hold it, and some local intellectual insisted it was more grey than black because the only authentic black ones come from Fiji.

Pedro erased the pearl count on the blackboard, chalking up the new total (mine made the 1,425th since 1978) and Captain Ezra persuaded us to stay and have another drink on the house. He never did elaborate as to why he didn't think we were the Bell Sands type, which I thought sounded like his idea of a compliment. Of course, he knew what went on there this time of year.

Since we didn't have that much farther to drive, Dan agreed to another Dixie. I accepted a smaller edition of Ezra's usual size Bloody Mary.

The pearl seemed like such a good omen for our trip. Even better, it appeared our concerns about Babe were without foundation because the next time I looked at the TV, the weatherman ("Sheeyut! Bet he ain't even a registered meteorologist.") was gone and a *Matlock* episode was just coming on. One of the early ones with, coincidentally, Linda *Purl*! As a bonus, just as we pulled onto the highway, the sun came out.

Being one myself, I should have remembered that small babes making noise don't take kindly to being ignored.

CHAPTER 4

Dan and I were in a real hillbilly mood by the time we departed from Captain Ezra's. A random scan of the radio dial netted us a delightful downhome station in Atmore, Alabama.

We covered the final miles to Crestview Cove regaled with an eclectic music mix that ranged from John Schneider's "It's A Short Walk From Heaven to Hell," to a vintage clip from the *Grand Ol' Opry*, "Taters Never Did Taste Good (When Chicken's On The Table)," by Little Jimmy Dickens, to the vintage country gospel tune, "Angels Rock Me To Sleep," by the Chuck Wagon Gang. Then the sun, beaming full force since we'd left Ezra's, suddenly retreated and jagged bolts of lightning slashed through a big pile of heavy pewter clouds that hadn't been there a moment ago.

A steady rain started to hammer against the windshield, and the radio sputtered with static, obliterating a Frankie Laine Festival just getting underway, beginning with "Moonlight Gambler." Dan muttered, "Damn!" and switched off the noise when it became obvious no amount of tuning could retrieve the station. Irritably, he flipped on the headlights and wipers. For a high-powered international lawyer, my husband harbors some unexpected affinities, and Frankie Laine is one of them. Dan had gotten hooked on the singer when we were going through *Tante* J's things after her death. He'd stumbled across *N'oncle* Hebert's collection spanning Laine's career from "Lucky Ol' Sun" to "This Time Lord, You Gave Me A Mountain," and that had been that.

Through a curtain of rain, we spotted an elegant pink billboard announcing the turnoff to CRESTVIEW COVE, MISSISSIPPI'S PREMIER BEACHFRONT RESORT COMMUNITY, five miles ahead. The Cove had been the brainchild of a shrewd California real estate developer who got in on the ground floor of post-Hurricane Camille reconstruction in late 1970. He envisioned an enclave that would be to the string of communities along Beach Boulevard what The Colony was to Malibu; exclusive waterfront residences protected by security gates and a twenty-four hour guard on duty in the entrance booth, plus round-the-clock vehicular street patrols. There were also branches of a national bank and the post office, as well as designer boutiques and an upscale grocer's.

Aerial photographs of the property were spectacular. Acres of pine and live oak on a slight rise curved around several miles of dazzling white sandy beach. There was a country club that boasted a championship 18-hole golf course, professional tennis courts, and riding stables. Not to mention the actual cove itself, that formed a perfect natural marina.

Luxurious California rancho-palazzo homes in stucco tinted peach, pink, apricot or cream with red tile roofs, were a radical departure from the Tara/West Indies architecture that formerly predominated as favorites among this area's affluent.

Crestview Cove was a huge success from the getgo. Many of the younger wealthy crowd who'd lived in Gulfport, Biloxi, or Longbeach, opted for some California-style beach life when their insurance claims finally got settled. And thanks to more rigid construction standards , the development survived several major hurricanes since Camille with substantially less permanent damage. After all, there's no such thing as hurricane-proof. If you live in the South near saltwater, you can count on having to bail out of at least two or three big ones in your lifetime.

Now, twenty-something years later, Crestview Cove was firmly established on the PGA circuit, and hosted two major tennis tournaments annually.

Mr. Shelby Bell had also gotten in on the ground floor with his Bell Sands Resort, a flagrant reproduction of the original Beverly Hills Hotel exterior, right down to its titty-pink paint. For the last five years, the Bell Sands had hosted the South's newest, richest, most glamorous and glitzy beauty contest, The Miss Gulf Coast Pageant. Founded by that former Miss America first runner-up, Mrs. Shelby Bell.

Of course, Dan had watched many golf and tennis events televised from the resort, but despite its close proximity to New Orleans, neither of us had ever been there before.

Consequently, we almost missed the Cove's deceptively unimpressive turnoff, which appeared to be nothing but a narrow, blacktopped, red clay lane leading through an overgrowth of sea oats and sawgrass to nowhere. Making it all the more surprising that the mile-long access was packed bumper-to-bumper with cars inching along like traffic on a Los Angeles freeway.

Living with a sports nut like Dan, I knew for a fact there was no golf or tennis tournament going on. So that left . . . a swift glance at his grim expression revealed he was thinking the same terrible thought, but he made no comment.

It took us at least ten minutes to reach the entrance gates. By now the water was being hurled down in buckets. Two armed, harassed-looking security guards in yellow slickers marked "Crestview Cove Protective Service" were ordering most of the traffic to circle the booth and head back out to the highway. One of them was about to do the same to us, until Dan identified himself.

The guard consulted a soggy clipboard and his face cleared. "Oh, yeah. Mr. Claiborne. Mrs. Bell's been callin' down all afternoon to see if you'd been checked through. Drive right in, sir."

"What's going on?" Dan asked stoically.

Shrugging, the guard spat into the downpour, a symbolic quenching of any last flickering hope. "Gotta buncha TV news people runnin' all over the place 'cause yesterday some broad started carryin' on 'bout gettin' kicked outta the beauty contest," he replied. "Sore loser, y'ask me. Gotta big lawyer threatenin' to sue somebody. Gotta buncha horny guys tryin' to sneak past us to get into the hotel to watch the judgin'. Gotta—"

A Mercedes behind us bleated impatiently, cutting short this seemingly endless litany and the guard transferred his attention.

Dan drove through the tall verdigris gates frowning. "*Gotta* real nasty feeling we're about to find out why we were so unexpectedly invited for those fun-filled days and nights at the beautiful Bell Sands, all expenses paid."

"Then let's turn around and head for the Broadwater Beach," I urged, not saying I told you so. "Whatever this is, we don't need any more trouble in our lives. I can well afford to lose Mrs. Shelby Bell as a client."

Dan shook his head. "Now, honey. You know we can't do that. At least, not till we see what she wants with us. Besides, I'll bet you're just itching to find out what's going on."

Well, I was. A little. But why on earth couldn't the woman have been honest about why she asked us here? Even though Mrs. Shelby Bell was my client, Mr. Shelby Bell wasn't, him being bald as an egg.

And he certainly wasn't Dan's, either. The lucrative Bell Group business was handled by one of Blanchard, Smithson, Callant and Claiborne's rival law firms.

Coral Reef, the main road, had cleared and we passed the first large beautiful homes backing onto the beach. To the lefthand side, more residences lined streets that ended in cul-de-sacs surrounded by a dense pine forest, and named for things beachy or piscatory: Starfish Way, Seahorse

Circle, Bluefin Court, Shell Place. When Coral Reef curved around a modified Taj Mahal that we recognized from television as the country club, it widened and the houses became even grander until there, rising from the mist and towering above them all in rosy splendor, was the Bell Sands Resort.

Live oaks festooned with Spanish moss formed a picturesque arch over the long circular drive leading to the entrance, but this tranquil effect was somewhat marred by a line of regional TV news mobile units parked along the shoulder. There was no one around when we pulled up beneath the overhang. Whatever was going on had moved inside when the rain got serious.

Above the tall entrance doors a giant banner proclaimed:

WELCOME MISS GULF COAST PAGEANT CONTESTANTS!

A sudden gust of wind whipped at the canvas, causing it to flap crazily.

We had been warned.

CHAPTER 5

No sooner did Dan switch off the ignition than Bell Sands staff, in jaunty maroon livery, materialized from nowhere and surrounded the car. With drill team precision, two of them simultaneously opened our doors, while another wheeled a tall brass luggage rack around to the trunk and began to unload our bags. That there had actually been enough room for the pieces we'd brought along, in addition to the cargo Dan hauls around in there on a regular basis, bore glowing testimony to the BMW's generous storage capacity.

As Dan took my arm and we started forward, a large, youngish man, who looked like a former football player, emerged from the hotel, holding a walkie-talkie to his right ear.

There is a certain physical type of male who no longer participates in sports to the extent he once did, but has not adjusted his calories to compensate, and this guy was it. Taller than average, just a tad too pink of complexion, with a layer of softness spread like butter over his big-boned, meaty frame. Beefcake has a mighty sneaky way of turning into poundcake.

I pressed snugly against Dan's rock solid bulk. Nothing squashy about him.

The man lowered the device and hurried toward us, impeccable in a maroon blazer designed to coordinate with the livery. A gold crest with "BSR" embroidered in black was affixed to his breast pocket.

"You'd be the Claibornes," he informed us, reaching to pump Dan's hand. "I'm Parker Bell, the manager. Aunt Tinker wants me to personally escort you to your suite. Follow me, please."

Dan raised his thick eyebrows a fraction. Suite? Knowing our hostess, we'd been prepared for a mediocre single at best. With twin beds. Whatever she wanted, it must be a big one.

It was clear why the woman always identified herself as "Mrs. Shelby Bell." Even in the South, where eccentric names are practically mandatory, "Tinker Bell" was way over the top.

Since Mrs. Bell was closer to Dan's age than mine, her tiara days were over by the time I reached puberty. And yet, in the context of Miss Gulf Coast, something about the name Tinker evoked hazy memories of an old beauty contest scandal.

"Parker Bell?" Dan repeated. "I thought I recognized you! Wide receiver, Ole Miss, 1984-"

Parker Bell didn't acknowledge Dan's overture as he swung the door open and motioned us to enter. But his face turned redder and his jaw grew rigid. Dan looked at me and shrugged.

"You're already registered so we can go straight on up. Things are a little too hectic just now for business as usual," Parker said, an understatement totally inadequate to describe the chaos that met our eyes.

The plush lobby of the famous Bell Sands Resort was swarming with people and vibrating with noise. Unbelievably beautiful girls, some wearing rhinestone tiaras and sashes printed with their titles, huddled together with older versions of themselves, cackling like angry hens at a small, uneasy-looking group of trendy men and women, several of them recognizable celebrities.

Most of the action though, was clustered in the middle of the room under the magnificent chandelier. Guys in baseball caps and jackets emblazoned with station call letters bulldozed forward with minicams at the ready, while flash attachments clicked and whirred and invisible hands thrust microphones into the air where they waved like eager phalluses.

Parker herded us toward the elevators, his size and menacing aura as he mumbled into the walkie-talkie helping to clear a path.

For a moment, we were close enough to glimpse the vortex of all this commotion.

She was tall and willowy, draped in taupe silk. A sash that read "Miss Tampa Tangerine" ran diagonally from left shoulder to waist. A sparkling crown set off long, black hair that fell in soft natural waves around a face so pale and perfect it could have been chiseled in marble. The artificially natural smile issued at birth exclusively to beauty contestants displayed teeth which gleamed in a way that struck me as carnivorous. Real man-eating equipment.

At her side stood a rangy older man attired in a tailored western suit; Brandon Battle, the notorious attorney. With bushy snow white hair and mustache, and skin the color of rawhide, he provided a striking contrast to the girl when he bent to murmur advice in her ear as questions were being hurled from all directions:

"Chessy, how will you be able to prove discrimination?"

"Miss Scarborough. Is it true you've got African-American blood?"

"Hey! What about the rumor you were sexually harassed by one of the judges?"

A fresh clamor broke out at that one, and my attention was caught by an elegant, expensive woman, who stood slightly removed, her coral lips curled in a malicious smile as she observed the scene. Coal black hair slashed with one dramatic silver stripe was piled high on her head, and her eyes were partially concealed by those peculiar glasses with green tinted lenses preferred by nine out of ten Latin dictators.

Dan was scowling. "Brandon Battle! Looks like big trouble for somebody."

"Three guesses *who*," I offered.

Parker had almost gotten us to the elevators when a voice exclaimed, "Well, slap me silly! It's the bride and groom!"

There stood Charlotte Dalton, our dear friend and

investigative reporter for WDSU-TV in New Orleans. Her chestnut mane like a prize filly's (which I groom every three weeks) was tucked under a man's broad-brimmed hat spattered with rain, and her paper-white face seemed luminous above the turned-up collar of a metallic gold trenchcoat.

Charlotte surveyed us wryly. "I know what *I'm* doing here." She waved an arm back toward the pandemonium. "But this is the last place on earth I ever expected to run into you two sex maniacs!"

Parker, who'd been holding the elevator open for us while emitting little huffs of impatience expostulated, "Ms. Dalton, please! The Claibornes are special guests of the Bell Sands!"

Charlotte nodded wisely. "So old Hell's Bell roped you into this mess, huh? Wonder what she's up to?"

Parker intervened a little desperately. "Mr. and Mrs. Claiborne. If you'll just come with me?" he nearly pleaded.

Dan took pity on him. "Sure, Parker. But first, would you kindly apprise Ms. Dalton here of our room number?"

"Suite 417," Parker disclosed unwillingly.

"Give us about forty-five minutes, hon," Dan told Charlotte.

"Sure you'll be finished by then?" Charlo took off giggling, further outraging Parker who had determinedly marched into the elevator, his ears a neon crimson.

He maintained a wounded aloofness during the short elevator ride. When we reached our floor, Parker unlocked the massive double doors to Number 417, handed the old fashioned brass key and a spare to Dan, then departed with perfunctory courtesy.

"Mercy me!" Dan exclaimed, looking around.

My suspicion increased at the sight of our lavish accommodations. The living room was cozily Euro-country in pickled pine with green and yellow flowered chintz. French doors opened onto a balcony that was built to give the illusion of being suspended right over the surging waves.

I surveyed the fresh flowers, chocolates, and basket of fruit, then rendered my verdict. "Big one, for true!"

Dan nodded. "Speaking of which. I need to get the sand out of my britches. It's starting to feel gritty down there."

"Now why is it," I wondered aloud, "every time I mention something 'big' you just automatically assume I'm referring to you? Or portions thereof?"

Dan slipped his hands under my arms and lifted me up to his eye level. "Well, aren't you?" he demanded, and kissed me with playful roughness. "*Aren't* you?"

He carried me into the bedroom where we encountered a view that was totally different from the first, but equally breathtaking. Here, long narrow windows looked out into thick pines and oak trees.

Our luggage stood in front of a large closet, between the dresser and chest of drawers. Two chairs decked in flirtatious green and yellow striped slipcovers were pulled up to a tea table, and a pickled pine armoire housed a complete entertainment center.

Dan dumped me onto the massive canopied bed, then turned on the radio, searching for our Atmore station. It was no use, but he did pick up some good jazz.

"I won't be too long, darlin'," he said, heading for the bathroom.

I heard him turn on the shower, and evidently dozed off a minute. Because next thing I knew, the smell of fresh soap and a tang of Dan's new cologne, D'Aventure, was teasing me awake, gentle as a feather tickling my nose.

He stood beside the bed with a towel wrapped around his waist. He let it fall open. "See what you get for letting me eat oysters in the middle of the day?"

"Mmm. I must be dreaming," I said.

Dan chuckled. "Well, Claire. Didn't I promise to make all your dreams come true?"

And proceeded to prove he was definitely a man of his word, engulfing, absorbing, ravishing, devouring, whispering, "Dream on, babylove, much as you want . . ."

The honeymoon had begun.

CHAPTER 6

"This was stuck in the crack of your door." Charlotte handed me a small envelope when I answered her knock, engulfed in one of the two maroon terry robes with the BSR crest that came with our room. As I tore it open, she knowingly eyed my freshly scrubbed face and hair, still damp from the shower.

> Dear Claire and Dan:
> Welcome! Meet us in the Bay Lounge for
> drinks at 7:30. Dinner at 8:00.

The signature was a touching little doodle of two bells joined with a bow.

Charlotte, who'd been reading over my shoulder, was incredulous. "*Our* Hell's Bell wrote *that*?"

"What?" Dan entered from the bedroom, looking fine as wine in the other BSR bathrobe. I showed him the note. "Straight out of *Alice In Wonderland*," he commented. "Apparently, we stepped through the looking glass somewhere between New Orleans and Crestview Cove."

Charlotte nodded. "Uh-huh, and smack dab into the

middle of the house of mirrors, as you are about to discover. Got time for a rundown?"

Dan consulted his watch and told me, "It's six-thirty now. How long do you think you'll need to get ready?"

I felt my hair. "Probably if I start blowdrying by seven it should be okay."

"I'll try to make this synoptic," Charlotte promised, flopping onto the sofa, Dan patted the arm of his chair, inviting me to perch.

"Once upon a time in Fort Walton Beach, Florida," Charlotte began dreamily. "A long, long time ago in the seventies, when Claire and I were just teeny, tiny little girls—"

Dan rolled his blue eyes and grimaced. "You made your point!" he grunted. "Now get on with it."

"Touchy, ain't he?" she chuckled. "Anyway, there lived a poor but beautiful maiden named LaWanda Jones who was a contestant in a regional Florida beauty pageant for the title of Miss Palmetto. Now, Miss Palmetto may not sound like much to you, but it happens to be a very important step toward becoming Miss Florida. And LaWanda wanted to win very, very badly.

"There was also another beautiful girl in this pageant whose name was—" she paused for effect. "—Tinker Taylor."

"Soldier, Spy?" Dan suggested. I guess no matter what last name you put with Tinker, it still sounds like a joke.

"Tinker *Elizabeth* Taylor!" Charlotte drawled. "I *swear*! Tinker was from a wealthy family in Pensacola. And she also wanted to win the Miss Palmetto crown. Almost as much as LaWanda."

She jumped up and began to pace the room, warming to her story. "The pageant was held in Tallahassee, and as the days passed it became clear to everybody that LaWanda and Tinker were running neck-in-neck. The smart money was on Tinker because, even though LaWanda was a dynamite tapdancer, Tinker was a state champion fire baton twirler. A skillfully wielded fire baton was almost impossible to beat in those days. And Tinker had mastered two at one time!

"But came the magic moment, and LaWanda was crowned Miss Palmetto. Tinker had to make do with first runner-up. LaWanda and her mother were overjoyed. You see, years back, the father deserted them and LaWanda's mother had struggled to make ends meet. Lord knows how she managed to get that girl so far down the beauty trail. Now, it would be goodbye to all that scrimping and saving. Hello to the good life!"

Charlotte stopped and stared through the windows at the darkening sea. "Only, it didn't quite work out that way," she said softly. "The very next morning, there was an announcement. LaWanda Jones was stepping down as Miss Palmetto, and her duties and privileges would immediately be assumed by Tinker Taylor."

It was starting to come back to me now. Even at that tender age, I had tried to keep *au courant* when it came to fashion and beauty. "Something about LaWanda being part Negro, wasn't it?"

"Right, Claire." Charlotte nodded, and resumed her

tour of the room. "Miss Palmetto was still unofficially open to whites only. It will come as no surprise that Tinker Taylor just happened to mention this juicy tidbit about LaWanda's pedigree within earshot of one of the judges, and major doo-doo hit the fan.

"What galls me is the hypocrisy. Everybody knows the unspoken truth is that the older and richer the Southern family, the more certain you can bet there's a touch of the tarbrush. It's just a matter of keeping the skeletons locked in the closet and your fingers crossed that that embarrassing blot of black ink won't turn up in *your* lifetime. The problem with LaWanda Jones was that she wasn't from a rich old Southern family.

"In fact, when the Miss Palmetto Committee checked her birth certificate, it turned out that mean old daddy who supposedly deserted them, never lived there in the first place. LaWanda Jones was illegitimate, and her mother had no idea where he was. Therefore, she couldn't prove the father *wasn't* black!"

Charlotte returned to the sofa. "Well, you can just imagine what happened. All of a sudden, the hotel was trying to throw Mrs. Jones and LaWanda out, there were threatening letters, obscene phone calls, the works."

"How were they able to get away with treating her like that?" I demanded, indignantly.

Dan interjected, "I can answer that. Although I would like to mention for the record, I was under twenty at the time."

"Which means Claire was not quite eight," Charlotte pointed out, and Dan shot me an alarmed glance.

"*Anyway,*" he continued. "The reason they were able to get by with dethroning LaWanda was that civil rights as we understand them today were barely older than you girls then, and let's just say not everybody was enforcing them? Remember, Dr, King had only been assassinated a few short years before.

"But what I remember best about that whole thing was that three famous lawyers all hotfooted it down to Florida, arguing about who was going to get to represent the Jones ladies for free! I guess by then any of those boys could've used the publicity for representing a client who hadn't done anything worse then being born on the dark side of the blanket for a change!"

Dan leaned forward. "Naturally, since I planned to enter law school, I followed the whole thing pretty closely. Daddy was interested too, and we were both selfishly disappointed when Mrs. Jones ended up with the then-unknown Brandon Battle from Atlanta and the thing was settled out of court. It was like it never happened. Even for those days, Battle got a damn good settlement.

"And though it wasn't supposed to matter, he clinched things by tracking down LaWanda's natural father, who turned out to be Pure D white trash and proud of it!"

I was losing the thread. "But—what on earth does some moldy squabble between LaWanda Jones and Tinker over the title of Miss Palmetto have to do with Chessy Scarborough's allegations against the Miss Gulf Coast pageant?"

Charlotte wriggled impatiently. "Well, I'm coming to that, only you've got to hear the whole backstory in order to fully understand and appreciate what's happening now."

"Go on, Charlotte," Dan soothed. "We're listening."

"That's better," she said. "Okay. Now, Tinker Taylor is pretty much an open book. She soon discarded her slightly tarnished Miss Palmetto crown for that of Miss Florida. Then went on to almost—but not quite—become Miss America.

"Afterwards, she returned home to Pensacola, where she was of course a big local celebrity, and had the smarts to parlay it into a combination baton twirling/charm school thing.

"Tinker met Shelby Bell at a country club dance. He'd taken a liking to Pensacola when he was in helicopter training at Ellyson Field, so he decided to move there after he'd survived his Vietnam tour. By their wedding day, Shelby was a civilian, already getting real rich and real bald."

Charlotte paused to marshal her thoughts, "LaWanda's story is a little murkier. We do know she went to New York, where she wound up modeling for Halston, and acted in several of those Warhol-type underground movies.

"After her mother died, LaWanda Jones flew off to Europe, and came back ten years later as Mrs. Scarborough, thanks to—of all things—a very wealthy, good ol' boy husband she'd found somewhere over there. And a daughter named . . .Chessy."

She laughed at our expressions. "See? I told you this thing went way back."

"How did you manage to come up with so much background information on these people so fast?" Dan asked, curiously.

"I didn't really," Charlotte admitted. "In fact, I'd totally forgotten the pageant was even going on! It's mostly courtesy of this society reporter on the Biloxi newspaper I went to Sweetbriar with but never much liked, Jan Windsor. She'd been calling and calling, and yesterday afternoon, I finally decided to call her back and get it over with."

Meanwhile, Chessy Scarborough had been eliminated from the pageant and started howling racism and sexual harassment. Nothing like it had ever happened during the entire five years Jan Windsor had been covering Miss Gulf Coast. Out of loyalty to her good buddy, Tinker Bell, Jan used Chessy's bio to run a computer check, hoping to find some dirt to dish on the girl.

Ironically, what she'd turned up instead was the mother's old Miss Palmetto scandal.

The well-meaning society reporter had no intention of getting out of her depth, but she couldn't resist mentioning what she'd found to Charlotte, whose phone call came through at just the right moment.

Charlotte—who didn't have a clue what Jan was rambling on about at first—soon realized a major story might be brewing. It hadn't taken much pumping to get Jan to divulge more personal details about Tinker, whom she'd known for ages.

Charlotte's reporter instincts told her to move fast, so she'd only delayed long enough to run a brief electronic search for additional information about LaWanda Jones.

And though it netted only the few sparse facts she'd shared with us, they were enough to convince her there was more to this episode than immediately met the eye.

"Put them all together, and they spell *Mothah!*" Charlotte concluded. "But I almost couldn't talk my producer into giving me a unit and crew, especially in this weather. Soon as we get here, the first person I run into is Brandon Battle, famous for winning big money for pretty little girls like Chessy. Suddenly, I'm a hero, because not one other station in New Orleans has a mobile unit on location!"

Charlotte looked at her watch. "Well, it's nearly seven so I'll wrap this up quick. Battle is a master at pitting factions against each other, and he's ever so subtly trying to instigate a media campaign against the Bells. Beginning with insinuations he was scattering around today, such as minorities employed at the Bell Sands are treated like slaves; or that Mrs. Shelby Bell is another Leona Helmsley and a bigot who wasn't content with ruining LaWanda's career twenty-three years ago; now she's out to destroy her daughter Chessy's, too!"

She shrugged. "It's a clever approach, I'll grant him that. And it could work because some of the Hollywood celebrities——who are here either as judges, or to entertain—— don't believe a word Chessy's saying, but those poor goons are in total confusion about the Politically Correct thing to do. Some of them have only recently decided beauty pageants are okay, after all!

"B.B. Battle might very easily manipulate a few into blabbing emotional crap to the cameras about how all America should boycott the Bell Sands, and encourage minority employees to walk off their jobs. Which is just about everybody, because the bellhops, waiters, chambermaids, cooks, beauticians and so forth are mostly black, Mexican, Latin,

Asian and Indian. Of course, that would wreck the pageant completely. Unless Chessy is reinstated as a contestant."

"The hotel staff can't strike unless their various unions call for it," Dan pointed out.

"Hey, maybe not legally," Charlotte agreed. "But you know something like this is potentially explosive. It can take on a life of its own, no matter what the truth may actually be. I can tell you this. I overheard somebody interviewing a desk clerk, who's black. She was trying to tell the reporter that the Bells were wonderful employers and the hotel was a wonderful place to work, and she's received two promotions in less than two years. And that reporter just cut her short and walked off. He'll keep asking until he finds a discontented minority employee, and he *will* find one. And if it's the right one, that's all it will take. At this point, Dan, it could go either way."

Dan nodded but made no comment. A legal dilemma like the Bells might be up against would give him the chance to square off against Brandon Battle, for whom he had absolutely no respect whatsoever. And provide a dramatic change from copyrights, patents and trademarks. A welcome one, I thought, studying his pensive face.

Charlotte stood up and stretched. "Oh. One more thing. Rumor has it the network doing the live broadcast of the pageant finals is bidding on the rights to LaWanda's and Chessy's story for a Movie of the Week!

"Of course, nobody thinks Hollywood's trying to capitalize on Chessy's itty bitty role in *Trading Down*, which comes out next month."

"Wait, Charlotte!" I called, as she headed for the door.

"How can Chessy claim racial discrimination in her case? Didn't they prove her grandfather was white? And even if he wasn't, I noticed several definitely dusky complexions amongst the pageant contestants when we arrived this afternoon."

Charlotte grinned. "Well, see. I was saving the best for last and I almost forgot about it! She's using the Q word, Claire."

"Q word?"

"Q is for 'quota'," Dan explained. "Which is not the title of a Sue Grafton novel, It means a certain ratio of one race to another, although it usually applies to a workplace situation."

I was baffled. "So? How is that relevant to Chessy? Is she saying she was eliminated because she was *white*?"

"No, Claire," Charlotte burst out laughing. "Remember those hateful, pig-ignorant Miss Palmetto idiots? Well, they were right about LaWanda Jones, except they got it ass-backwards.

"Because she was passing, after all. Only, not on her daddy's side. On her *mother's* side.

"Honey, LaWanda's maternal granny was a high yellow!"

CHAPTER 7

Since we hadn't yet gotten around to unpacking, I fished out the easiest fancy things from my garment bag—a short, brown linen sheath and bronze sequined mules.

I'd underestimated how long it would take to dry my hair, so I wound up twisting it into a topknot, a style that really showed off the heartshaped canary diamond pavé pendant and earrings, Dan's wedding gift to me.

The foyer outside our suite was paneled in full-length mirrors, and when I caught sight of his reflection, I fell in love all over again.

Unlike some men, Dan enjoys dressing up. Lately, he'd given a lot of thought to finding a different look for those festive nights when a suit or tuxedo was too much, but casual simply wouldn't do.

This was the first time I'd seen him in one of his hot new outfits, which consisted of a deep indigo coat, matching trousers, and collarless pewter shirt buttoned to the top, all in textured silk. Plus, some very Uptown cowboy boots.

The colors turned his blue eyes smoky and dangerous.

They captured mine in the mirror, and I could feel myself melting like a candle.

Dan's image surveyed mine approvingly. "You look just like a small iced cappuccino, baby," he said, huskily.

"Well, now." I pressed closer to him. "That must mean you're feeling a bit warm and thirsty."

"Oh, yeah. That's exactly how I feel." He pulled me tightly against him to confirm the truth of this. "As you can plainly tell. That's what——" he suddenly broke off and let me go.

Puzzled, I looked up at him, but he jabbed agitatedly at the elevator button, avoiding my gaze. "These things must be running in slow motion."

"Uh-huh. What's wrong, Dan?" I demanded.

He sighed. "Okay, Claire. I'm wrestling with a very bizarre little problem right now."

Glancing down at me warily, he added, "About us, sweet thing."

Us? My heart plummeted at least fifty feet. But I wasn't prepared for what followed.

"Sometimes. . ." Dan hesitated, " . . . sometimes, it flat scares me, how much love I feel for you, Claire. I can't remember what I ever did without you, and I can't bear the thought of not having you." He slid his hands up and down my bare arms. "We ain't the usual thing, baby. That's for damn sure."

Dan studied me seriously. "I'll even go so far as to say I believe we were specially created to be together. Never nobody else, Claire. No how, no way."

The elevator pinged, startling us. Inside, I pressed my

hand against his freshly shaven cheek. "Oh, I absolutely agree, Dan. So what's the problem, *cher*?" But I was starting to get a glimmer.

Looking embarrassed, Dan said, "Well, all the above being true, what if I *had* met you when I was nineteen and you were——dear God, like Charlotte said, *seven* years old, and—" he shook his head miserably. "See what I'm saying?"

"Dan Louis! You hush and listen to me!" I ordered. "The very fact you'd even worry about something like that is ample proof you're a man of honor who'd never dream of doing such a thing.

"And while I acknowledge there is most definitely a certain delicious sugar daddy/babydoll facet to our love life at times, may I remind you—nothing happened until I was twenty-eight and you were nearly forty. Last I heard, that qualified us as consenting adults.

"And, honey. Did we ever consent!"

Dan gave a relieved laugh. "Oh, you can say that again, darlin'!"

"I'd be charmed to—consent, consent, consent . . ."

We were still consenting when the elevator bumped gently to a halt.

After the chaos of this afternoon, it was strange to find the lobby practically deserted. About the only people around were Charlotte's cameraman, Buddy Gaines, engaged in putting moves on a pretty desk clerk, and a few media types lounging near marble pedestals supporting outsize floral arrangements.

The reporters perked up a little when they saw us, but

their interest fizzled when we turned out not to be "anybody."

The Bay Lounge was tastefully nautical—not one coiled rope barstool, artfully draped fishnet, or bright plastic crustacean anywhere in sight.

Instead, rich mahogany, cordovan leather, Turkish rugs and highly polished ship's brass replicated the sitting room of a luxurious Victorian yacht.

At one end of the lounge, a quiet game of billiards was in progress beneath windows shaped like large portholes, which undoubtedly provided a magnificent daytime view of the Gulf.

At the other, the Shelby Bells awaited us in a curved, high-backed leather booth. "Well, don't you both look so *nice!*" Mrs. Shelby gushed mechanically, as her husband stood to shake hands.

"Greetings, my boy!" he thundered at Dan. "And your lovely little wife!" I did hope he wasn't planning to address me in the third person all night.

My feelings about Mr. Shelby were ambivalent. At first, I'd found him very appealing in a wide but solid, comfortable way. His baldness only served to enhance his particular type of masculine attraction.

However, it was difficult to have any meaningful exchange with him, due to his annoying tendency to boom unnecessarily, as if creating a kind of noise barrier to conceal some private agenda.

I reminded myself that Shelby Bell was a man who'd not only flown dangerous helicopter missions over Vietnam, but also made a fortune in three different areas—cattle, oil and real estate. It would be a mistake to forget the powerful intellect that lurked beneath the dancing bear.

As we slid into the booth, a waiter appeared and set an icebucket holding champagne into a stand within easy reach of Mr. Bell.

"Tinker and I are going to have some bubbly because it always cheers her up!" he announced heartily. "I hope you'll join us?"

I looked over at his spouse, whose bottom lip jutted out, her initial animation gone. She surely did need something.

When Dan and I agreed that champagne sounded fine, Shelby nodded at the waiter, who deftly popped open the Veuve Clicquot and poured. Out of habit, we hesitated politely with our full flutes, expecting one of the Bells to propose a toast, but Mrs. S.B. tossed hers back in a single gulp, and thrust out her glass for a refill before the waiter could get the bottle back into the bucket.

It was wonderful champagne. "The widow's champagne," I mused, and the other three looked at me uncomprehendingly. "*Veuve* means 'widow' in French," I explained, indicating the label on the bottle. "In 1805, Clicquot's twenty-seven year old widow took over the family vineyards, and her creative techniques revolutionized the wine industry. I always suspected she intended this fine champagne to celebrate old Clicquot's departure, without which she wouldn't have gotten her big chance!"

The Bells just stared at me blankly, and Dan pressed his lips together, trying not to laugh. I aimed a wife-to-husband look at him which meant, in any language, "Okay, smartass. Let's see you do better!"

Moodily, Mrs. Bell hoisted her replenished drink, taking more sedate sips this go-round. I noticed the ordinarily smooth, big brunette tresses were slightly mussed and flattened, and her face looked flushed. Somehow, it was getting easier to think of her as Tinker.

Finally, Mr. Bell took a deep breath and adjusted his heavy Cary Grant hornrims. "Well, I guess you folks saw all the commotion when you got here today."

"Bitch!" Tinker snarled, and lapsed into silence again.

Dan thought it was time to take the wheel. "Why don't I just tell you what we've heard, and you tell me if we heard it right,"Dan suggested. "Okay?"

"Fine," Shelby rumbled, and hastily poured himself another drink before Tinker could demand more.

The Bells slugged steadily away at the remaining champs, listening intently as Dan recapped Charlotte's information.

"Well, sugar. That's *fine*, far as it *goes*," was Tinker's assessment when both Dan and the Clicquot were done. If nothing else, drink had loosened her tongue. "But there's a *bunch* more to it!" She waggled her shapely finger at Dan. "See, I never really thought LaWanda was well, *passing*. But I did know for a solid gold fact she went down on one of the judges."

Tinker nodded in satisfaction at the effect her revelation produced. "Mind you, such things rarely happened way back then. In those days, a woman who got caught doing something shameful could not count on landing herself a big agent and a movie deal, I promise you!

"Anyway, even now, they'd never dare try that kind of shenanigan at Miss America. When I was in Atlantic City, us girls were constantly chaperoned, and good as *chained* to our mothers, or some old she-dragon of an official. And never, ever were we allowed in the same room alone with a M-A-N, precisely so nobody's mother could accuse somebody else's daughter of, say, exercising undue influence."

She chuckled reminiscently. "Listen. Just turn a bunch of those pageant mothers loose on Saddam Hussein, and I guarantee he will cease to be a problem!"

However, the near-paranoid policing of Miss America was not enforced at state and local pageant levels. Far from it. Blind eyes were knowingly turned. On both sides. Which partly accounted for what happened to LaWanda Jones.

"Entering beauty contests is an expensive proposition," Tinker admitted. "New formals, bathing suits, hair, makeup and whatnot every time you turn around.

"Now, suppose a girl happens to be from a hogdirt poor family who has sold granny's gold teeth because they're staking everything on her winning some title or other. At the very least, she'll certainly have better odds of finding a rich husband. Why, that girl might even get the idea it sure couldn't hurt to be, well, a little bit . . . *nice* to the judges."

Tinker shrugged. "Which is my roundabout way of leading up to that fateful Miss Palmetto contest. I just wanted you to know some of the background."

Miss Palmetto, she explained, was a pivotal regional competition on the way to becoming Miss Florida. "So at that point, you're starting to get the pick of the litter. Everybody knew it was going to be me or LaWanda.

"Well, I'd been hit on by judges before, of *course*, but they were all the kind you could just giggle and rap on the wrist with your fan, if you know what I mean." She demonstrated by fluttering her lashes and tittering, "Now you big *naughty* man! You are just *terrible*! I just *know* my friend Imogene's very own *daddy* would never bother me!"

Tinker resumed her normal voice. "Only it didn't work like that with this judge. He plainly told me I could kiss that Miss Palmetto crown goodbye if I didn't kiss his you-know-what? I looked him right in the eye and said I'd rather kiss a *frog* 'cause at least there was a fifty-fifty chance of *it* turning into a prince!"

Dan and I erupted into laughter, and Shelby grinned. Tinker looked gratified at the response, then picked up her narrative.

"Understand, there was a conspiracy of silence among the girls about judges like that. Oh, we warned each other who to watch out for, but agreed never to tell our parents. Because, if they even believed what we said, they might not let us enter any more contests! So, we figured we could handle these things ourselves.

"But I was worried because I sensed LaWanda was desperate enough to do anything—even that—to win. Only, I didn't have a clue as to what was driving her. At least, not then." Tinker toyed absently with her empty glass for a moment.

"Sure enough. LaWanda did The Number on him. I

know this because I watched through the keyhole until I had to run and throw up! And I couldn't tell anybody about it.

"What I did was repeat something I'd overheard my parents say. That LaWanda looked just like the actress, Susan Kohner, who played a girl who was passing in that movie, *Imitation of Life*."

Tinker gazed at us unblinkingly. "I know it was wrong. But I never in a million years expected they would dump her, I swear! Gosh, I was only a kid, and I was just so darn hurt and mad. I mean, those were the days you had to be a virgin to wear your *circle* pin on the left side. It was like a badge or something, and you couldn't lie or it would *rust* right in front of everybody! And here LaWanda got to be Miss Palmetto because she did *that*?"

She looked down at the table. "It was terrible what happened. Because it seems like other people had been quietly speculating about LaWanda, too. There was just that tiny *something* about her, you know? But nobody dared utter a word until I vented my spleen. Then honey, the place went up in smoke *that* fast!" She snapped her fingers. "That old fart like to have had a heart attack when the story got back to him!

"Next thing I know, I'm Miss Palmetto, and the *next* thing, LaWanda's accusing me of ruining her life, and all those famous lawyers are on her side. Well, I marched myself straight into that judge and told him if me or my family wound up going to court over this, I'd sure as God made fried grits call a press conference and tell the world what a disgusting pervert he was. Then I dropped the bombshell that I had personally eyewitnessed what he made LaWanda do to him."

Tinker heaved a sigh, clearly almost out of steam. "Also, I offered to return the Miss Palmetto title to LaWanda, seeing as how it was my big mouth that triggered the whole stinking mess in the first place. But she and her mama decided to grab the money and run. Which I don't blame them.

"Well, twenty-odd years and not one peep from LaWanda until last Tuesday night, when Shelby and me were greeting the pageant arrivals at the big welcome cocktail party. This fancy woman in Chanel and spooky eyeglasses slithers up and says, 'Well, Tinker. You haven't changed. Not even your hairstyle. I guess you don't remember me, though.'

"I look her head to toe and say, 'Well, LaWanda. So we meet again.' It was kinda like a weird dream, you know?

"And then she said, 'Tinker, my dear. Now you are going to pay.' "

CHAPTER 8

Red meat and red wine revived us all. Both were unexpectedly excellent, for the Bell Tower Restaurant menu ambiguously classified its fare as "continental cuisine."

"It's lots easier to surprise people with something way better than they thought they were going to get, than the opposite," Tinker explained her simple marketing strategy, tucking into a slice of butter-tender Châteaubriand with fervor.

Shelby, who had retrieved his personality en route between the Bay Lounge and the restaurant, began to expound. Not only was the beef served at all Bell Sands eating facilities completely free of growth hormones, but it was humanely raised and slaughtered. Plus, it was specially bred to contain the lowest possible fat content and still be edible. "If what we're eating now had any less fat, it would be a briefcase!" Shelby joked, with an elan befitting one of the richest men in three states.

The Bell Tower's burgundy, pink and green decor was vaguely Santa Barbara mission with a dash of mama mia;

Italian tiles, heavy dark oak, and murals featuring Spanish galleons, the ruins of Pompeii, ladies in mantillas and dandies on horses. Somehow, it worked. Our secluded banquette on the mezzanine level commanded a view of the whole dining room. Every table was taken, and the pleasant medley of laughter, conversation and scraping of silver on china, indicated a good time was being had by all.

Including those celebrities specially imported for Miss Gulf Coast. Seated around the largest, most conspicuous table, they were happily aware of being the center of attention. Fickle and vulnerable to every roll of politically correct dice they might be—even to the point of resigning as pageant judges or dropping out of the entertainment lineup—but tonight, while the situation was still in flux, they were enthusiastically availing themselves of Shelby and Tinker's free food.

Tinker observed the scene below with a sardonic expression. "Strange how it doesn't go against their so-called principles to continue to accept my hospitality!" Her dark eyes glittered. " *'He who has eaten my bread has lifted up his heel against me.'* " she intoned.

"Now, honey. It's going to be okay." Shelby patted his wife's beringed hand soothingly.

"You were quoting from the Psalms just now, weren't you Tinker?" Dan inquired.

"Any *real* Baptist can quote *anything* in the Bible," Tinker declared. "But I'm kinda surprised at you recognizing it. Aren't you guys Episcopalians or something?"

Dan laughed. "Last time we were in church, they did read from the Bible."

"Not the same thing," Tinker insisted.

When coffee and dessert arrived—chocolate bread pudding with chocolate custard sauce for Tinker ("Shoot, I'm not the one who's got to parade *my* fanny around in a bathing suit!"); apple pie for Shelby, creme brulee for Dan and mixed berries drenched in Grand Marnier for me—Shelby reached inside his coat pocket and produced two big cigars that glowed with a rich chestnut burnish. Wordlessly, he offered one to Dan, and laughed with gratification at his reaction.

"This is the real thing!" Dan exclaimed. "I almost hate to smoke it, Shelby."

Shelby Bell's colorless eyes sharpened behind the heavy glasses. "Nonsense, my boy. There are plenty more where these came from, and I'll see to it that you are amply supplied. Provided you and your pretty little wife here will help us out, that is."

"Oh, for heaven's sake, Shelby!" Tinker's shovelful of chocolate halted midway to her mouth, "The girl is *here*! Her name is *Claire*!"

Shelby smiled at me warmly. "I'm sorry, my dear," he apologized. "That's what comes from working mostly around oil and cattle men. Tell the truth, about the only ladies in my life are my wife and secretary."

I returned his smile. He really was an adorable Daddy Bear. Dan rolled the contraband cigar sensuously between his palms "Shelby, this smoke is just icing on the cake if you'll excuse the mixed metaphor. I'd already decided to offer any assistance I possibly could before you plied me with fine wine and Cuban tobacco."

The two men had begun performing the esoteric ritual dance of cigar lighting, when Tinker advised, "Maybe you better reserve your decision till you hear what we could be up against, Dan." She added to her husband, "Shelby, honey. You'd better get *on* with it?"

Shelby and Dan fired up and puffed ecstatically, causing a haze of illicit silver incense to rise and hang above our heads. I can't tolerate cigarettes under any conditions, but I love the smell of a good cigar.

After a moment, Shelby said, "I guess the quickest thing in the long run would be to tell you how we operate the Miss Gulf Coast pageant that makes it different, and we believe superior, to any other. Including Miss America."

Poor little JonBenet notwithstanding, both Bells were staunch defenders of beauty contests, opining they provided—in a unique way—access to many glamorous career opportunities perhaps not otherwise available.

"I, for one, am mighty tired of those feminists trying to get rid of beauty pageants because they're supposedly so demeaning to women," Tinker declared. "But it's okay if *they* demean women who don't agree with *them* on the subject?

"Shoot, I thought the whole point of getting liberated was about more choices, not less."

Which was not to say, she acknowledged, there wasn't plenty of room for improvement; witness her personal Miss Palmetto ordeal. That's why, a few years back, she decided to design her very own dream pageant.

While Miss Gulf Coast might not be the most traditional of beauty contests, it certainly sounded like the most fun.

And lucrative, for all concerned. Tinker made no bones about the pageant's objective, which was to give each participant her very best shot at money and fame.

And if the $20,000 entry fee sounded hefty, consider that it covered roundtrip business class airfare, ten days in a hotel mini-suite plus all meals, long distance telephone calls and FAX, alterations and drycleaning, beauty services and gratuities—just to name a few.

It also paid for a Broadway choreographer to rehearse them for dance routines they'd be performing on live national television with big name entertainers.

Additionally, every contestant was guaranteed to be seen by more famous people over a period of several days than she could ever hope to audition for in years.

Compare twenty grand with the cost of renting an apartment in Los Angeles or New York, then spending months of heartbreaking pavement pounding, trying to get in to see even a handful of those decision makers who'd be at Miss Gulf Coast, and it was cheap at the price.

A wide variety of sponsors—airlines and automobile manufacturers, cosmetic companies, and designers of everything from swimwear, sportswear and evening gowns to sunglasses—bought television advertising, paid substantial promotional fees, and supplied complimentary products, which helped underwrite additional expenses like first-class flights for the celebrity judges and star entertainers.

Then there were impressive cash prizes for the three big winners. Miss Gulf Coast's share alone was $100,000 and a luxury car. "And we're not talking some sad little hatchback," Tinker said, turning up her nose. "This year, it's a Jaguar!"

Even with such high overhead, Shelby revealed that Miss Gulf Coast had turned a larger profit each year. Which meant things could only get bigger and better as their audience grew. "In fact, Dan," he remarked casually, "I'd like to get your thoughts about our expansion plans. We're contemplating adding the titles of Miss Atlantic Coast and Miss Pacific Coast, and franchising all three under the banner of Tri-Coastal Pageants, Inc."

Dan laughed. "Sounds interesting, Shelby. But let's take one thing at a time, shall we? I still don't quite know what precipitated your current crisis."

"Fair enough," Shelby conceded. "Tinker, honey. Why don't you fill in the rest of the background?"

His wife's eyes had regained much of their customary sparkle. "Well, as you can see, Miss Gulf Coast is a completely different kind of pageant. For example, instead of emphasizing the competitive angle, we like our girls to treat this more like a vacation at some fun resort!"

To that end, the Bells removed as much stress as possible by conducting the most important phase—the interview—on the very first day of judging, following a week of rehearsals, costume fittings and local publicity appearances. Any contestant eliminated at that point was informed immediately. The same held true for each subsequent phase, rather than keep anyone in suspense.

However, as Tinker expressed it, "There's no such thing as a loser at Miss Gulf Coast. We refer to them as, 'non-contenders'."

Though non-contenders were out of the running for the crown, they retained all their rights and privileges, and still participated in every competitive event, "so they won't feel left out," and lots of the dance numbers.

Moreover, they would also get to appear in evening gowns and bathing suits—along with the ten finalists—on the night of the television broadcast, thus ensuring everybody had an equal shot at any modeling contracts that might be up for grabs.

But best of all, each non-contender got to perform her talent solo in front of a live audience which was, in Tinker's words, "just crawling" with celebrities and showbiz types.

"Only now, since most of the pressure's off, they'll probably do better than some of the finalists," Tinker said. "Why, two of last year's non-contenders wound up as regulars on a soap."

Of course, only the ten contenders would perform their talent portion on the live television broadcast.

It sounded to me like the Bells had created the closest thing to a perfect world for their pageant.

But Chessy Scarborough had caused trouble in paradise, right away.

Again, Tinker had broken pageant tradition by restructuring the way interviews were handled. Instead of trotting those poor girls, one by one, into a roomful of people like lambs to the slaughter, she'd created a more intimate atmosphere, designating two judges to one contestant at a time.

The Miss Gulf Coast charter stipulated a minimum of eight judges, instead of the usual seven. Because, in Tinker's opinion, the possibility of a tie only made things more interesting. This year, there happened to be two honorary celebrity judges, as well.

"Since we had thirty contestants, that meant each pair of judges was assigned six girls apiece to talk to on Monday," Tinker said.

"Which finally brings us to what happened." Shelby sighed, not sounding quite so relaxed as he had. "The two honorary judges Tinker mentioned are Franny and Freddy Franks, the husband and wife comedy team. They're also headlining as entertainers.

"However, each had been matched up with someone else for the interviews. Franny was paired with me."

"Franny's one of my favorites," I said.

"Ours, too," Shelby replied. "And a delightful woman. But very unhappy, just now." He signaled for fresh coffee.

"I'd say that's putting it mildly," Tinker drawled. "Unfortunately, we hadn't tuned into *Hard Copy* lately, or we'd have been better prepared.

"Just before Franny and Shelby were supposed to interview Chessy Scarborough, Franny excused herself to go to the bathroom. Next thing anybody knows, she and Freddy are having themselves a big old screaming match in the hospitality area, which is conveniently located outside the gentlemen's and ladies' lounges. So naturally, the maximum number of people witnessed their brawl."

We fell silent until the waiter finished pouring our coffee, then Shelby took up the tale.

"Freddy seemed none the worse for wear afterward, because he joined his assigned partner for their next interview. But Franny was completely unable to continue, and went up to her room.

"Certainly I was very concerned about Franny, but otherwise I didn't give her absence a second thought. We were on a tight schedule, and the interview had to take place right then."

He puffed pensively on his cigar, frowning. "I had no way of knowing what a terrible mistake I was about to make."

Tinker explained that each of the six interview rooms were equipped with a tripod-mounted video camera. The hotel employed a part-time audio visual guy named Jimmy, who handled rudimentary taping for various events.

For Miss Gulf Coast interviews, Jimmy would focus the lens on the woman's head and shoulders, lock the camera into place, and go on to set up the next subject.

"After that, it just runs automatically until Jimmy comes back and turns the thing off," Tinker said. "I suppose a chimpanzee could do just as well. And the one time a human witness would've come in handy, he was somewhere else."

Dan and I exchanged intrigued glances. This was beginning to sound interesting.

But Shelby seemed loath to continue, until Tinker prodded, "Oh, go on and *tell* them, honey!"

Her husband ran a big, blunt hand over his slick dome. "I still can't believe what happened. Jimmy had already adjusted the camera to Chessy, and was just leaving when I walked into the room. Out of habit, Jimmy closed the door behind him.

"I re-introduced myself to Chessy," Shelby continued, looking down at the table, "and explained that Mrs. Franks was unable to join us. And then, thank God, something told me to offer her the opportunity to be interviewed by another couple. But she said no, this was fine with her."

So Shelby had begun the interview. But gradually, he realized that while Chessy was responding to his questions, she was staring at him in a very strange way. Without knowing why, he became extremely uneasy.

And then, it happened.

"She flashed me!" he muttered.

Dan was incredulous. "You mean—?"

"Shot him the squirrel, as we used to say in Pensacola," Tinker clarified, succinctly.

Shelby took off his glasses and rubbed his eyes, as if to erase the image. "It was just like that scene in *Basic Instinct*. Only Chessy remained absolutely frozen-faced. Just by watching the video, you'd never guess what was going on . . . down below."

A tide of emotion surged across his face, outrage mingled with disbelief and a touch of hilarity. "Then, she did it again. And a third time!"

"Well, what did *you* do?" Dan inquired, interestedly.

Shelby had pulled out a white handkerchief and was patting his face. "I didn't refer to the incident," he replied. "In fact, I didn't speak to her at all."

"That's because he was totally incapable of speech!" Tinker giggled.

Shelby gave her a cross look, then continued. "I stood, opened the door, and walked out."

"Very wise," Dan approved. "Anybody see you?"

With a shrug, Shelby said, "I don't know. There were a few people in the hospitality area, but I was too upset to notice who." He wrinkled his brow. "Now that I think about it, though, LaWanda Jones—Scarborough, rather—was having coffee with Brandon Battle."

"How convenient," Dan commented. "Did either of you mention to anybody at all what Chessy had done?"

"Hell, no!" Shelby exclaimed. Tinker also denied it, saying at first, she'd thought it was a hoot, but not one she cared to have get around.

"Now, remember," Tinker added, "that happened on Monday. Tuesday morning—which was yesterday—all the judges watched all the taped interviews, then we started thrashing it out.

"Not a pretty sight, let me tell you, Because after a week of being around these women, that's when our impressions and preferences are the most raw and honest."

Shelby said, "The point is, Dan, no matter who else the judges argued over yesterday morning, just about everybody but Freddy Franks took an instant dislike to Chessy Scarborough!

"Which is a mystery, since they couldn't have known what happened. Because, when you compare her looks to the others, she is probably the most classically beautiful of them all."

Tinker put in. "Mind you, neither of us had a clue Chessy Scarborough was LaWanda's daughter. I still thought of her as LaWanda Jones."

Dan had let his cigar go out and was studying the Bells,

chin propped on folded hands. "Now, I find that real difficult to believe, Tinker. A woman from your past turns up out of the blue, threatens you right under your own roof, and you don't make it your immediate business to find out why she's here?"

She flushed. "But I did. After the cocktail party last Tuesday night, I asked Parker to check on her first thing the next morning. But whether you understand this or not, I was so busy these last few days, I nearly forgot about LaWanda." Tinker shrugged. "Apparently, Parker did."

Shelby contemplated the glowing stump of his cigar and eloquently said nothing.

Tinker raised her brows. "Well, honey. He's *your* nephew."

Dan looked puzzled. "Wait a minute. When Parker Bell played for Ole Miss, everybody said he was bound for the pros. Suddenly, he quits school and drops out. Now, years later, I stumble over him here. He turns out to be your nephew, Shelby, manager of a big resort hotel. And yet you're both implying he's basically incompetent."

"Dan, of course Parker's not *the* manager," Shelby said. "We gave him a manager title because, well . . . it makes him feel more important." Grinding his cigar butt into the ashtray, he added, "Parker's not even really my nephew. He's the stepson of my widowed brother Kenneth, who died a few years back. I promised him I'd look after Parker, and I have,"

Shelby sighed. "Poor boy. He got off to a bad start. His daddy was killed in a hunting accident when Parker was no more then five or six years old. He was about twelve when my brother married Alva, his mother."

Which had been a disaster. Apparently, Alva was a honkytonk girl who ran around on Kenneth with some brutal characters. Not too surprisingly, she ended up gunned down in a barroom brawl.

"As you've probably guessed," Shelby said, "Parker got into some pretty bad trouble at Ole Miss. He and another football player fought over some girl, and Parker injured him . . . severely. Really, the school had no choice but to expel him. I don't think he's ever forgiven himself for wrecking what might've turned out to be a great career. He can't bear to be reminded of those glory days."

Dan shook his head. "What a shame. Now I understand why he acted so strange when I told him I recognized him."

Shelby went on. "Well, after he left Ole Miss, I got a friend of mine in Jackson who owns an electronics manufacturing plant to hire him, strictly as a favor to me, but Parker actually worked out fine and stayed there for several years. After Kenneth's funeral though, he seemed at a loose end. We happened to need somebody to manage the gym for insurance purposes, so I offered Parker the job, which turned out to be perfect for him. He knows all about the latest exercise equipment, and he can also show the guests how to use the machines if need be."

Tinker nodded, "Plus, he's real good when it comes to catering to celebrities, like delivering flowers and champagne and all to their rooms. Frankly, it looks more impressive for the hotel when he does it instead of some little waiter or bellboy. And a guy his size is mighty handy to have available when we need some extra security. He does so love to roam around with that walkie-talkie of his!"

Shelby spread his hands. "I guess every family's got at least one special case, but what can you do? Obviously though, he was not the right person to entrust with Tinker's errand to get information about LaWanda."

"It seemed a simple enough task to me at the time," Tinker snapped.

We declined a half-hearted offer of more coffee. Clearly, our hosts were ready to call it a night. Dan requested contract samples, and any other information they considered relevant, delivered to our room, then we took our leave.

Once outside the Bell Tower, we could hear the thump of a live band somewhere in the distance.

"Feel like dancing, baby?" Dan invited. "I wouldn't mind showing you off in that little brown dress."

Following the music to its source, we arrived at the Beach Club, which was seeing big action. We love to dance together and squeezed onto the crowded floor, boogying every number until the band took a break.

Buddy Gaines hailed us from the bar, and surrendered his stool to me. "Just to prove I'm a real Southern gent, no matter what lies Charlotte's told you!" he declared with a grin, and turned to go.

"Stick around, Buddy," Dan urged. "Let me buy you a drink."

Buddy shook his head. "Ain't no point, Danbo. Things are strictly water, water, everywhere and not a drop to drink. Or in this case, beautiful girls everywhere—" he waved a hand around the room "—and they all got mammas watching 'em like hawks.

"A man can only take just so much. I shall now retire to my room to watch *The Rockford Files*."

After Buddy's departure, Dan ordered a Remy Martin, which we shared while watching some of the celebrities carrying on. When the band started up again, Dan drew me back onto the floor.

It was a set of slow oldies this time. Somewhere around Peaches and Herb getting reunited, the big pin popped out of my hair, and it tumbled down onto my shoulders. Dan pulled my head against his chest and hummed softly along with the music as we danced. Suddenly, another couple crashed into us—hard—knocking us apart.

The woman staggered right into Dan's arms, while the man, who seemed as startled as we were, apologized.

It was Brandon Battle, and he'd been dancing with Chessy Scarborough. And when I saw how she was mashing herself against Dan, I knew she'd choreographed the whole thing.

"Oh, my goodness! I'm so sorry!" Chessy exclaimed. Then glanced at me over her shoulder, smiling coldly.

She knew I knew.

And she didn't care.

CHAPTER 9

The Bell Sands gym, the Bar Bell, was large, well-equipped and already jumping when I arrived a little after ten o'clock the next morning. Those Miss Gulf Coast contestants certainly took the "physical fitness" phase seriously.

Almost every machine was occupied by a gorgeous female grimly determined to hone her already fabulous body to impossible perfection.

A few equally dedicated males focused entirely on their bench presses, but the other guys swaggered around, trying to look macho in their weight belts, pretending to do power sets while checking out the ladies. Parker Bell was one of the latter, seeming mesmerized by the hard-pedaling womanflesh astride a long row of LifeCyles, while butter-flying a hundred seventy-five pounds with little effort. I realized there was still plenty of brawn beneath his surface layer of softness.

A step class I could hear revving up in the next room sounded appealing, until I spotted three of those new super treadmill machines positioned in front of the tripleglazed (and laminated to prevent shattering, Tinker had assured us) plate glass windows looking onto the ocean. One was vacant, and I made a beeline for it before anyone else could climb aboard.

From my window, a slice of the marina was visible, and I caught a glimpse of two people trying to haul down a wind-crazed mainsail. Meanwhile, the Gulf erupted with breakers far as the eye could see, and the sky was dark.

This morning on the news, our friend, the weatherman, had announced a storm warning from Key West to Morgan City, Louisiana, pointing anxiously to a considerably larger blob on the satellite picture. While tropical disturbance Babe had been dithering between the Atlantic, Caribbean and the Gulf of Mexico, she had definitely put on weight.

A flock of seagulls swooped past the window and landed at the edge of the frothing surf, staring intently out to sea as if waiting for something. Maybe they already knew what Babe had decided to do.

There was printed information in all the hotel rooms about evacuation procedures should they become necessary, but in recent hurricanes, because of its structural superiority, the Bell Sands had actually been used as a shelter, despite its proximity to the water. For that matter, if Babe did come our way, the only effective escape routes would be to the north. Even then, you'd have to travel considerably inland for it to make a lick of difference, since there's not anything that could remotely be defined as "higher ground" much before Lucedale.

Only the seriously stupid insist on throwing boozy hurricane parties and drunkenly defying powerful natural forces—like those poor idiots during Hurricane Camille back in 1969 when the tides were twenty feet over normal and two hundred and fifty-six people died that didn't have to—but sometimes it's safer to stay put and keep a prayerful vigil. In which case, you've got to stake your life that your contractor and building inspector didn't rip you off.

The Bell Sands emergency information sheet boasted the entire community of Crestview Cove was built to exceed the highest specifications, not just for hurricanes, but fires and earthquakes. Probably only a Los Angeles real estate developer would've thought to include the latter contingency.

I picked up my pace on the treadmill slightly, pondering the situation Dan and I had walked into. Aside from the possibility of riding out a hurricane, that is.

Certainly, we believed Shelby and Tinker's story. So, when she heard it, would Charlotte, giving her a big jump on the other reporters if this thing hit the fan. As Chessy Scarborough, aided and abetted by her mother, the former LaWanda Jones, and attorney Brandon Battle, seemed bound and determined it would.

While I could appreciate the poetry of LaWanda taking sweet revenge against Tinker by using Chessy to wreck the pageant, why had she waited until this year? Miss Gulf Coast had been around for five, and Tinker T. Bell was well known to be its driving force.

According to Shelby, Miss Tampa Tangerine was just the latest in Chessy Scarborough's long line of titles. She could have participated in any previous Miss Gulf Coast. Anyway, a contestant didn't have to hold a previous title to make her eligible for this pageant, provided she was at least 18, paid the $20,000 entry fee, and was a bona fide resident of any officially recognized Gulf Coast community between Galveston and the Florida Keys.

The most likely answer as to why LaWanda hadn't acted before now, was that she'd simply bided her time until Tinker's beauty pageant became important enough to destroy.

Brandon Battle's presence was clear warning she had no intention of stopping at a mere eye for an eye. For example, they couldn't possibly have known ahead of time that Franny and Freddy Franks would have a bitter fight which resulted in Shelby and Chessy ending up in a room alone together, but Battle instantly recognized the ammunition that unfortunate, nasty little twist of fate had provided them with.

Nor could they have anticipated her getting knocked out of the running in the first round, yet Battle immediately produced an ace (of spades, as it were) in the hole—Chessy's weensy little drop of African blood.

Obviously, this trio was totally prepared to meet any contingency.

Wily old B.B. was certainly living up to his dubious reputation. In twenty-four hours, he had skillfully wielded legal smoke and mirrors to distort every circumstance into reflecting racial discrimination and sexual harassment against Chessy, and play up Tinker's sorry history with LaWanda.

Following that unwanted close encounter with B.B. and Chessy last night, Dan and I had abandoned the Beach Club for the sanctuary of our suite, only to find a large manilla envelope of Miss Gulf Coast materials propped against the door.

One of the items was a video cassette of last year's pageant. Out of curiosity, we'd postponed our intended soak *a deux* in the giant bathtub to watch it.

As Tinker had promised, Miss Gulf Coast was indeed the most fun and entertaining of all beauty contests. And we were both pleasantly surprised at the program's high production values and slick direction.

If LaWanda and company got their way, Miss Gulf Coast would be ruined. Not just this year, but forever. The Bell Sands Resort could become the Southern equivalent of the Helmsley Palace, and Tinker's final crown, the new Queen of Mean.

I was momentarily diverted by the thought of Jaclyn Smith playing Tinker Bell in the miniseries.

Long after I'd fallen asleep last night, Dan had pored over the sample of pageant entry forms and contracts with a fine-tooth comb, jealously nursing the last of his genuine Cuban stogie like a hobo eking out a salvaged cigarette butt.

Over breakfast this morning, he'd informed me that Miss Gulf Coast was uniquely discrimination-free; not even a race box to check on the preliminary application!

And though there was a minimum age of 18, the pageant imposed no maximum. If some sixty-year-old lady felt like strutting whatever stuff she had left, she was entirely welcome to do so.

The only rigid requirements, beyond minimum age,

were proof of Gulf Coast residence and pre-payment of the entry fee.

Without question, Brandon Battle had also thoroughly studied the same documents, and knew that the greenest law student could prove "no cause" to any charge of discrimination.

So what other approach would he be likely to try?

"Obviously, since there isn't an iota of truth to any of this, he intends to keep threatening the Bells with every permutation of nuisance suit, hoping to get them to offer a big settlement to avoid going to court," Dan said, gazing out at the sky and water, which looked like one solid sheet of ominous steel grey.

"I expect next he'll try to prove a quota violation. But if he can't, well, he just might be able to claim a lack of equal opportunity. He could allege that an African-American woman would not have an equal opportunity to pay the $20,000 entry fee."

"But, that's crazy!" I objected. "Chessy *did* come up with it. If I were African-American, I'd be terribly insulted. And for that matter, what about all the poor white girls who couldn't come up with the entry fee? How are they different?"

"Calm down, darlin'," Dan advised. "I'm just telling you what he *could* do, what there's legal precedent for.

"He could even file a class action on behalf of all those other African-American girls—eighteen and older, legal residents of a Gulf Coast community—who couldn't have afforded to enter if they had wanted to. A charge like that could take years to fight, and run into millions of dollars."

"Even if it's not true?"

Dan nodded. "And, are you aware that you white girls are different since you automatically have more access to sources for such funds, *because* you're white?"

I told Dan I'd never make a lawyer because I couldn't relate to such convoluted thinking. He replied soberly that unconscionable abuses—by both sides—opened Pandora's box and unleashed the current flimflam practices that had so quickly eroded the original noble intent of equal opportunity.

"The tangled mess we've got now makes it criminally easy for shysters like Battle to slide in and use the confusion for their own gain, which has basically undermined many valid cases. Again, on both sides.

"Look, the exact same thing's happening with sexual harassment," Dan pointed out. "Women with real problems are suffering because of dishonest opportunists who jumped on the latest legal gravy train,"

He laughed grimly. "Here, we've got both issues. And God forbid this thing goes to court, because I warn you, Claire—it will get very, very ugly.

"The perception of a rich, white Louisiana lawyer, defending rich, white clients against accusations of racial discrimination and sexual harassment by a beautiful girl of color? Please!"

Dan had then spoken long distance to Foley Callant— who'd just gotten back from New Orleans from Lake Charles—giving him the rundown. Foley is Blanchard, Smithson, Callant & Claiborne's labor relations expert. He was intrigued by the simmering situation, and briefed Dan as to some things the Bells could do to protect their legal position if a chunk of their staff went on strike on Chessy's behalf.

When Dan casually mentioned that Charlotte Dalton was here, Foley said, "Whaddya know, I just happen to have a few days free! Maybe it would be better if I were on hand, in case anything blows. Don't tell Charlotte, though. I want to surprise her!"

Foley and Charlotte, our two best friends, were madly in love, but it had been a rocky road. Charlotte was still reeling from the wonder of finding the right man after a string of disasters, while Foley attempted to extricate himself from the financial complexities surrounding his divorce from the flighty Belinda.

What's more, they were going the abstinence route, Charlotte having decided every woman deserved to have at least one honest-to-God Wedding Night in her lifetime.

"How do you plan to arrive?" Dan had questioned. "By submarine? I seriously doubt the airport's going to be operating by the end of the day and I understand Highway 90's in gridlock."

"Hey, you need me, bubba!" Foley said. "This sounds just like the kind of thing that could get Leighton to tearing his hair out!" He chuckled mischievously. Leighton Blanchard, the most senior partner of the law firm, always claimed he wanted to be on the frontier of the "New South," but invariably went into a tizzy every time an unconventional situation arose.

Foley had signed off with, "Besides, I need to see my woman. I'll get there. Believe it!"

Now I smiled, thinking of how happy Charlotte would be to see Foley so unexpectedly.

Suddenly, my mind veered back to the distasteful subject of Chessy Scarborough, and I realized there was a question no one had yet asked.

Since Chessy didn't know ahead of time she'd wind up alone with Shelby, how come she arrived prepared to do a Sharon Stone impression on the spur of the moment?

CHAPTER 10

"Hello? Hel*lo*! You gonna walk to Mexico on that thing, or what?"

An irritable, unpleasant, and oddly familiar voice seeped into my consciousness, distracting me from an equally unpleasant memory of Chessy Scarborough's triumphant smirk after she'd hurled herself into Dan last night.

The front of my pink leotard was drenched, and no wonder. Blinking red numerals on the display screen informed me I'd traveled nearly ten miles.

A moment later, I realized the hostile voice had actually been addressing me. Freddy Franks, ostentatiously Hilfigered for working out, was standing to the left of my treadmill.

The comedian's coarsely attractive face bore no traces of levity as he scowled at me. "Yeah, I'm talking to you, Miss Sweetcheeks!" he snapped. "That's my treadmill."

Freddy ignored my pointed glance at the two other identical treadmills, both now vacant. He shook his head. "No. I specifically ordered that fat cracker in charge to have this treadmill available for me at exactly 10:30 every morning. Which it now is."

He thrust a diamond-weighted Rolex beneath my nose for verification, adding, *"This* treadmill. The other two've got the wrong *feng shuei."*

In fact, I was more than ready to get off, but his attitude made me want to act perverse.

"Not the wrong *feng shuei!"* I gasped, in mock horror. "Quick, somebody! Call 911!"

A pair of nearby gymbunnies giggled, and Freddy grimaced angrily. Some comedians have no sense of humor.

Just then, Parker Bell came bustling up. "What's the problem, Mr. Franks?" he asked, obsequiously.

"Whaddya think's the problem?" Freddy barked. "I tell you I gotta have this machine at 10:30 because I'm on strict circuit training. You guarantee me priority. Okay. It's 10:30. But the person on my machine is not me. Ergo, *you* are the problem, pal." Parker's naturally pink complexion suffused with red. I doubt whether he knew what ergo meant, but he definitely realized he'd been insulted by one of his beloved celebrities.

I couldn't help but feel sorry for him. No reason Parker should pay for my baiting Freddy Franks. Switching off the power, I said sweetly, "There's really no problem at all, Parker. Why, I wouldn't dream of disrupting Mr. Franks' *feng shuei!"*

Parker said, "Huh?" And Freddy glared as I dismounted the treadmill.

I crossed over to the mat area and began concentrating on some floor stretches, while Freddy boarded "his" machine. Evidently, he felt the need to somehow justify his bad behavior.

"My personal trainer in L.A. says it's critical to program your body timewise, like a clock," he confided loudly to a couple of impressed females. "My routine never varies. Three times a day, it's five minutes on the treadmill, fifty prone quad presses, fifty pec flies, fifty lat pulls . . . hack squats . . ."

I tuned him out, wondering why certain celebrities consider it their privilege to throw childish tantrums in public when they have to wait more than ten seconds for anything, be it a ski lift, restaurant table, or piece of gym equipment.

Due to the recent, unusually steady popularity of New Orleans as a movie location, Dan and I have met several stars, With a few notable exceptions, that old adage, "The bigger they are, the nicer they are," holds true.

Freddy Franks could not be defined as big. Medium, maybe. And that was mainly thanks to his wife, Francesca.

Because of their offbeat routines featuring a sincere, traditional Italian-American wife and mother, encountering the nightmare nineties, while coping with her terminally-hip, Jewish husband, the pair had been billed as, "The New Stiller and Meara."

But it was Franny who had achieved cult heroine status among American women who totally identified with her depiction of a natural-born, contented, slightly wacky housewife, variously harangued by her *uber* feminist friend, Rena, her apparently demon-possessed teenaged son and daughter, and a husband desperately clutching at any flot-sam of youth to keep him from sinking in his midlife crisis.

The bit they'd done on Jay Leno—where to please Freddy, who keeps nagging her to dress younger and sexier, Franny bravely buys an extremely short, lowcut black dress and major Wonderbra for the big, important party he has wangled an invitation to, but when she appears in the slinky outfit, looking great and ready to go, Freddy jealously refuses to allow her to leave the house—had given them a huge boost up the perilous comedy ladder.

Initially, Shelby and Tinker were delighted when the Franks agreed to perform on all three nights of the talent show.

Again, Miss Gulf Coast had crossed new pageant frontiers by making the most potentially embarrassing aspect of such contests relatively comfortable and enjoyable for all concerned. Each set of ten amateur acts would be substantially cushioned throughout by star entertainers.

This year's lineup featured a hot, male country singer; a rising Latino rock band; a nouveau-retro dance duo, *à la* Brascia & Tybee; a trendy ventriloquist; a perennial female vocalist; and the comedy stylings of Franny and Freddy Franks.

But, as Tinker explained, despite one critic's assessment that Freddy's solo act was, "like Don Rickles, without the love," Freddy's attitude indicated that he considered Franny's contribution merely incidental to his personal success. And, seemed to suffer delusions of equality with Billy Crystal.

Because, upon learning that a certain comic, famous for

the ability to ad-lib on his feet, was hosting the pageant, Freddy had demanded that he be given the emcee role instead, threatening to pull himself and Franny out of the show entirely if he didn't get his way.

Evidently, cooler heads—not to mention lawyers and agents—prevailed, because here they both were at the Bell Sands.

Or at least, here Freddy was. I hadn't yet caught a glimpse of Franny, but I'd already seen way too much of Freddy.

And I was about to see even more.

Freddy, having finished the required five minutes on the treadmill of contention, began his prone quad presses on a weight machine directly opposite the floor mats.

I was in the middle of a wide-straddle ankle-grab, pressing my torso forward and down, when Freddy caught sight of me. He did an exaggerated double take. "Whoa! You're little, but you sure are stacked! ... ten, eleven, twelve ... Wanna come up to my room and stretch out like that where it'll do us both some good? ... seventeen, eighteen, nineteen ..."

He didn't bother to lower his rasping voice, and I was mortified because quite a few people overheard.

But somebody else had heard him, too.

Dan, who'd just arrived for our scheduled workout together, a little later than he'd intended.

He was seething as he reached down to give me a hand up from the mats, but managed to control his anger long enough to walk over to the machine where Freddy was lying and say quietly, "Please apologize to my wife."

". . . thirty-five, thirty-six . . ." Freddy, engrossed in quad presses, barely bothered to glance up. "That your wife? . . . forty, forty-one . . . Hey, I'da never guessed!" Then he added, very suggestively, "Aren't you kinda big to be playing with dolls? . . . forty-five, forty-six . . . shit! What the hell are you doing?"

This in response to the additional twenty-five pound steel donut Dan had slipped onto the right side of Freddy's stack. As Freddy struggled to push up the unexpected extra load, Dan added another twenty-five pounds to the left side. "I don't know how you're accustomed to addressing the ladies of Los Angeles, Mr. Franks. But we don't talk to our women that way here. Especially other men's wives."

Casually, Dan stuck ten more pounds onto the right side, forcing Freddy's knees practically into his throat.

This particular machine was one of the older, standard models, which required the weight bearing bar to be elevated high enough to slip back into its notch before a user could withdraw.

Cursing and purple-faced, Freddy had just barely managed to heave the bar back up, when Dan shoved on ten more.

Once again, Freddy found himself folded like a stack of laundry. "I'll sue you, you bastard!" he wheezed.

"Be my guest," Dan invited, with a grin. "Oh, wait. Did I mention I'm an attorney?"

I could see Freddy's quads shaking like pine needles in a strong wind, but he was unwilling to plead for mercy before a gymful of macho men and strength-training women.

Fortunately for his fragile ego, due to the rock music blaring from the step class, plus the hum of multiple machines and clanking of weights—only a few were actually aware that Freddy and Dan were having a moment. Parker Bell, who'd immediately recognized the situation, was wisely staying out of it.

Dan gazed down at the immobilized Freddy. "Now. About that apology?" he suggested, thoughtfully toying with a shiny metal disk emblazoned with a big "20."

"Okay! Okay!" Freddy gasped. "I'm sorry, man. Really!"

"That's more like it," Dan approved. Effortlessly, he slid several heavy weights from either side of the bar at once, releasing the pressure so suddenly that Freddy was caught off- guard, and nearly toppled backward into a reverse somersault.

Dan turned to me, looking a little sheepish. "I hope I didn't embarrass you too much, darlin'. But I just saw red. Guess I'm still an unenlightened caveman at heart, after all!"

"Personally, I'm thrilled to bring out the Jurassic in you," I assured him, stroking his tense forearm. "It's not every girl's got her own great big old Danosaurus galloping to the rescue."

"Well, thanks for making it sound so good, Claire." He took a deep breath and smiled wryly. "After that little episode, I need a workout worse than I did before."

I spotted for Dan through a series of bench presses. As he began a set of shoulder flies, I noticed that Freddy had recovered sufficient aplomb to start on his fifty lat pulls.

A beautiful woman stood in front of the comic, watching him haul the cable up and down.

The two were engaged in deep discussion, but Freddy's strident, trademark whine was conspicuously inaudible. Nor was there the slightest hint of his usual suggestive leer when he looked up at her.

Instead, the arrogant Freddy Franks looked almost humble and pleading as he spoke softly and urgently to Chessy Scarborough.

CHAPTER 11

If you have a rich and/or sexy husband some woman will, at some point, try to take him away from you.

Dan and I were married—the first time—barely three weeks after we met. It had been Mutant Ninja lust at first sight, which finally ran out of steam after a feverish seven months during which we did nothing but party and screw ourselves silly. When the novelty wore off, neither of us had known how to take our relationship into the next phase. We were both too scared of what might happen if we started talking about it. Which inevitably paved the way for the absolute worst to happen.

One terrible night at a party, Dan had too much to drink and I stumbled over him and a Tulane cheerleader in the bushes, That same night I suffered a miscarriage. I hadn't even known I was pregnant. It was a very sobering time, and Dan told me later he had felt like he would die of shame.

After the divorce, we discovered not only was the physical desire still intense, but we really did love each other. So Dan and I committed ourselves to four abstemious months (made barely tolerable by prolonged sessions of very heavy necking and even heavier phone sex, much of it at transatlantic rates) to give us the chance to focus on learning as much about each other as we could.

As a result, we became wonderful friends who could discuss (or argue) any subject, co-designers of Eclaire, and partners in crime when people we knew started getting murdered. Then, at long last, we had celebrated with a beautiful formal church ceremony, a blowout reception with two bands, and consummated with a Wedding Night.

The point I'm trying to make is, that Dan, while exuding luscious masculinity, also has such an aura of power and authority—and, because of what we've been through, sends such a definite message of total unavailability—the ordinary adulteress is too intimidated to put a move on him.

But the sight of Dan in cropped tank top and gym shorts is heartstopping. And Chessy Scarborough was no ordinary adulteress.

This had been our first workout together in months, and I'd found the combined forces of sweat, rock music, and Dan's muscular thighs and arms pumping iron, intensely erotic.

So much so, that I made a suggestion he felt compelled to take me up on right away.

But Chessy stepped quickly in front of us as we hurried from the gym, effectively blocking our exit.

"I just wanted to apologize again for bumping into you last night," Chessy told Dan. Me, she ignored completely.

Tall, poised and confident in black and red Spandex, she could've been an athletic vampire. Tendrils of glossy black hair had escaped their ponytail to frame a dead white face, in which her lips gleamed a bloody crimson.

Chessy continued, "But what I'm more sorry about than anything else is that we didn't just go ahead and keep on dancing together while we were at it. You see," her gaze roamed speculatively over Dan's broad body, its fur damply matted with exertion, "I'm a professional dancer, and I really like the way you move."

Very deliberately, Dan cupped his big hand around the back of my neck and returned politely, "Why, thank you. I love to dance . . . with my wife." He looked down at me with a fatuous smile. "Isn't that right, baby?" One blue eye closed in a mischievous wink.

I gazed adoringly up at him and gurgled, Stepford-like, "Oh! Yes, darling!"

Chessy realized we were needling her and didn't like it one bit. The red lips thinned angrily and she let those enormous dark eyes, nearly on a level with Dan's, drop and linger challengingly below his elastic waistband.

"Perhaps you'd find it threatening to . . . partner a woman who doesn't have to stand on your shoes to . . . um, line up?"

First Freddy, now Chessy! I was getting mighty tired of these innuendoes about my size. I'm five-two, but you'd think I was some kind of midget.

Before Dan could reply, I snarled, "Perhaps you'd find it threatening to get a bikini wax. Without the . . . um, wax?"

Dan threw me a surprised look, then broke into a huge belly laugh.

I couldn't believe Chessy had really expected Dan to

immediately plop into her greedy hands like a big old ripe, juicy plum. Which he most definitely was, but not hers. Mine.

Looking outraged, Chessy quickly sidled away from us, straight into the willing arms of Parker Bell. This time, her move hadn't been premeditated.

"Oh, Parker!" Chessy welcomed the face-saving encounter with an enthusiasm the poor guy was plainly unaccustomed to receiving from her. "I need your help!"

Parker Bell frowned at us. "You okay, Chessy?" he growled protectively.

Chessy tossed her ponytail and cooed, "I am . . . now. Parker, sweetie. Will you spot me on a butterfly superset?"

We left her squeezing her cleavage at Parker on the pec machine, obviously getting a kick from tantalizing him with the thrust and swell of snowy flesh.

Back in our suite, Dan was still laughing about my threat to Chessy when we lowered ourselves into that long-awaited hot, swirling whirlpool bath.

"Oh, Claire. I never realized I was married to such a sharp-tongued little hussy!" He caught his breath as I started to nibble on one of his fingers. "But sometimes, that tongue feels just like velvet . . ."

CHAPTER 12

The noise of heavy rain pounding against the windows woke us from a sweet little nap. Snuggling under the covers, we could watch sodden pine trees thrashing helplessly outside, while tracking the storm's progress on the television satellite map.

The weatherman, whose panicky eyes belied his fixed grin, announced merrily that tropical storm Babe had just been upgraded to hurricane status.

Charlotte called to ask what we were doing for lunch, grumbling about not being invited to partake of a potluck luncheon the Junior League was giving for Miss Gulf Coast contestants.

I smiled, remembering Dan's reaction when I'd read him the listing from today's schedule of events:

POTLUCK BUFFET LUNCHEON
HOSTED BY
THE JUNIOR LEAGUE OF BILOXI/GULFPORT
Members will prepare their own special
recipes from the league's recently
published cookbook, *Sea and Shore,* in

> honor of the Miss Gulf Coast
> candidates. Each one will receive a
> complimentary copy as a memento of her
> stay in our area.

"Only in the South!" he'd chuckled.

We were both feeling too lazy to go anywhere to eat. Dan had already planned to order some food from room service, and told Charlotte she was welcome to join us.

Meanwhile, I consulted the pageant schedule again. Tonight, of course, was the kickoff talent show, featuring the first ten non-contenders.

Before that, though, from three o'clock to five this afternoon, the Southeastern Colonies British Club would host a tea. This was no ordinary tea, however, but yet another facet of Miss Gulf Coast's screwball charm, because it was an actual category that had to be totally unique in pageantdom. Contestants would be judged for ". . . competence in hostessing and hospitality skills, including the companion arts of conversation and the handling of formal tea service."

According to the program, the breakdown of this event would be two judges and a British Club member to every four contestants, seven per tea table.

Charlotte arrived shortly after room service had delivered our load of ultra-lean burgers, fries, and Cokes, proudly displaying a copy of the *Sea and Shore* cookbook she'd managed to snag.

"Just listen to these recipes!" she exclaimed, paging gleefully. " 'Red Snapper Pudding.' My gosh, here's something called, 'King Mackerel Hollandaise,' Can you believe it? Oh, I love this one! 'Miss Mamie's Oyster Specialty'."

Charlotte put the cookbook aside and attacked her hamburger with enthusiasm. "So, what have you two been up to?" she inquired, adding hastily, "that's fit for my delicate ears, I mean!"

Between us, Dan and I filled her in on Shelby and Tinker's side of the story while Charlotte continued eating, listening intently.

When we were done, she nodded judiciously. "Uh-huh. That sounds pretty straightforward to me. But, while it's a serendipitous opportunity to strike back at Tinker, are either of you picking up just a tiny whiff of overkill? Or is it just me?"

Charlotte's question struck a responsive chord with me. Without realizing it, I'd been thinking along the same lines. "It does seem like an awful lot of extraneous emotional, legal and financial wear and tear to go through after twenty-plus years," I agreed.

Dan pensively swirled a french fry around in ketchup before giving his answer. "That all depends on your point of view," he said, finally. "Remember, LaWanda still believes Tinker deliberately set out to humiliate her publicly.

"And, exactly because it was so long ago, her trauma has had plenty of time to grow even bigger than it was to start off with."

Charlotte started to speak, but he forestalled her. "However, having said that, I do find it interesting how Brandon Battle's still connected to LaWanda after all these years. On one hand, I can appreciate his showmanship in seizing this opportunity to distract attention from that big Hollywood palimony suit he just lost, and remind everybody of the civil rights case that launched his career. Which, for the record, was settled, not won.

"On the other hand, Charlotte, I can see why you'd feel like somebody's dropping an anvil on an ant."

"Maybe the LaWanda/Tinker thing is just a smokescreen," I ventured. "Except I can't imagine for what."

Dan seriously considered this. "It could be, Claire. Only, if they're willing to go to so much trouble and expense to create a smokescreen of this magnitude, that means they've got something very, very big to hide."

"Obviously, we need more background information on all these people," I said.

"That reminds me." Charlotte wiped her hands on a napkin, then extracted a notebook from her omnipresent woven black satchel. "I was diddling around on Jan Windsor's computer earlier. Very casually of course, since I didn't want her to realize I'm more interested in her electronic facilities than in hearing about her current interior decorating crisis.

"But I did manage to pop out one little nugget. Suddenly, Jan and I are such dear old friends, know what I mean?" Grinning unrepentantly, she leafed through her notebook.

"Here it is. Okay. Remember me telling you after LaWanda got mixed up with the Warhol loonies, she went on to Europe? Well, seems like she hung out with an even stranger crowd over there.

"Because that rich old country boy husband of hers had evidently been in the old country to lay low until the heat was off. So when he brought LaWanda and Chessy back to the States, he must've thought it was safe.

"Little expecting to be conveniently shot in a deer hunting accident shortly thereafter, I'm sure."

Charlotte closed her notebook and looked at Dan. "Are you ready for this? There were hints at the time it was the Gillis faction of the Redneck Mafia that arranged to turn Eddie Scarborough into venison."

Dan, who'd been lounging on his spine, sat up straight and grinned. "Are we talking about Eddie Jack Scarborough, here? And LaWanda's his widow? Well, well, well!"

The Redneck Mafia, which back in Prohibition was officially known as the Gillis Gang, eventually saw a bloody split between the Gillis and Scarborough families.

Over the years (when they weren't too busy killing each other off) heirs on both sides had successfully parlayed old bootleg fortunes into more modern and sophisticated avenues of crime.

As time passed, the term "Redneck Mafia" was loosely applied to any organized criminal activity in the Gulf States definitely known not to be Italian, Latin, or, most recently, Asian.

However, the original authentic Redneck Mafia still existed. Galveston was rumored to be Gillis headquarters, while the Tampa area supposedly ran rife with Scarboroughs.

They were said to be most powerful up and down the

Gulf Coast, while Mobile provided access to smaller operations in the southeastern Atlantic states.

And despite that homey, good-old-boy nickname, the Redneck Mafia, whether Gillis or Scarborough, was as deadly as a nest of water moccasins.

Clasping his hands behind his head, Dan leaned back and beamed at Charlotte. "Come, on, girl! Don't you remember who represents several men alleged to be kingpins in the RM?"

Charlotte's forehead puckered in concentration, then she bounced excitedly up from her chair. "Dan, you're right! Brandon Battle was the lead defense attorney in that St. Petersburg trial!"

While they tossed around big names of various lawyers and gangsters—though it wasn't exactly clear who was which—I began to think closer to home.

Over two decades after Brandon Battle had won a settlement for LaWanda Jones, he was still very much part of her life. Maybe it was gratitude. Maybe it was something else entirely.

Brandon Battle did legal work for alleged Redneck Mafia bosses. It was suspected that LaWanda's alleged Redneck Mafia boss of a husband was executed by his Redneck Mafia rivals.

The recurring theme in the life of LaWanda Jones Scarborough seemed to consist of two main notes: Brandon Battle, and the Redneck Mafia.

"Maybe . . ." I mused aloud, ". . . maybe they got their hooks into LaWanda as far back as Miss Palmetto."

Dan and Charlotte broke off their discussion and

glanced at me in surprise, which I was gratified to watch turn into respect when I'd explained my line of reasoning.

"Real good point, Claire!" Dan said, observing me with an expression I'd never yet seen.

He went on, "Well, ladies. I think we've unexpectedly accomplished an amazing amount of work, here. We've managed to pick a thread loose. But now, we need more so we can grab hold and pull."

Charlotte saluted. "Okay, chief. I'll get on it right away. Although you realize the price of continued proximity to Jan's computer is probably going to be me accepting her invitation to address the local chapter of our sorority's alumni association."

Dan laughed. "Let's hope it doesn't come to that. I got roped into a similar situation once in Alexandria. All they wanted to talk about was the terrible things they did to three Ivy League boys who'd had the misfortune to transfer to LSU."

"Oh, well! Iyam so glayud that Iyam a Kayappa, Gayumma!" Charlotte declared bravely, gathering up her things. "I'd better hurry on over to Jan's office so I can finish up before the talent show tonight. I wouldn't miss that for all the rednecks in Tallahassee!"

She paused, her hand on the doorknob. "Oh, Claire. I almost forgot. I ran into Ricky Gomez from the beauty shop earlier. He said to tell you to stop by and say hey."

The door no sooner closed behind her than the phone rang. Dan picked up. "Foley!" he shouted. "You're here? Hey, you just missed your lady friend. You want us to get her back, or you still want to surprise . . . okay. Come on up."

He put down the receiver and grinned. "Neither rain nor sleet nor storm can stop Foley on the trail of his one true love. You know what that wild man did? He hijacked some poor bastard at Moisant airport to helicopter him right onto the Bell Sands roof!" Reaching for the telephone again, he added, "I'd better get in touch with our gracious hosts and see if they can't find room at the inn."

"Somehow I think they'll manage," I predicted. "And while you guys are filling each other in, I'm going to run down and see what Señor Ricky wants."

Dan opened the door for me. "Better take the extra key, baby. I might just trundle Foley over to meet the Bells in person. But I will definitely be back here in time for hors d'oeuvres."

"Mmmm. And what are we having?" I wondered, toying with the dangling ends of the drawstring to his sweatpants.

Dan caressed my derriere. "Anything your little heart desires," he assured me.

"Hey! You two are going to be doing this shit the whole time, I'm outta here!" a somewhat dampish Foley Callant yelled from the hallway. "Hey Claire, you cute thing!" He strolled past us into the room. "Hey Danbo, you big disgusting horny toad, you!"

I laughed. "Don't worry, Foley. I was just leaving."

Foley shucked off his Burberry. "Good thing, too," he grumbled, in mock irritation. "Cause darlin', we all know if you're in grabbing distance of that guy, he's gonna grab you and ain't nothing else going to ever get done!" He grinned, his big frame bursting with energy. A few raindrops glistened on his thick, wavy strawberry blond hair. Light blue eyes twinkled in a handsome freckled face.

It was incomprehensible to me how Belinda could've ever cheated on this fabulous man even once, say nothing of that parade of scrawny, funky artist types she'd seemed to go for. The only exception had been the last—a hunky Native American potter.

Foley had come home and discovered them recreating that instantly classic scene from *Ghost*, complete with Righteous Brothers music, and that had been the last straw. Though most men would've run out of straws way before then if they'd been married to Belinda.

I looked at Dan and Foley standing side by side. "See you later, you two great big old rich, gorgeous honeypots, you. Bet Charlotte and I have to beat bees off with a big stick tonight!" Waving goodbye, I headed down the hallway.

"But see, we don't put out no honey for nobody but our little queens!" Foley bellowed at the top of his lungs. To my right, a door opened suddenly, and a woman's startled face peered out to see what the commotion was.

Dan and Foley's laughter followed me all the way to the elevator.

CHAPTER 13

During my descent to the lobby, I thought about Ricky Gomez, the self-proclaimed Jose Eber of the Gulf Coast.

Ricky was from a wealthy, aristocratic Mexican family in El Paso, and the general consensus among his many female clients was, "What a waste!" He had a compact, magnificently defined body, pale olive skin, luminous aqua eyes, a pearlescent smile, long, thick, glossy brown hair. And, he was gay as a goose.

We had trained together in New Orleans at the Institut de Beauté, directly under the famous Marcel Barrineau, and Ricky had never forgiven me when Marcel chose me to be his personal assistant. Bitchily, he'd claimed it was because Marcel, a notorious raving heterosexual, had specific ideas as to the range of duties his protégé would perform.

And yes, Marcel had tried his "smooth operator" approach on me. But once he took my no for an answer, the experience of working alongside a true genius was something money couldn't buy.

I wondered what Ricky wanted all of a sudden. I had

already stopped by Bella Salon on my way to the gym this morning to say hello, but he'd been pretty busy and acted kind of snippy when he saw me.

When the elevator stopped, I took a wrong turn and wound up in front of the gym. Glancing in, I saw Freddy Franks trudging away on that treadmill, right on schedule for his 2:30 circuit training. I remembered he'd bragged he trained three times a day, every four hours, which meant his last session would be at 6:30 p.m., when he said he had the place all to himself and that's the way he liked it, uh-huh. Reminding myself to tell Dan we should avoid coming to the gym at those times, I stepped quickly away before Freddy noticed me.

The Bella Salon was empty, except for Ricky Gomez himself, looking like a time-traveling Aztec prince in a maroon and gold-crested Bell Sands baseball cap. He was moodily watching an old *Loveboat* and waved a languid hand when I walked in. "*Que pasa*, Claire. Don't you think Gavin Macleod is *mucho gusto* handsome? I just saw him in *Love Letters* in Pensacola a couple of months ago, and he is still *muy hombre*! Gavin is one of the few men on earth who looks better bald than he would with hair, *si*?"

I watched Captain Stubing, who was lecturing Dr. Bricker about something. "I think so too, but then I'm partial to those big Daddy-Bear types. For that matter, I think Shelby Bell is a doll. And by the way, Ricky. Save the phony salsa for your customers, or I will *drownez-vous* in the gumbo, *cher*."

Ricky flicked off the TV with a remote and regarded me sourly. "Good hairstyle, Claire," he commented, without a trace of accent. "Marcel's handiwork, no doubt? Going to need a trim any day though," he meowed, with satisfaction.

I climbed into the client's chair next to his station and swiveled to face him. "Ricky, you can go into your Great Bitch routine, or you can tell me what you want. Or, I can leave."

"I'm sorry," he sighed. "It's just, my life's soooo complicated right now."

"You wouldn't have it any other way," I cut in ruthlessly. "Specifically, what?"

"Well, I don't really expect you to understand, Claire," he pouted. "I mean, you've got it made. Your own shop in a town where people actually still care about style. Me, what do I have? I'll tell you what I have," he answered himself, contemplating his flawless reflection in the mirror.

"From February to October I am merely a glorified employee of an expensive hotel that caters mainly to wiry women with shoe leather for skin who live in sun visors and tennis skirts or golf outfits, and aren't interested in anything but a blunt cut and maybe a few highlights for some real excitement. And all their husbands in madras Bermuda shorts want is a little bit off the top and sides and be sure and clean up the ear and nose hair."

I chuckled at Ricky's scathingly apt description of his clientele, and he spun his chair around. "Claire, the only chance I ever get to do anything really creative and fun is during the Miss Gulf Coast Pageant. I look forward to this all year long! You know, I've even gotten a couple of film jobs and some fashion mag credits because of it?

"See, if there's a big tennis or golf thing, I can get by

fine hiring some freelancers to handle the overflow. But for the pageant, I not only need as many freelancers as I can get, I can't make it without my two best stylists, Jerome and Trini. And Viola, the manicurist. Those gullible sluts."

"How so?" I inquired cautiously, somehow knowing I wasn't going to like where this was headed.

"After Chessy dropped her bomb Thursday, some of that Hollywood crowd started carrying on like the Ku Klux Klan was burning crosses on the beach. Those jerks plainly didn't give a damn whether she was telling the truth or not! They're just scared to death they'll wind up on the wrong side. Do they want to hear that the Bells aren't bigots or that Shelby wouldn't harass a piece of lint? Does anybody ask questions about Chessy's spooky *madre* who looks like Cruella deVil? Of course not!

"Well, that afternoon one of the white celebrity chicks—Marlowe Goodkidd—shows up for her manicure with Viola—who's black—and wants me to drop everything and do her hair immediately. She got real miffed when I pointed out a lady was sitting in my chair at that exact moment, so Trini volunteered.

"God, some of those showbiz people make me want to upchuck, the way they waltz in and expect you to kiss their Rolex! Anyway, Goodkidd started advising us minorities of color to stick together and boycott the pageant to teach racists like the Bells a lesson. You notice how she wanted to make damn sure she got her snowy ass all polished up before that happened?

"So Trini was lapping it up, fawning all over her, and Jerome, the homeboy, does whatever Trini does, and Viola's going, 'Uh-huh, girlfriend!' Next thing you know, the big star invites all three of them to L.A. to do her hair and nails for some disgusting sitcom pilot!"

"No!" I protested. "They couldn't have fallen for that!"

"No?" Ricky grinned maliciously. "It gets better. You know, it's in the contract that all the beauty stuff is supplied by the pageant? I figured I ought to warn the Bells what could go down. Good thing I did, because yesterday morning, all three of those cheap whores call in sick and the freelance people are afraid if they come in they won't be able to get home if there is a hurricane." Ricky Gomez tilted his baseball cap to the back of his head and flashed me those beautiful teeth. "But you' re here, Claire!"

In my heart, I think I had known what my mission was going to be from the moment Dan told me the only non-union shop in the Bell Sands was the beauty salon. None of the other employees could be so easily stampeded into an illegal strike; they had too much to lose. But if the Bells weren't able to deliver on their end of the contract, even in one area like beauty services, they could find themselves up to their ears in lawsuits. There seemed to be a diabolical cunning behind all this, that knew exactly how to take instant advantage of the circumstances and people to hand, such as fear-ridden actresses. Ricky's three employees weren't the only gullible sluts.

Ricky was openly laughing at me. "Aw, come on Claire. It'll be almost like old times," he teased.

I shook my head helplessly. "What kind of schedule are we looking at?"

He jumped out of his chair and went to the reception

desk, motioning for me to follow. "Here's the book. Today's been kind of slow, but tomorrow afternoon, *ay chihuahua!* A weave, a prelight and tone, several haircuts and some manipeds."

"Ricky, read my lips!" I ordered. "I do not do nails."

"But, Claire!" he whined. "Neither do I!"

I leafed through the book incredulously. "And just who is supposed to handle the big old arm, leg and bikini wax-o-rama before the bathing suit competition?" I demanded.

Ricky squeezed his eyes shut in pain. "Oh, my God! I forgot all about that! I don't know whether Ludmilla will show up or not," he moaned.

"Well you better find out," I said crisply. "Get ahold of yourself, Gomez, and face facts. There is no way the two of us can handle the volume alone. Not if we started right this minute and worked twelve hours a day until Saturday night!"

"You're right, you're right!" he whimpered. "What are we going to do, Claire?"

"What's with this we, Mexican? I'll have to think about it. Right now, it seems pretty hopeless." But I was getting the germ of an idea. I just didn't want to mention it to Ricky yet.

"Excuse me. Are you still open?" Franny Franks entered the shop hesitantly. She had obviously been crying, and she looked awful. Swollen eyelids, puffy red nose, and in dire need of cut and color to freshen her auburn hair.

Franny looked at us defiantly. "Please don't bother to pretend you don't notice. Everybody in the hotel must've heard about Freddy and me by now.

"Well, can you do anything with?" Her long eloquent hands she was so famous for using to express herself in comedy routines effectively described her condition. "After all, the show, as they say, must go on."

Before either Ricky or I could respond, a man who identified himself as a network executive strolled in and demanded that his hair be cut exactly like Robert De Niro's in *Mistress*.

"I didn't see that film," Ricky said sulkily. But Dan and I had. We'd both thought De Niro's 'do looked so good, that Dan had seriously considered letting his hair grow. That style was very deceptively simple, though, and I wanted to develop a real good technique before I tried it out on Dan.

I beamed at my unwitting guinea pig and indicated a chair. "How about a few of those highlights like he had in the movie to go along with that?" I offered.

"And a mole for your right cheek?" Ricky muttered under his breath, and Franny Franks managed a wan smile as he fastened a cape around her neck.

I misted the guy's hair with water and parted it in the middle to get a sense of how it grew. As I circled the victim's chair studying his profile, Ricky started doing a disco step and whistling *Deja Vu*.

CHAPTER 14

Franny gradually relaxed under Ricky's ministrations. Noticing the large television set, she requested that he turn it on, confessing she'd become hooked on the channel that specialized in reruns. Which was where Ricky kept it permanently parked, anyway.

We were all enjoying a particularly absorbing *Perry Mason*, when interrupted by the weatherman, whose panache and sartorial splendor had visibly deteriorated since his last appearance.

Making ineffectual gestures at the satellite picture, he informed us that the hurricane watch was now a hurricane warning.

In contrast to the former California weatherguy's emotionalism, a dispassionately analytical spokesperson from the Miami Hurricane Bureau calculated that, if Babe stayed her course and the wind velocity continued to build at its present rate, she would make landfall at Mobile, Alabama within the next forty-eight hours.

Mobile was not much farther than a good, hard spit from Crestview Cove.

Despite this grim prospect, I was rather pleased with the results of my De Niro experiment. Once I got started, I realized the only way to achieve that kind of volume and movement with a man's hair was to approach it like a woman's short bob.

The network executive had been pretty happy, even though it wasn't as long as he wanted. Tell the truth, the project turned out a whole lot better that he had a right to expect, given the raw material.

At four o'clock Ricky was still working on Franny, both so engrossed in *Charlie's Angels* they barely noticed me leaving. There were no windows in Bella, so it wasn't until out in the corridor I saw it was already dark as night.

The rich, sedate tones of string quartet music caught my ear as I passed by one of the ballrooms, reminding me the British Club Tea was in progress. Unable to resist the temptation, I pushed one of the doors open a crack to peek.

Groups of tables, loaded with finger sandwiches, *petits fours*, silver tea services and delicate china, were surrounded by ladies in hats and elegant gentlemen, perched on gilt chairs. It was easy to distinguish the British contingent, because most of the women sported dowdy twinsets or tweeds, and fabulous pearls, while all the men looked like either Alistair Cooke or Alfred Hitchcock.

There was Tinker Bell, the soul of decorum in a blue-veiled and feathered chapeau, wielding her teacup and saucer as to the manor born.

It was a thoroughly delightful scene, confirmation that

Miss Gulf Coast was one of a kind. Eat your heart out, Atlantic City.

"Now, if this isn't a most fortuitous coincidence. Just the young lady I wanted to see!" The voice behind me dripped like thick brown gravy over mashed potatoes. I turned, unsurprised to find it belonged to Brandon Battle.

At close range, it was plain that his image of the great outdoorsman was far more Rodeo Drive than rodeo. Everything about him was too calculated. The white hair and mustache were carefully groomed to look as if they weren't, the intensity of those narrow brown eyes was artificially enhanced by contact lenses.

And yet, from behind all the facade, emanated a formidable intelligence it would be foolhardy to overlook. I imagined many had found that out to their sorrow.

"Miz Claiborne, my card." Battle proffered a rectangle of creamy parchment.

I accepted it, saying, "Why, thank you Mr. Battle. But if I should happen to need an attorney, I've already got the best on permanent retainer."

He laughed with false heartiness, displaying a set of equally false teeth and said waggishly, but with intentional offense, "Spoken like the good little wife I'm sure you are, ma'am."

I bit back a sharp retort. Let him think I only spoke blonde.

"Oh, Mr. Battle," I simpered. "I surely do try. But, my goodness! I can't imagine why a famous man like you was hoping to run into me?"

From his contemptuous blink I could tell he'd bought

my lil' ol' act. His voice grew even greasier. "Well, it's like this, Miz Claiborne. I was wondering if you'd do me a great big favor and have your husband contact me? My room number's on the back of that card. I believe he and I have some important business to discuss. You won't forget to do that now, will you?"

Producing a dazzling, lights-on-but-nobody-home smile, I trilled, "Of course I won't, Mr. Battle. 'Bye now."

I hurried away, both angry and chilled. Brandon Battle was a mean old nasty granddaddy rattlesnake. No wonder the cracker crooks and high-priced kiss-and-tell palimony diggers flocked to him! For one fleeting moment, I worried that Dan might be out of his league, but quickly dismissed the thought. Maybe it was just unrealistic hero worship, but I believed Dan was more than enough mongoose to handle that serpent.

When I got off the elevator, I found Parker Bell standing in front of our door, fiddling with the gift card of an elaborate floral arrangement.

"The card fell out of the holder and I was trying to get it back in," he explained.

"Don't bother, Parker," I said, reaching to take it.

His ruddy skin darkened. "It's not for you," he mumbled, seeming embarrassed.

Just then, Dan opened the door. "I thought I heard voices out here," he began, and smiled when he saw the flowers. "Why, Claire! For me?"

Parker thrust the bouquet of flowering ginger, eucalyptus and those red things with suggestive appendages Charlotte calls "little boy flowers," into Dan's arms and abruptly departed.

"Apparently so," I said, closing the door behind us. "But I can't claim any credit."

"Probably from the Bells," Dan remarked, scanning the gift card. His face changed, and he handed it to me wordlessly.

I felt violated and nauseated as I read:

Dear Dan:

I'll be dancing just for you tonight.

Chessy

Dan took the thing from between my fingers and ripped it into fragments. Then he wrenched open the French doors and heaved everything off the balcony. Taking me in his arms, he muttered, "Oh, honey. I'm sorry about that. This makes the third time today something's tried to get between us."

I tilted my head back to look up at Dan and said, keeping it light, "Three strikes and they're out!"

He didn't smile. "Don't try to fool me, Claire. I saw your face just now, and I won't stand for anybody hurting you."

"Come on. Sit down with me, baby." I coaxed him over to the sofa. "Listen, Dan. You said it yourself. It's pretty obvious what we've got ain't normal. Certain kinds of people are just going to take that as a direct, personal sexual challenge. It's a drag, but that's the deal. And so what? However!" I paused for effect. "That bitch sends you flowers again, and she'll be pushing up daisies!"

"Whoo!" Dan laughed. "I just love it when you go all

coonass and aggressive! Hey, where've you been all this time? I thought you were only going down to see Ricky?"

I stretched out and propped my legs on the coffee table. "Wait'll you hear this!" I proceeded to fill him in on Ricky's predicament, and that Tinker Bell obviously had such an eventuality in mind when she requested I bring along my "darling little tool kit."

Dan ruefully agreed. "She is one shrewd lady, as I am quickly finding out. Honey, you don't have to do all that work, it's just not right,"

"Dan, of course I do. You aren't exactly sitting here on your so very fine butt, are you? Analyzing contracts and maybe going to court and all? This is a serious situation. If they don't live up to that beauty services clause, it could open up a whole other can of worms, right?" He nodded. "So, we're going to function as a team. Shoulder to shoulder."

Dan grinned. "I can think of a few more interesting positions." He reached for me, but I stuck Brandon Battle's card into his hand.

"Whatever you've done so far, it's certainly stirred up something," I told him, and recounted my strange meeting with the lawyer.

Dan's eyes gleamed with animosity. "I'll call that sonofabitch an hour after I'm good and ready. This is very interesting, in light of what Foley and I discussed with the Bells this afternoon."

"Foley was able to get a room?" I asked.

"Right next door to Charlotte's. But she still doesn't know he's here yet, so don't tell her if she calls."

I promised I wouldn't, then dropped the big one on him. "Dan, about my helping Ricky? There's just no way the two of us can handle all the work by ourselves. But I got to thinking, If Marcel could send a few of his students out here before the weather gets any worse, do you think the Bells would comp the whole thing?"

"They won't have any choice," Dan retorted, his hand already on the phone. "Between Foley and me, we've saved them a chunk of money in legal fees alone. I am not having you worn out over this mess."

He picked up the receiver and asked the switchboard to connect him to Shelby. "Hey, Shelby. It's Dan. Listen. Claire's just brought up a problem that you and I, being insensitive male hogs, didn't even think about and it could have backfired real bad. But she's got a good plan about how we can handle it. Maybe."

Quickly, Dan put him in the picture and listened, then gave me a thumbs-up. "Uh-huh, That's what I thought you'd say. We're going to have to work fast, then. Okay. I'll let you know. Right."

Dan hung up. "Whatever you need, you get. About twenty people checked out today to try to beat the storm home, so there's plenty of room." He grinned at me. "Blanchard, Smithson, Callant and Claiborne are going to have ourselves a big slice of the Bell Group's business before this is over. Believe it."

Marcel, whom I tracked down at his new shop on Esplanade Avenue, greeted my S.O.S. with an enthusiasm entirely inappropriate to the occasion.

"Claire! Of course I will help you! Beauty queens, Mrs.

Shelby Bell *and* Ricky Gomez, you say? Wonderful! I just happen to have several students who need to be punished— yes, I know the weather is terrible, am I deaf and blind? It is now five o'clock. You can definitely expect some helpers before midnight. At least four, possibly six. I am Inspector Barrineau, on the case! *Au revoir*, Claire!"

I was vaguely disturbed. Yes, I needed help desperately, but I hadn't expected Marcel to respond so . . . joyously— that was the only word for it—blithely committing some of his people to an arduous and, weatherwise, potentially dangerous situation. That handsome, sleek silver fox never did anything for no good reason.

For instance, when I first opened Eclaire, I'd been so touched when he graciously recommended me to one of his longtime clients, Tinker Bell. Of course, I soon discovered why.

Come to think of it, Marcel was morally obligated to pull me out of this jam, since I wouldn't be in it in the first place if not for him.

Dan called Shelby back, and they arranged the details. Then Dan said, "Claire, I want to give you a fast rundown on the legal end. Foley had a brilliant idea how to spike Battle's guns. There's going to be an announcement made before the talent show that because of some unexpected problems with the interview tapes—which is true—all contestants will be reinstated.

"In other words, they're going to start everybody from scratch, as of tonight!"

I laughed. "Old B.B. won't have a leg to stand on!"

"Don't count on it," Dan cautioned. "That one's got

more legs than a centipede. I already have a suspicion what he'll do next, but we'll just have to cross that river when we get there."

The phone rang again. It was Charlotte, sounding disgusted. "Guess what happened after I endured three-quarters of an hour of Jan Windsor's redecorating plans, complete with fabric swatches?" she inquired rhetorically.

"When the woman finally goes away and leaves me alone with her computer, I hadn't been at the screen more than ten minutes before all the terminals went down because of the storm! Although I did manage to turn up one or two juicy tidbits, but—she broke off. "Hang on, Claire. Somebody's at the door."

I smiled when I heard her yelp of surprise. "Foley! Baby! Honey! Oh, shoot. Wait a minute, let go . . ." She came back on the line breathlessly. "Claire, guess—"

I laughed. "I know. Consider it your reward for those fabric swatches."

"Hang on," she said again. "What, honey? Foley, please! Don't *do* that! Okay, I'll tell her. Claire? Foley said he reserved us a table for dinner in the Beach Club at seven. Wear something gorgeous, I am. 'Bye."

Dan raised an inquisitive eyebrow. "Barnacle Bill has arrived?"

"With a yohoho, from the sound of things! Oh, Charlotte said the computers conked out before she could get more than a couple of items."

The wind was picking up. We could hear its low moan and see glints of phosphor on the pitching waves, flashes of lightening in the dark sky. I drew the heavy curtains across the French doors, shutting out nature's violence.

But there was no way to shut out the violence that was about to strike from within.

❦ ❦ ❦

"Yum, yum, yum!" Dan growled, when I entered the sitting room in my short, flouncy spaghetti strap dress of juicy red chiffon. With such dresses, Dan has a certain way of sliding a slow index finger underneath one thin strap until I'm all over goosebumps. That's why I wear them.

"Who wants dinner? Let's get right to dessert!" He kissed me and smacked his lips. "Dee-licious. Strawberry shortcake!"

"Hey, no more cracks about my height!" I warned, bestowing a final kiss before applying soft red lipstick. "Ummmm . . . if you keep doing that, I'll smear this stuff," I said when he came up behind me and started running his finger beneath my left strap.

His mirrored reflection smiled at mine. "You won't have to, baby. I'll smear it for you . . . damn!" he said, when the phone rang. "I'll bet it's Foley wondering where we are . . . hello?"

In the mirror, I could see Dan's eyes pop wide open and his jaw drop. "WHAT?" he shouted. Dan listened some more, shaking his head. "We' re on our way!" he barked, then slammed down the receiver.

"Honey, what's wrong?" I demanded, alarmed at his expression.

Dan rubbed a hand over his face. "That was Shelby. Freddy's dead!"

CHAPTER 15

Vertical blinds had been pulled tightly closed across the windows of the Bar Bell gym, and a piece of cardboard on which was scrawled in red—CLOSED FOR REPAIRS— stuck to one of the swinging doors with masking tape.

At Dan's knock, Shelby Bell peered out furtively, then whispered, "Hurry. Don't let anybody see you come in."

Freddy Franks would certainly not be winning any prizes for Most Beautiful Corpse.

Fried, tossed, and sliced, basically described his condition. Shelby explained that the treadmill Freddy considered to be his personal property had short-circuited, which resulted first in the machine speeding out of control, then electrocuting him. As the speed continued to increase, Freddy's body had been thrown backward to smash into the mirrored wall behind him, causing multiple lacerations.

There was an unpleasant odor of burned-out machine innards, mixed with another smell I didn't care to contemplate.

I hid my face against Dan's chest.

The Biloxi Police, singular, was already on the scene in the person of Chief Troy Hepkins himself, who had responded to the radio dispatch while en route to his house to change clothes because the Bells had invited him to attend the talent show tonight.

Chief Hepkins was a wide, bluff man, with sandy hair clipped close to his head and a countenance that looked as if it were unusually affable. At the moment, though, it wore an expression of extreme displeasure as he listened to the plaintive voice of Parker Bell.

"But I taped that sign to the machine!" Parker protested, indicating another piece of cardboard similar to what we'd seen on the door, lying beside the reeking carcasses of Freddy and his treadmill.

Even from where I stood, I could plainly read the large, red, block-printed message: DANGER. DON'T USE.

"This afternoon, somebody told me it was starting to speed up and stop, speed up and stop, and they'd almost gotten thrown off," continued Parker. "I knew something was wrong so I unplugged it and put a sign up until I could get around to taking it apart later."

He shook his head in bewilderment. "When I came in about seven to straighten the gym like always, I found Mr. Franks, lying there like that." Parker's face puckered like a giant baby's. "I just don't understand why he'd go ahead and use the treadmill when that sign was on it."

Shelby, who'd been listening intently, sighed with relief. "Thank God, it's not that bad," he said in a stage whisper, then looked ashamed. "Well, it is for Freddy

Franks, poor fellow. I mean, it was just a terrible accident after all."

Dan gave Shelby a considering look. "What else did you think it might be, Shelby?" he asked, quietly.

Shelby yanked off his big glasses and polished them industriously with his white hanky. "I-I'm not sure, Dan, " he muttered. "At this point, the way things have been going . . ." he shoved the glasses back onto his face, his eyes flickering warily behind the lenses. "I guess I'm getting conditioned to expect the worst."

"The worst being what?" Dan prodded.

Shelby darted a furtive glance over his shoulder at Chief Hepkins, still questioning Parker, and hissed, "For God's sake, Dan! Tinker and I were having big trouble with him. After you and Foley Callant left the office this afternoon, he called and threatened to yank himself and Franny out of the show tonight, because he didn't think he was getting proper VIP treatment. His complaint involved that very treadmill, in fact."

"I'm afraid that was my fault," I confessed.

Shelby waved it away. "No fault involved, Claire. Look, our gym is very well-equipped, we've got at least three of everything. But for some reason, Freddy insisted on access at will to one particular machine, and considered it a slap to his prestige that we didn't make it off limits to everybody else."

"I do know the answer to that," I said, and explained Freddy's *feng shuei* theory.

"Anyway," Shelby continued, "when he started that business about pulling out of the show, I threatened him with breach of contract. He threatened me back, saying his Century City attorney was top gun. I told the bastard to fire away, because my attorney was right here on the premises.

"Well, he got kind of quiet when I said that, then asked if you were a big guy with dark hair. I told him yes. Then somebody knocked on his door and I held on while he went to see who it was.

"When he came back, he totally changed the subject and started demanding to have cold champagne sent up to his room immediately. I said I'd be happy to have a whole case delivered, but he damn well better be ready to go on when his name was called tonight."

Shelby pulled out his handkerchief again and blotted his neck. "I guess the Lord called his name first."

Dan shook his head. "If I were the Lord, I'd take mighty strong offense to the things folks accused me of doing. And you still haven't answered my question, Shelby. Why did you immediately assume a human hand assisted Freddy to that spotlight over yonder in the sky?"

Shelby shrugged. "I suppose because he was such a total jerk. Freddy Franks seemed bound and determined to go the extra mile to offend everybody. He was a loudmouth who thought he rated special privileges, over and above the substantial perks we take sincere pleasure in providing for our celebrity guests. Though I can't imagine why, because we often have far bigger names than him staying with us.

"Maybe it's because he recently finished shooting a movie, which I hear is expected to be a big hit. Apparently, it was his first feature film role. But I don't pretend to understand that Hollywood stuff.

"I'll confess right now, though, I was personally ready to tear his head off for how he humiliated his wife in public. Ask anybody who was at the welcome cocktail party and they'll tell you he started in on her that night and hasn't let up since.

"And you know that horrible fight I mentioned he and Franny had Wednesday morning? What I didn't say is there were rumors floating around that Franny had gone to use the ladies' room and caught Freddy in the middle of a wall-banger with one of the contestants." He stopped and looked faintly shocked at himself. "Forgive my graphic language, Claire. I'm very upset."

"Of course, Shelby," I said, graciously. "Incidentally. Did those rumors also include the name of that lucky girl?"

"No." Shelby shook his bald head. "Apparently, he made unwelcome advances to several of the young women."

I could well believe that. However, this one didn't sound like it had been so unwelcome.

There was something else I wanted to ask Shelby about his account of this afternoon, that didn't quite jibe with what little I knew of Freddy, but my train of thought was derailed when Parker strode purposefully past us without speaking and went out the door.

"Hey, Shelby!" Chief Hepkins ambled over, a few beats behind Parker.

When Shelby had introduced everyone, Hepkins re-marked, "Well, I'm just about done here. Looks pretty damn simple to me. Ah, thank you, son," he added to Parker, who had quickly returned with a folded white sheet.

"I asked him to sneak this out of one of your linen

closets," Hepkins explained. "No reason to get the maids all upset and talking, know what I mean? That's right, just spread it over him, son," he instructed Parker, who complied. "Okay, son. You go on about your business while I talk to your uncle and these folks, now."

Parker looked contritely at Shelby. "I should've just gone ahead and moved the machine out of here. Then, this wouldn't have happened," he mourned.

"Now don't blame yourself, Parker." Shelby gave him a reassuring pat on the back. "How could you know somebody would just totally ignore that warning sign? And don't forget," he called as Parker trudged slowly away, "Mr. Franks is the one who plugged it back in."

His words created an ugly little visual in my mind that made me shiver.

"Got to wait for the coroner to make it official," Hepkins told Shelby, "but I can just about bet we're looking at your basic death by misadventure here."

"No betting allowed on dry ground, especially not hotel property, Troy!" Shelby Bell joked weakly. "At least, not yet."

Hepkins grinned. "Can't catch you, can I, Shelby? You big old law abider you!" His expression suddenly sobered. "Oh, good evening, ma'am," he greeted Franny Franks respectfully.

Ricky Gomez had worked some of his best magic on Franny this afternoon. She hadn't seemed to care what he did. Therefore, being Ricky, he had arbitrarily taken carte blanche and done everything possible. Since he'd still been at it when I left Bella after finishing with my De Niro wannabe, this was my first glimpse of the finished product.

Now, instead of that poor Pitiful Pearl who'd walked into the shop, she looked absolutely stunning. Had Freddy seen the new Franny before he died? Ricky had given her a soft perm, then cut the hair a few inches shorter, layering it in wisps and curls around her face, and added some subtle red and gold highlights to the auburn base.

Shelby stepped forward and took her hand. "I'm so very sorry, Mrs. Franks. Franny. This is my attorney, Dan Claiborne, and his wife, Claire . . ." her eyes widened a little when she recognized me, ". . . and Biloxi's fine chief of police, Troy Hepkins."

Franny shook hands all around, then said, "Chief Hepkins, I would like to see the body now, please."

Hepkins gave an involuntary shudder and glanced quickly behind him at the heap beneath the sheet Parker had brought from housekeeping. "Uh . . . I don't think that's such a good idea, Mrs. Franks . . ." He trailed off because Franny had simply walked over to the body and lifted a corner of the sheet.

She stood there a moment with her back to us, head bowed. Then she let the fabric drop back and looked at us uncertainly. "I . . . need to sit down, please," she murmured and both the Chief and Shelby rushed forward to assist her to a long bench just inside the door. "What—what happens now?" she asked vaguely.

Hepkins explained about the coroner, then added, in view of the circumstances, if the airport was open tomorrow, she would be allowed to take Freddy back to L.A. after the coroner had examined the body. Or if it wasn't, he would provide ground transportation to New Orleans where she might still be able to catch a flight.

"I don't anticipate any difficulties from our end except maybe with the weather, Mrs. Franks," the chief assured her.

"Thank you, Chief. May I please go back to my room now?" Franny inquired, adding to Shelby, "Please forgive me, Shelby. But I'm afraid I couldn't be too funny tonight."

"Good heavens, of course not!" Shelby expostulated, mortally offended at the implication he would even dream of requiring her to perform. It occurred to me that Freddy had gotten them out of the show tonight after all. "I'll take you back up, Franny."

Chief Hepkins watched them go, and sighed. "I guess you folks better go on ahead and do whatever you got all dressed up so nice to do. If the coroner ever gets here, maybe I'll still be able to go home and change in time to get back and see a little bit of the talent show, anyway. I sure was looking forward to that."

Dan clapped him on the shoulder. "It doesn't start till nine o'clock, and it's only about seven-thirty now. Maybe you'll make it after all, Chief."

I was glad for the chief's sake when a little grey bird-like gentleman hauling a black leather doctor's bag scuttled past us as we turned down the hallway toward the Beach Club.

I started to say something, but Dan gave my arm a gentle squeeze.

"Keep your voice real low, baby," he said softly, although nobody was nearby. "Walls have ears."

If only Shelby and the chief were able to implement their plan of shipping Franny and Freddy out of town by whatever means tomorrow, with no one the wiser until they were back in L.A.! And preferably, not until after the pageant was over, but that might be too much to hope for.

At least, nobody would be terribly surprised at tonight's discreet announcement that the Franks' were unable to appear. Insiders would immediately assume they knew why.

The rest of the audience wouldn't give it another thought after the next announcement was made, about the reinstatement of all contestants as contenders.

However, when the couple continued to be no-shows, questions would be raised, And the minute the press discovered they'd been hoodwinked, all hell would break loose.

"Dan," I whispered. "This whole thing's just a little too strange."

A couple was walking along the corridor toward us, and Dan slid his arm around my waist as he bent to murmur in my ear, "I agree, darlin'. But right now, we've got other fish to fry, and we can't do that if Biloxi's finest should take a notice to treat Freddy's abrupt demise in the Bar Bell as suspicious.

"You may recall, someone very close to you was witnessed making physical threats to him on those very premises?

"And while I don't think for one second that Chief Troy Hepkins is anybody's fool, he hasn't been around here the past few days, so there's no reason to ask questions when what he's got looks like a perfectly good accident."

I nodded. "And we really don't know it's not. But I used

that same machine this morning myself. And it seemed fine." Then, I remembered something else. "Dan! I saw *Freddy* using it this afternoon on my way to the beauty shop! For his second circuit." I could feel a little bubble of hysteria rising in my throat at the thought that Freddy's third and last had given a whole new meaning to the term, "circuit training."

"Of course, I really can't believe Franny did it, never mind she had that dazed look of a woman who's just been told she doesn't have cancer after all."

"Like a kid on Christmas morning," Dan concurred. "But legally, our perceptions do not count as evidence."

"Depending on what time Ricky finished with her, she might've been able to plug in the machine and hide the sign before Freddy came back down to work out," I mused. "Bella Salon is right around the corner from the gym."

"Although that would mean she'd have had to know there was a problem with the treadmill in the first place, as well as what the probable damage would be," Dan pointed out.

"You know, Dan. Shelby Bell did a whole lot of talking, but he never did directly answer your question about why he right away assumed Freddy had been murdered."

He nodded grimly. "It did cross my mind that he might be trying to protect somebody."

I goggled at him. "You don't mean Tinker?"

"No," Dan said quietly. "I mean Franny."

"Hmmmm! Well, he certainly was exceedingly attentive and gallant towards her," I agreed. "But unless he's getting ready to pitch a big old mid-life crisis which involves dumping Tinker and running off to Hollywood with Franny, I can't see why he'd bother. Although, stranger things have happened."

"You're right," Dan said. "As a lawyer, I've found there is usually only one person that people will go to any lengths to protect."

"That being?"

He laughed cynically. "Numero uno, who else?"

CHAPTER 16

I have a friend in New Orleans who refuses to attend funerals because she claims everybody there is thinking, "Thank God it wasn't me!" She's probably right, but I'm not convinced that's a bad thing. If it's true that in the midst of life we are in death, it must be equally true that, in the midst of death, we are in life.

All I know is, when I walked into the Beach Club, it was as if I had suddenly plugged into an electric socket and a power surge shot through me from head to toe. The beat of the music, the sound of voices, the melange of smells of food and liquor and perfume—everything was almost unbearably intensified.

The sensation of Dan's fingers resting lightly on my bare back, gently steering me toward the table where our dearest friends sat waving to us, seemed to penetrate right through skin and muscle and bone to make the tips of my breasts feel like strobe lights flashing through the thin fabric of my bodice.

I was alive!

I stopped and turned to ask Dan, "Are my nipples lit up, *cher*?" My words sounded a little slurred to me.

His jaw dropped. It's not often I'm able to catch him off balance like that, and another jolt of that same power buzzed through me.

Dan's eyes jumped down to my bosom. "Like Las Vegas," he confirmed in a hoarse voice. "My God, Claire! I've got to have you. Right now!"

"Oh, please," I begged. My heart was pounding in my throat.

"Come on!" He grabbed my hand and yanked me back out of the club and we managed to catch an empty elevator just as the doors were closing. A voice calling, "Wait! Hold it open!" fell on deaf ears.

Dan crushed me tightly against his body. I raised my left leg, hooking it over his right arm and he said, "Flamingo—"

The elevator, a rocket of stainless steel shooting us up to the fourth floor in seconds . . . our red and black reflections multiplying in the smoky glass mirrors, rushing into infinity . . . through the door . . . and it was hard and fast and furious and everything it had to be because it was life against death.

Thank God it wasn't us!

As we once again walked toward Charlotte and Foley's table, they observed our sedate approach with the jaded air of watching a video replay.

"Strange thing happened a short while ago," Foley drawled when we were seated. "Two people looked just like y'all were on their way over here then, boom. They suddenly disappeared!"

Dan pressed his full lips together and studied the menu, not meeting Foley's eye. "Sorry about that," he apologized offhandedly. "Just some business needed taking care of right away."

Foley snorted, "Monkey business, you mean. Don't you think so, Charlotte?"

"Mmmm," Charlotte nodded dreamily, slurping up the remains of her drink through a straw. She looked like an angel in red and gold brocade. I realized Foley, who was just a tad less large than Dan, had commandeered odds and ends from his friend's wardrobe; last night's blue silk jacket and a cream silk shirt. Whichever trousers he'd managed to finagle were concealed by the tablecloth.

"Well," Foley complained, "you were late before then, anyhow. Thought I told you seven o'clock and it's getting on for eight now. There's a limit to the amount of macadamia nuts my stomach can handle." He indicated a serving bowl cleverly fashioned from half a varnished coconut shell, empty now but for a few Mauna Loa fragments.

"We've got a real good excuse," Dan told him. "But first, let's order some drinks and a couple of hot appetizers."

A waiter glided up to the table, traditional in austere black and white except for his Japanese sunglasses. Dan said, "We'll have the crabcakes with jalapeño sauce, a double order of fried Maui onion rings, and the miniature hushpuppies with corn relish. Ten minutes ago, please."

Foley grinned. "Talk to me, bubba!"

Dan glanced up from the menu. "Anything else? No? Okay, then." He spoke to the waiter. "Be straight. How good is this bartender?"

The waiter made a circle of approval with thumb and forefinger.

"Uh-huh?" Dan queried skeptically. "Well, you ask him if he can make a Negroni. If he comes back with 'Say, what?' instead of informing you he makes the best damn Negroni in the whole damn state of Mississippi, forget it! Otherwise, bring us two. Right, Claire?"

"Perfection," I murmured, giving him a soft-focus look. I was preoccupied with the way that recent little bite on my neck, hidden beneath my hair, was throbbing so deliciously.

"You quit that now," Dan growled out of the side of his mouth, then raised his voice. "Foley, Charlotte! What are you guys drinking?"

Foley consulted Charlotte, which took a moment or two because he had to kiss her first. But the kiss kept going so without looking at the waiter, he lifted his empty glass, then held up two fingers.

"Oh, right. Two more Harvey Wallbangers." The waiter melted away.

Dan and I looked at each other and laughed, remembering Shelby's description of what Freddy was doing in the ladies' room with a Miss Something when Franny caught them. Though on second thought, it really wasn't that funny. Quick as the lightning outside, another thought skipped through my head, and just as quickly, was gone.

Foley looked up and snuggled Charlotte against him. "Go ahead and laugh. Harvey Wallbanger's a damn good drink! Besides," he looked down at Charlotte and rubbed his thumb lightly against her lips, "we wanted to celebrate with something kinda silly."

"Celebrate what?" I zoomed a quick look at Charlotte, wondering if she *had* after all? She grinned and shook her head, holding her left hand across the table for our inspection.

"Oh, my gosh! Charlotte, it's gorgeous!" I gasped at the heavy chunk of rubies and diamonds on her ring finger. The old-fashioned setting had belonged to Foley's grandmother, smaller stones spiraling concentrically around a big center diamond, and mounted on a modern wide gold band. Foley proudly revealed he'd thought of that touch all by himself.

"Congratulations!" Dan jumped up and went around to hug them both, and I stood reaching across the table to make it a football huddle. Our drinks arrived and they were fine. We made toasts and listened to Foley and Charlotte.

"Well, honey. I was flat surprised!" Charlotte giggled.

"Gaped at me like a stuck flounder!" Foley said. "But see, I explained I wanted her to buy me a big old wedding ring, like that piece of corrugated pipe Danbo's got, and it wouldn't make any sense unless we went ahead and got married. Hell yes! Big old ring, big old Christmas Eve wedding, and a great big old you-know-what!"

Charlotte looked at him coolly. "So you keep telling me."

"Good one, Charlotte!" Dan roared, and we clowned around some more until the waiter showed up with our appetizers.

"I don't think you'll have time to order dinner if you want to catch the show, sir," the waiter warned. "But I could bring you some more appetizers if you like."

"Well I need some damn food!" Foley fretted. "Just

bring us something fast and good, and another round of drinks."

The waiter was delighted to be given his head. "I know just the thing," he said enthusiastically. "Our Tasty-Platter serves eight generously. Grilled chunks of tender marinated beef, jumbo garlic shrimp, chicken livers coated in crushed black pepper and sauteed in butter—"

"Damn it!" Foley thundered. "Don't just stand there telling me about it. Go get it!"

"Yessir!" The waiter hurried off.

"Okay, you two," Charlotte said, diving into the onion rings. "What happened to make you so late?"

Dan and I exchanged looks. Right into the midst of life, here came death again.

One point in favor of talking in a noisy place is that nobody else can overhear what you're saying. Between us, Dan and I filled them in on everything from the Ricky Gomez Beauty Crisis to my encounter with Brandon Battle, to Freddy's so-called accident.

Foley mopped up some garlic butter with a tiny hush-puppy. "Don't like the sound of this, Danbo. You got a handle on a connection here?"

Dan shook his head. "Not yet. But I know there is one."

"Oh, yeah." Foley agreed. "Absolutely."

"You did good, kid!" Dan congratulated the waiter when he brought the check. "You managed to get us loaded and stuffed in less than forty-five minutes!"

The sunglasses glinted as he snuck a peek at the tip. "I know my job, sir."

"Smartass!" Foley laughed as he and Dan helped extricate us womenfolk from our chairs. "I like that in a waiter."

"Oh, Dan." Charlotte said. "I brought along the printout of what little I got before the system went down." She patted the woven leather satchel. "Looks great with this outfit, huh? But I didn't think it was smart to leave it in my room."

"The whole thing'll take you about two seconds to read," Foley said. "But it's enough to make me suspect we're sitting on a bundle of Pure D dynamite."

"In that case," Dan retorted, "let's get busy and find us a Pure D match!"

CHAPTER 17

The Liberty Grand Ballroom was patriotic and palatial. Crystal chandeliers and candelabra wall sconces gleamed like fistfuls of diamonds flung upon rich reds and royal blues.

Eight hundred gilt-framed, red and blue striped opera chairs were arranged in a segmented fan shape facing the large stage, hung with heavy peacock velvet, gold-fringed curtains.

Tiered seating for two hundred additional spectators had been erected at the far end.

The incoming crowd was composed of hotel guests, contestants and their entourages, and residents from the surrounding communities. A sizeable delegation, who seemed to answer to the security guard's description of "a buncha horny guys," had apparently bought out the entire bleacher section. Despite the weather, the place was packed.

Charlotte, Foley, Dan and I were escorted to the VIP row directly behind the judges' panel, all present and accounted for except the two Franks. When Shelby Bell introduced us to the remaining six celebrity judges, I took special note of Marlowe Goodkidd, the sitcom actress Ricky Gomez had told me about.

Marlowe's attractively humorous features were gradually settling into a brittle cast, and insecurity flickered behind her eyes.

I remembered her jumping into the Hollywood confessional sweepstakes by announcing her addiction was neither drugs, alcohol or sex, but gambling. Whether sincere, or just picking a sin category a little less clogged with celebrities, Marlowe was a spokesperson for a gambler's twelve-step program between crashed sitcom pilots.

By the chummy manner she displayed toward the Bells, one would never guess she had successfully urged mutiny against them the day before. The actor's indispensable chameleon skin would provide camouflage until she knew which way the wind blew in that situation.

But whatever happened, it was a safe bet those three stooges she'd duped into leaving Ricky Gomez twisting in the wind could just whistle for their big trip to L.A. for her sitcom plot.

Across the aisle on Foley's right, coiled like two expensive and lethal reptiles, were Brandon Battle and LaWanda J. Scarborough. Battle had donned a sort of western tuxedo for the occasion, while LaWanda was elaborately Escada in green and black taffeta pieces with stripes and dots in complicated juxtaposition.

Once, she turned and seemed to look directly at me, although I couldn't be sure. It was eerie how those tinted lenses didn't actually conceal her eyes but so effectively masked their focus.

On the other side of our section, to Dan's left, sat Chief Troy Hepkins, unexpectedly dapper in a charcoal suit. Tinker told me later that the chief—early fifties and a widower—was relentlessly pursued by a hoard of Mrs. Hepkins hopefuls.

The remaining seats in our particular latitude were occupied by Crestview Cove residents and other locals— many longtime friends of the Bells—and the next few rows from one end of the room to the other were filled with the twenty pageant contestants not performing tonight, along with mothers, chaperons, and supporters.

The only videotaping allowed was by the pageant's production company, but still photographers were firing shots from endless ammo clips of film.

An excited murmur rose from the audience as the orchestra started to tune up.

Parker Bell was pacing in the wings, stage left, walkie-talkie at the ready. During the last hour, he'd apparently pulled himself together enough to resume normal duties. Or maybe he just needed to be surrounded by all those definitely live and lovely bodies to blot out the picture of that terrible dead one.

Foley frowned in the big man's direction. "Hey Danbo. That couldn't be Parker Bell up there, could it?"

"Uh-huh," Dan confirmed. "He's Shelby's nephew. Kind of. Only don't let him know you recognize him. Shelby says he doesn't like to be reminded of Ole Miss."

Foley laughed shortly. "I guess not! After all, he shoved

some guy's head in along with a load of laundry while the washing machine was still running!"

"Ouch!" Charlotte squawked. "I can't imagine Parker doing that! He seems so bashful and straightlaced!"

"Where'd you hear this, Foley?" Dan asked.

Foley swiveled a cautious eye toward Charlotte. "Well ... Belinda knew the girl the brawl was about," he said. "She was homecoming queen and all, and actually bragged how she got two big old dumb football players fighting over her! Just goes to show you the kind of friends Belinda had.

"Obviously, the boy's mellowed out over the years, but I guess he still loves to hang around them beauty queens!"

At stage right, occasional glimpses could be had of Ricky Gomez in his official Jose Eber hat, prancing like a high-strung colt, seeing to last minute recalcitrant locks.

A sudden, surprised spatter of applause grew until it became an ovation, when the famous comedian emcee appeared unheralded on stage in front of the curtains, holding a sheet of paper.

"Well, where the hell were you all when my last movie bombed?" he kidded, and the audience roared. "Seriously, folks. The show has not started yet, okay? Hey, I haven't been introduced, nobody's played my theme song—don't you people know anything?" Laughter.

"Listen. The only reason I'm here right now is that I've been asked to make some important announcements by our gracious hosts and founders of the Miss Gulf Coast Pageant, Shelby and Tinker Bell! Stand up and take a bow!"

Shelby and Tinker rose and waved, acknowledging the applause. Tinker looked fabulous in strapless silver sequins, and Shelby's tuxedo was trimmed surprisingly with a cummerbund and bow tie to match her dress.

The comedian suddenly fired off a barrage of juicy one-liners that had everybody cracking up, which ended as suddenly as it had begun.

He gave a theatrical sigh of relief. "I'm sorry. I just never know when these attacks are going to occur! Now, will you please settle down and pay attention so I can make these announcements?" He consulted the paper. "Well, I've got good news and bad news. Let's get the bad news out of the way first,

"I'm very sorry to tell you that America's favorite funny couple, the George and Gracie, the Ricky and Lucy, the Stiller and Meara of the nineties, Franny and Freddy Franks are unable to perform tonight." Big groan from the audience.

"I know. I know. But what can you do? However. Here's some news that's going to make everybody—especially several beautiful girls—very happy. Due to certain technical complications, every previously eliminated contestant in the Miss Gulf Coast Pageant is hereby reinstated to full competition status!"

Thunderous applause from the audience, squeals and joyful tears from the girls.

But those serpents on the far right seemed turned to stone. Only the silver streak in LaWanda's hair seemed to writhe like a live thing.

Dan leaned forward to observe their response, then sat back in satisfaction. "I knew they didn't give two hoots about Chessy getting back in the contest. Now, it's their move."

CHAPTER 18

The move came during intermission.

Up until then, the talent show had provided a pleasant, if temporary, escape from certain gruesome realities. Such as the pitiful, sheet-covered remnants of Freddy Franks, lying in the gym.

But even if poor Freddy had lived twice as long, it's doubtful he would've ever attained to such ready wit as the guy he'd tried to replace.

The emcee concluded his hilarious opening monologue (focusing on the contrasts between Catskill and Gulf Coast resort hotels) with a song and dance number—a specially-lyricized "One" from *A Chorus Line*—performed with to-night's ten contestants.

Chessy, strutting and kicking on legs up to her armpits, was the best. I felt queasy when I remembered her note to Dan.

In its own way the eclectic talent show was evocative of those Sunday nights when, as a little girl, I watched Ed

Sullivan with *Tante* Jeanette on the latest model TV set from the appliance store.

The country hunk urged the crowd to its feet so he could teach them a simple dance step, named after his latest hit, "Country Mile."

Our Hollywood visitors were discernibly taken aback when the gonzo ventriloquist appeared on stage, carrying two black dummies (even the terminology presented an immediate problem) one considerably darker than the other, both terribly nervous about being in Mississippi.

Soon, however, he had as many people rolling in the aisles as were dancing in them earlier. Particularly the blacker dummy's "reaction" when the ventriloquist told it to, "lighten up!"

As to the amateurs, in my opinion, Miss Captiva Island was going to be tough to top. That dusky beauty performed a sexy rap version of "Tramp" (papa wuz)—on a trampoline. Just the visual pun was brilliant.

Having forgotten Chessy's title, I was unprepared for the veiled figure that floated on stage in a gauzy harem outfit when Miss Tampa Tangerine was announced. No tap shoes required for this number, a sinuous, barefoot interpretation of Rachmaninoff's *Scheherezade*.

Then, one by one those veils began to drift into the audience, but in such a ladylike way, nobody was offended.

Except me, of course. I knew who she was really taking them off for.

I hunched rigidly in my chair, willing myself not to look at Dan as Chessy, still veiled of face but now down to a barely-there jeweled bustier and the billowy sheer harems, undulated into a backbend that brought her head to the floor, and the house to its feet.

Not until she flipped off the face veil as a grand finale did I turn toward Dan, only to see he was resting his forehead against one hand, shielding his eyes from the stage. He opened his fingers a crack and peered out at me. "Is it done yet?" he whispered, and grinned at my expression.

Leaning over, he kissed my left ear and said, "If asked, I wanted to be able to say truthfully, I did not watch her performance."

My eyes stung with sudden tears, causing his smiling face to blur. This man was one of a kind. I'd have to think of a real special way to say thank you . . .

Chessy's act had been the last before the break, and we were all glad to stand and stretch.

No one was allowed to approach the judges, who were scribbling final notes and marking cards.

Foley and Charlotte joined us to mingle and chat with the locals. We heard the latest weather report (pouring rain, Babe still headed for Mobile, expected to hit late tomorrow night); listened to them debate the pros and cons of evacuating inland at this point (very few pros); and learned about the problems with some of the larger boats in the Crestview Cove marina.

Several were tossing on their moorings in the increasing wind, swinging around and whacking into adjacent smaller craft. Shelby and Tinker's *Wedding Bells' Blue* was among the offenders, and all said vessels must be adequately secured by sundown tomorrow evening or a fine would be imposed.

"Mr. Claiborne, I believe we need to talk. I did tell your wife that this afternoon." Brandon Battle's buttery voice intruded into our enjoyment of a spirited argument between two serious pageant freaks who were rooting for different girls.

More or less as a quartet, Foley, Charlotte, Dan and I revolved to face Battle and LaWanda.

Dan smoothly forestalled either of them by performing introductions. "Good evening, Mr . Battle. I understand you've already met my wife, Claire?"

B.B. inclined his head, rattlesnake eyes glittering at me coldly as Dan continued, "And may I present Mr. Foley Callant, a senior partner of the law firm of Blanchard, Smithson, Callant and Claiborne, and his fiancée, Ms. Charlotte Dalton of WDSU television in New Orleans."

There was no escape for Battle, who was snared in the Southern Manners Trap. With bare civility, he reciprocated. "A pleasure," he lied. "And this dear, lovely lady is Mrs. LaWanda Scarborough. My friend and client and the actual mother, if you can believe it, of Chessy, our charming Miss Tampa Tangerine."

Charlotte, apparently with one Harvey Wallbanger too many under that gorgeous gold belt remarked, as stiff, insincere handshakes were exchanged, "Oh, I can believe Mrs. Scarborough's an actual mother all right!" She caught herself. "I mean, she looks so much like her daughter!"

Formalities concluded, Battle took off the gloves and got right down to brass knuckles. "Very clever move on your part to suggest reinstating all contestants, Mr. Claiborne. Or Mr. Callant. But it won't do your clients any good. Miss

Chessy Scarborough has not only suffered extreme mental anguish as a result of discrimination, but she has experienced severe humiliation as a result of being sexually harassed by one of the judges. Your client, Shelby Bell."

Foley grinned. "Yeah. She sure danced like she felt humiliated as all hell tonight."

LaWanda spoke for the first time, her expression unreadable behind those green lenses. Her voice was as soft as Battle's, but deeper. "Are you a psychiatrist as well, Mr. Callant? I assure you, Chessy's therapist will testify otherwise."

"Oh," Foley returned, "I'm sure he—or she—will. If it comes to that."

Battle showed his chalky teeth in a shark's grin. "Now you sound a mite more reasonable than your partner, young man. Because none of us really want things to 'come to that', do we?"

"Don't count on it," Dan warned, and I knew he was sorely tempted to challenge Battle to a courtroom duel. However, he had to consider the best interest of the Bells.

Battle's grin dissolved as quickly as it had come. "I have every reason to expect this to be settled out of court," he snapped. "And unless you want to see your clients' names dragged through the mud, you'd best expedite the process, rather than hinder it."

Dan smiled. "Really? As for dragging the Bells' names through the mud, you haven't exactly been holding back pending a settlement, have you now? And haven't you been telling everybody all you wanted was for Chessy to get back into the running for Miss Gulf Coast? Well, she is. What is the problem here?"

"But," Battle returned the volley, "the judge who sought to obtain Chessy's . . . favors, shall we say? still sits on the judging panel. That is unacceptable to us. And if he is removed, the panel of eight specified in the pageant contract will be incomplete. This is also unacceptable." He smiled and spread his hands open. "You see?"

Foley laughed. "You've made yourself crystal clear, sir. In fact, transparent might be a better word."

Battle's countenance grew dark with anger. "Have you forgotten who you're dealing with here?" he demanded. "I have won millions of dollars for my clients with far less to go on than this!"

Suddenly he began to croon in a low, throbbing voice, "The shameful advantage that has been taken of an innocent, vibrant, lovely young lady of color in the lush, flowering bloom of womanhood, by an undemocratic, unequal establishment.

"Furthermore, vile attempts were made upon her—ah—virtue by a wealthy white man who promised—" Abruptly, he switched off the courtroom drama and added, smugly, "Et cetera."

"Very impressive," Dan acknowledged wryly. "But I think you're getting this so-called case all mixed up with another one down in Florida twenty-something years ago."

LaWanda drew herself up, turning her blank eyes upon Dan. "Well, you are the clever boy, aren't you, Mr. Claiborne? Of course, since you are so clever, you will also be able to understand that I, as Chessy's mother, am determined not to let her suffer as I suffered at Tinker's hands.

"It is infamous, the way this woman has reappeared to ruin my life, and I am prepared to fight her with every weapon at my disposal." She paused and added throatily, "The stakes are so very high."

B.B. Battle was getting restive. He didn't like to hear the sound of anyone else's voice go on that long except his own. Taking LaWanda's arm in what seemed to me a less than affectionate manner, he soothed perfunctorily, "There, there, dear. You mustn't let these people upset you like this."

Battle started to lead LaWanda off, but halted when Dan called after him, "I'm curious, Mr. Battle. Exactly what kind of settlement do you envision would compensate Miss Scarborough for these terrible events in her life?"

Battle's teeth and eyes glinted beneath a big chandelier. He waved an arm that seemed to encompass the entire hotel and said, "Oh, I have a feeling that Miss Scarborough's trauma will run very, very deep. Emotional wounds like those inflicted upon her tender spirit may never heal." He smiled again. "Good evening."

We watched them head out of the ballroom, no reason to stay now that Chessy had done her stuff. Dan and Foley looked at each other.

"Well, counselor," Foley remarked. "That was fairly enlightening, wouldn't you say?"

Dan nodded thoughtfully. "I'd even say, more so than they intended."

CHAPTER 19

Despite the continued originality of the contestants' acts—the all-too-aptly crowned Miss Honeydew ("I'll just bet she *does*," sniped Charlotte) from Catonment, Florida with her dreamy, Peggy Fleming-style ice skating routine, but executed on Rollerblades in a scanty costume; Miss Butterbean of Pascagoula and her selection of Hawaiian melodies played on pedal steel guitar; and the truly remarkable demonstration by Miss Dauphin Island Deep Sea Fishing Cruises on how to bait up for, play, and land, a two hundred pound marlin (while almost wearing a leopardskin bikini)—Dan and I were getting pretty burnt out.

After passing Dan the manilla envelope of information pirated from Jan Windsor's computer, Foley and Charlotte had vacated somewhere around Miss Fairhope Mustard Green's more traditional offering of a Big Tearjerker Hit, "I Will Always Love You."

When the Male Country Star returned for an encore to fill the gap left by Franny and Freddy Franks, we slipped away as well.

Back in our suite, Dan poured us brandies from the decanter provided by the Bells, and switched on the radio. Soft, midnight jazz muted the sound of rain lashing against the windows. He sat on the bed and leaned against the pillows.

"Don't move," I instructed. "I'll be right back." In the bathroom, I located the bottle of almond-sesame oil in my travel bag, and slipped into a lacy black teddy.

Dan smiled when I walked back into the bedroom. "Now that was worth waiting for—" he began, but I put my fingers against his lips and made him sit still while I undressed him.

"Uh-uh!" I said, stepping away when he reached for me. "Lie down on the bed. On your tum, chum."

Dan narrowed his eyes at me speculatively and drawled slowly, "Oh, yes ma'am. I am definitely getting interested to find out exactly what you've got in mind."

"Mmmm, so I see," I laughed.

"Ah, now you're revealing an unsuspected cruel side to your nature, Claire," he said, rolling onto his stomach. "Well, this better be good, is all I got to say."

Beginning at his toes and working my way up to his ears, I massaged the oil into his body until he was practically delirious.

"Turn over," I commanded, and he obeyed. "No!" I scolded, slapping his hands away when he reached for me again. This time, I started at the forehead and worked my way down, ignoring his pleas, which soon became angry demands.

There were things I just didn't know how to tell him any other way, and I had to say them uninterrupted.

Dan snarled and fought and thrashed for control, but fortunately, I had picked up some valuable pointers from Miss Dauphin Island Deep Sea Fishing Cruises about playing a two hundred pound marlin, and I put them to excellent use.

Then, when he least expected it, I let the line run out, leaving this ferocious creature suddenly and completely free to take his revenge.

CHAPTER 20

I had suspected Mr. Marcel Barrineau of ulterior motives when he so nobly insisted on galloping to my rescue in his trusty Range Rover (the Corniche being snugly tucked away in his New Orleans garage) nearly 150 miles along a waterlogged coast in what could be the prelude to the most major, Gulf-driven hurricane since Andrew.

And I was right. Dan and I heard the whole story not long after Shelby rang from a house phone at around 7:15 the next morning, with the good news that the coroner had released Freddy's body.

Chief Hepkins himself was providing an escort for Franny and her late husband to the Gulfport Municipal Airport. Taking advantage of a momentary lifting of cloud cover, the control tower had cleared the eight o'clock hop to New Orleans for takeoff. From there, Franny, with any luck, should be able to get a flight back to L.A.

Shelby concluded by alerting us that Marcel and his cronies had arrived at around 1:00 a.m. and that the gym (minus one treadmill and a slab of mirror) was now open for business, should we want to beat the crowd.

Dan shifted on his elbow, just managing not to yelp and said, "I think we'll be confining ourselves to the whirlpool today, thank you, Shelby." He tried to glare at me but it turned into a grin instead. "Yeah," he continued to Shelby. "Eleven, your office. Fine."

He hung up and lay on his left side, head propped on his hand, watching me in the morning's leaden light. "About last night," he growled, starting to edge nearer but winced and stopped. "Woman, you hit me like a train wreck! I guess I'll live, though. Provided I don't make any sudden moves, that is."

"Your loss," I taunted, with sheer bravado. If somebody had yelled "Fire!" I doubt I could've budged.

"You know I'm gonna pay you back!" he threatened.

"And what do you call that? " I wondered, indicating the tattered shreds of silk lying at the foot of the bed—all that remained of my black teddy.

"Self-defense," he informed me, "in response to your unprovoked act of aggression."

I gazed at him. "You provoked me, Dan Louis. Well as I thought I knew you—in every way—the last couple of days I'm finding out I've barely scratched the surface. Something just came over me, and I suddenly felt like I would explode from the love I felt.

"I needed to show you, tell you, give to you. And because you always want to be the giver, I just had to make you take it, make you love being inescapably on the receiving end."

Dan had been watching me intently as I talked, and his blue eyes grew misty. "God, you are unbelievable, Claire! Yes, you're right. You had to make me take it, because I wouldn't have. At first, when I thought you were just being cute and sexy and teasing, it was fine and I was absolutely getting turned on. But when I suddenly realized what you were really doing, I actually got angry.

"It was like I almost couldn't accept knowing you love me as passionately as I love you. Then something inside told me to just let go, to just receive, because this was true and real and for me, from you. And it would take us someplace way beyond where we've been yet."

"Then it sounds like we both needed last night to happen when it did," I commented.

"Timing is everything," Dan agreed, smiling. "Come here, you."

"Can't!" I admitted. "I was in that same train wreck, remember?"

The question was academic anyway, becoming even more so when the phone rang again. "That was Marcel," Dan informed me, replacing the handset. He hauled himself up with a groan. "Better roll out, darlin'. Marcel has, and I quote, 'ordered much coffee and various tidbits from room service,' to be delivered here in about twenty minutes."

Marcel has a charmingly pedantic speech pattern which gives the *faux* impression that English is not his first language. He did come by this appealing little trick quite honestly, however. Being a direct descendant of one of the first families of Loyalists to settle in New Orleans, he also speaks fluent French.

To save time, Dan and I shared a scalding shower followed by an ice cold rinse, which restored at least some movement to our arms and legs, so when Marcel showed up right on the heels of room service, we were chastely wrapped in our maroon bathrobes.

Marcel breezed in like a shaft of white light, without the slightest sign of having whipped his Rover for miles along storm-tossed Highway 90 or of having snatched less than four hours sleep. His handsome olive face radiated health and careful pampering, the boyishly styled (by me) silver hair gleamed thickly, and his tall, lean frame lounged comfortably in costly sneakers and one of his favorite cashmere sweat outfits—in pale charcoal this time.

"Claire, Dan!" he exclaimed, bestowing energetic embraces. "You look," he hesitated and lifted a black eyebrow knowingly, "somewhat, ah, depleted. In need of sustenance." He tipped the waiters and shooed them out. "See, I have ordered enormous amounts of coffee, though one is not sure what one will receive in response to this request in places other than our own city.

"And here," he lifted covers from dishes, "are muffins—both English and corn—scrambled eggs, because I simply gave up explaining 'baste' to the person on the telephone. Sliced fresh fruit, bacon, avocado, tomato, butter, jam and cream cheese."

He looked at us expectantly. "Have I done well?"

Dan grinned. "Great. But what are you and Claire going to eat?"

Marcel nodded sagely as we settled around the coffee table. "Ah!" he sighed, buttering a muffin. "It is always so when a man has been living for an extended time on love alone. One ravenous appetite sated, another to take its place.

"At least," he added sourly, "I seem to recall."

I managed to swallow my mouthful of bacon and avocado without choking on a laugh. Marcel Barrineau has been married and divorced twice, dated most of the beautiful single women in New Orleans, and always had a talented and succulent young student from his Institut de Beauté training as his apprentice.

If he was claiming forgetfulness in the ways of love, it could only be as a result of his turbulent relationship with Detective Sergeant Nectarine Savoy, NOPD, whom he had met in the course of a murder case we'd all been involved in.

Nectarine Savoy was a stunning octoroon with copper-gold hair and blue eyes, who had been a famous international high-fashion model until her best friend, another model, had become the victim of a still-unsolved murder case.

Nectarine quit modeling and returned to her hometown of New Orleans, where she had risen to her present rank in the police force.

Marcel, adroit eel in the game of romance as he was, had fallen unexpectedly hard for Nectarine, and soon found himself a pickled eel.

Nectarine had fallen pretty hard herself, and their chemistry was obvious to the most casual observer. But so far, she hadn't succumbed to Marcel's expert wooing. He'd even gone so far as to take a bloodtest, and practically carried his clean bill of health in his teeth, dropping it at her feet, wagging his tail hopefully.

Still Nectarine resisted. In fact, she told him she didn't want to see him anymore. Charlotte, who knows her better than I do, confided Nectarine was really in love with Marcel. But, given her racial mix and Marcel's social position, she didn't see a snowball's chance in hell for marriage, although Marcel regularly squired her to all the ritziest Uptown do's without the slightest flinch.

Nectarine felt if she allowed herself to get involved any more deeply in something that had no future, the whole thing would be an even bigger heartbreak.

Naturally, having her pride, Nectarine told Marcel none of this, instead pulling her African Queen aloof act on him.

Naturally, Marcel, having his pride, went shopping among his students for a new protégé, and found one named Dolly.

That's as much as I knew until now. As it turned out, he was telling us, with Dolly he'd gotten hold of a tiger by the tail.

"My judgment is indeed slipping," Marcel mourned, pouring himself another cup of coffee which he conceded was not terrible. "As you know, I select my assistants very carefully. Talent with hair is the most important thing, as I could not tolerate to work alongside, or otherwise associate closely, with someone who does not show promise of becoming brilliant. And then, of course, the other . . . attributes.

"If she is not interested in a discreet liaison, well, that sometimes happens, does it not, Claire? And did I not continue to train you? Did I ever once threaten you would not remain for the full three-month apprenticeship if you did not, um, cooperate?"

"Yes, yes, and no," I agreed, around a mouthful of corn muffin. "The noblest Frenchman of them all. So what happened with Dolly?"

Marcel looked genuinely puzzled. "As to that, I am not entirely certain. Following my little tradition (which I may say many find very charming) I invited Dolly to Antoine's for dinner to announce she had been chosen to be my apprentice.

"She listened most attentively, and asked intelligent questions. Dolly is, of course, quite talented in addition to having naturally curly brunette hair in abundance, and a more, ah, robust stature than I normally find appealing.

"She also happens to be extremely ambitious and an ardent, no, militant feminist. She told me, 'Look, Marcel. I've heard rumors about you and your apprentices. Yes, I'll accept the job because I think I deserve it, and frankly, it'll look good on my resume. But if during the course of our work your hand accidently grazes my boob even once, I'll hit you with a sexual harassment suit so hard it'll shrivel your pathetic penis!'

"I do not see cause for such levity," he added severely, as Dan and I howled.

"Whoo! Sorry, Marcel!" Dan apologized. "Go ahead."

"Well that, as you can imagine, was as instantly quenching to any romantic notions as a bucket of cold water. Suddenly, Dolly did not seem so robust anymore, but rather somewhat too large. And I was genuinely alarmed by this attitude that she was just waiting for me to put a foot or some other appendage wrong. How was I to instruct such a person? It was all a dreadful mistake, but what could I do? If I were to withdraw the offer, she would certainly claim it was because she spurned my advances. Which, I hasten to point out, I had not yet made."

"Oh, you can believe she would," Dan agreed. "I'm beginning to think someone could operate a very lucrative law practice doing nothing but defending against sexual harassment charges."

"And then?" I prompted.

Marcel shrugged. "I sent her home in a taxicab. But in the three weeks since, a very strange thing has happened. Dolly has been winking at me, making suggestive remarks, calling me at home late at night, and contriving to turn up at various bars and restaurants I patronize on a regular basis." His brow furrowed. "It is either she is trying to force me into a compromising position so she can sue me, or she is suddenly genuinely interested."

He shuddered. "Either way, I am a nervous wreck. And to make matters worse, the luscious Grapes is seeing someone else with increasing frequency."

From the beginning of their acquaintance in July, Marcel had been calling Nectarine by the names of almost every other fruit. That she was seeing another guy was something Charlotte hadn't mentioned. "Really!" I remarked with interest. "Who?"

Marcel made a face. "Some phoney criminal attorney by the name of Duke Abbidis."

"Oh, come off it, Marcel!" Dan ordered, nabbing the last corn muffin. "You know well as I do the Abbidises are an old quadroon family. Though I must say," he chewed thoughtfully, "I do find it hard to picture Nectarine running around town with an oily customer like Duke."

"Exactly!" Marcel agreed eagerly. "He has been married several times, and has a reputation for being a philanderer. I am convinced that Apple's good name will suffer."

Dan and I gaped at him. In describing Duke Abbidis with such righteous indignation, Marcel had also furnished a nearly exact description of himself! How interesting that Marcel should find an (admittedly magnified) reflection of his own behavior so distasteful.

"I have been intimate with no one since that ill-fated affair of Angie," Marcel went on self-pityingly. It was during the investigation of Angie's murder Marcel had met Nectarine Savoy.

"Nothing is the same anymore," he fretted. "The diseases one can contract, the caliber of woman one meets. And then when one does encounter a lady of high quality and offers one's love, she spurns me."

Dan put a consoling hand on his shoulder. "You got it bad, son!" he diagnosed.

Marcel studied his perfect manicure a moment then looked up and sighed. "You are right, of course," he admitted. "And that makes everything more complicated. One cannot offer a woman like that anything less than—" he interrupted himself hastily. "I mean, what with Apricot now on vacation and keeping frequent company with the odious Duke Abbidis, and this business of the demonic Dolly, my nerves are simply screaming. That is why, Claire, your cry of distress was to me an answer from God. I could quickly round up several pairs of willing and skillful hands by promising credit for extra hours, put Dominica in charge of my station, and escape."

Dominica, Marcel's second-in-command, was a forceful, chunky Italian woman with a fierce visage. She had been the terror of the Institut when I was a student and I figured she would make short work of Dolly.

After unloading his woes, Marcel listened avidly to our recitation of everything that had been going on here—from Chessy's accusations against the pageant and Shelby; her flagrant overtures to Dan; Freddy's mysterious "accident"; Battle's threats against the Bells—and commented that there must be something in the water.

He took notes as I estimated what needed to be accomplished between now and Saturday night, seeming to view the whole mess as a refreshing challenge.

Around nine o'clock he stood. "I will now say *au revoir* and go to take care of a few personal things before I seek out Ricky Gomez for a conference. The only thing I wonder, Dan, is what do you plan to do about the judging situation? Of course, I know little of contracts, but it seems this Battle person has some sort of point about the number of judges?"

Dan told Marcel he was right. "I had anticipated that move," he said. "But nothing could be done until he made it. And frankly, now that he has, I'm not sure how to counter him. Foley and I have been concentrating on some other angles, but we need to come back with the right answer fast. It can't be just anybody, either, because then he can claim the person is unqualified."

Marcel stood with a hand on the doorknob, smiling in a superior way. "Possibly you require someone who was once an internationally famous model, who moved in the higher circles of society, and partied with royalty?"

Dan and I jumped up from the sofa as one. "You mean?"

Marcel nodded. "Yes. Raspberry."

I said, "Nectarine is here? Now?"

Dan demanded, "How did you convince her to come to *Mississippi* with you in this weather when she won't even see you back home anymore?"

"Oh. As to that." Marcel studied the ceiling. "She did not exactly know she was going out of town until it was too late. You see, after much persuasion, the lady had agreed to join me for a drive.

"When I picked her up I had with me my four volunteers, explaining that I needed to drop them off. I simply neglected to say where.

"It did not occur to her to question our destination until we passed through Bay St. Louis. By then, as I said, it was too late. And she is too much of a lady to make a fuss in front of strangers. But after we arrived, *ay yi yi!*"

Dan shook his head. "Marcel, you don't understand. You *kidnapped* a police officer and transported her across state lines. In a near-hurricane! She could have you arrested! And you have the gall to stand there and volunteer her as a replacement judge for a beauty pageant? I ain't asking her, pal, believe it! Especially if she's armed!"

Marcel considered. "Since in her extreme displeasure last evening she did not threaten me with a firearm, I assume she did not bring a gun. An unfortunate circumstance if there is indeed a murderer at large.

"And as for judging the pageant. Papaya did not calm

down until I managed to explain that not only was I desperate to see her away from the distractions of our lives in New Orleans, but that you and Claire were in a predicament over complications arising during this beauty pageant. She was very interested, especially in the racial aspects.

"At this point, she would be highly insulted if you did not avail yourself of her presence."

Dan grinned. "My God, what a grenade to explode in Battle's face! We couldn't ask for a more perfect replacement for Shelby!"

Marcel inclined his head complacently. "Somehow I felt I was doing the right thing, even though it was, technically, a crime. I must have been an unwitting instrument in the hands of God to you, as you were to me."

He consulted his watch. "Ah, the boutiques will be open. I must now take Cheremoya down and buy her many beautiful and expensive things as it is entirely my fault she arrived with nothing."

On that note, Marcel departed, singing about God moving in mysterious ways, His wonders to perform, in a resounding baritone.

CHAPTER 21

Right after Marcel left, the phone rang. It was Shelby again, with the news that Chief Hepkins had contacted him to report Franny's plane had just taken off for New Orleans. Guilty or not, she was safely out of reach. At least temporarily.

Dan and I sat around like lumps for awhile, trying to digest our unaccustomedly huge breakfast and indulging in wild speculations.

I couldn't forget how awful Franny had looked when she'd walked into the salon yesterday afternoon. What on earth had happened to inflict such visible emotional ravages? At the time, I'd simply assumed she and Freddy'd just finished another round. In fact, Franny herself even called attention to her appearance and insinuated that was the case.

But if so, was that final episode so devastating that she had arrived at the desperate and irrevocable decision to eliminate her mate? From what little I'd heard of their situation, death might be the only way she could get rid of Freddy—until he was good and ready.

Clearly, nobody wanted him without Franny. And he was certainly aware of all the husband/wife teams who'd split, then fizzled out as solo acts. He simply couldn't afford to let her go. How he must've hated her for that! Freddy Franks' ego, his "you-owe-me" attitude, were way too enormous to hide. In order to save face, he would keep a grip of steel on his wife, unless and until his movie role was praised. Then, it would be adios baby time.

Maybe Franny had simply been abused beyond endurance this trip, saw an unexpected chance, and grabbed it, Or perhaps there had been a kinder, gentler man who reminded her of what she'd been missing . . . which brought us back to Shelby again. Somehow though, I just couldn't believe his chivalry would stretch so far as to wipe out an inconvenient and unpleasant husband, even if he had toyed with the notion of a romance with Franny.

Plus, as Dan pointed out with a laugh, if the merest thought of a dalliance had fleetingly crossed Shelby's mind, Tinker would've spotted it right away and put an immediate stop to such nonsense!

It was much easier to imagine *Tinker* greasing up that frying pan for Freddy, but why would she? Maybe he'd threatened her precious beauty pageant in some way——beyond blowing hot air about canceling out.

Could he have seen a chance to use the potential crisis the Bells were facing with Chessy's allegations, to blackmail Tinker into ensuring him a solo star turn on the final night when the pageant would broadcast coast-to-coast-to-coast? Freddy and Franny Franks' ardent public support of the Bells in exchange for what? A smear campaign if Tinker refused?

"This stuff is getting us crazy and nowhere at the same time," Dan said finally. He rose stiffly. "Well, I better start dressing now, if I'm going to make that meeting at eleven."

"The fun never sets at the Bell Sands Resort," I observed, and stretched out on the sofa.

When Dan came back into the sitting room, he was carrying the single sheet of computer paper from the envelope Charlotte had given him last night. "Forgot all about this," he said, handing it to me. "Foley was right. It's just enough to suggest there's something going on behind the scenes around here."

I perused the brief newspaper excerpts. The most recent, headlined "HIGH ROLLERS SHOOT TO TURN GULF COAST INTO A NEW RIVIERA," was about a group of prominent business and professional men who had formed a lobby to get an on-shore casino gambling bill, similar to Louisiana's, introduced before the legislatures of Florida, Alabama and Mississippi. Brandon Benjamin Battle's name headed the list of lobbyists. So far, their effort had succeeded in Mississippi, and the bill was expected to be put to a vote before the Thanksgiving recess.

Unlike the current gaming law—which required all gambling be conducted on vessels in the water, either at sea, or floating permanently moored to a dredged-out site—proponents claimed the new bill would stimulate the construction of deluxe resorts along the coastline, raise oceanfront property values, and allow existing hotels to maximize their profits by opening their own in-house casinos.

Opponents argued the reverse would occur, that if a "dry land" bill passed, casino operators would immediately abandon their floating games and move to areas of highest traffic and population, thereby defeating the purpose for which the original law was written in the first place—to increase tourist trade for the Mississippi beaches.

Both sides of the controversy were coming out swinging and the reporter concluded, tongue-in-cheek, that it was a crapshoot.

The other was dated 1983, and concerned Eddie Jack Scarborough 's deerhunting accident. Actually, it was a double tragedy. Because the man responsible, Jerry Hutto, was so devastated about killing his buddy, he'd stuck the same shotgun in his stomach and blown a hole right through his guts. The account was incomplete, but it did contain a significant piece of information; among those named as being members of the hunting party were LaWanda Scarborough and Brandon Battle.

CHAPTER 22

At high noon, upon the advice of Dan and Foley, Shelby and Tinker Bell threw an impromptu brunch for the press in the hotel lobby.

It seemed like quite a tall order to fill at virtually the last minute, with Hurricane Babe on the way. Nevertheless, between 11:30 and twelve o'clock, long tables filled with Southern goodies—spicy pork sausage patties on hot buttermilk biscuits, cream gravy, sweet and sour green beans with bacon, potato salad, fried chicken and individual pecan pies—had been set up on one side of the room.

Tables on the other side formed a bar with all the makings for mimosas, bloody Marys, mint juleps, and almost everything else. I wondered if Foley and Charlotte were still sold on Harvey Wallbangers, which made me recall what Shelby told us about Freddy's rumored shenanigans in the ladies' room. Maybe that had been the final blow to Franny's soul, and she'd gone over the edge. Not to mention, all the way to L.A.

But wasn't there also a more direct connection between

Freddy and liquor, too? Oh, yes. Something bothered me about the champagne being sent to his room . . . no, it wouldn't come.

Word about the brunch spread among the media already at the hotel as if it had been communicated by jungle drum. And, thanks to the increasingly valuable Jan Windsor, some local newspaper and TV reporters braved the elements to show up as well.

In less than forty-five minutes since its inception, everyone involved with the pageant, including many of the contestants, were swarming over the food like white on rice.

Tinker, with professional savvy, gauged the exact moment when the food had been tasted and savored, and half the room was already on their second drink.

"Ladies and gentlemen!" she called over the microphone Charlotte and Buddy Gaines had hastily rigged up for her. "I have an important announcement to make." The buzz died down and Tinker smiled at the crowd as if she was getting ready to twirl those fire batons and *win* this sucker. "As most of you know, this is the fifth year of our beloved Miss Gulf Coast Pageant." Applause. "Thank you very much. And many of you have been coming back every year, right from the get-go. I see lots of familiar faces out there today.

"But this time, we have met with a number of unexpected difficulties. From the weather, which we can do nothing about—" Laughter. "—to some serious legal complications, which we are making every effort to rectify."

The room grew still. She had their undivided attention now. "I don't need to go into detail and embarrass all the parties concerned. But since an objection has been raised to the continuing presence of a certain member of our judging panel, and the pageant bylaws state specifically the selection of a winner shall be determined by a minimum of eight judges, we were faced with either being forced to cancel the entire pageant—" A groan of objection. "—or come up with a qualified replacement."

Tinker dimpled charmingly. "Now where, you might ask, could we locate such an individual at the last minute, practically in the middle of a hurricane? And the answer, of course, is that it's impossible."

The crowd stirred and murmured uncertainly.

From my position behind Dan, two steps up on the staircase to the mezzanine, I saw Brandon and Chessy standing together, looking pleased. Parker lurked nearby, gazing hungrily at Chessy. If LaWanda was around I didn't see her.

Tinker timed her pause to the second. "However! The impossible has happened! They say it's an ill wind that blows nobody good, right? Well, *honey*. This wind is as good as it gets!"

Tinker smiled, both fire batons twirling faster now. "This woman is a famous international beauty in her own right. You've seen her on the covers of expensive magazines and read gossip about her in the cheap tabloids. Oh, I'm sorry. Nobody in here reads *those*, right?" Laughter.

"She has not only worked hard to fight discrimination in the fashion industry, but has been successful in her second career—fighting violence in the streets of her city, as a New Orleans police officer.

"Ladies and gentlemen. May I present the newest member of the judging panel for the Miss Gulf Coast Pageant—the very glamorous, the very beautiful, the very courageous, Miss Nectarine Savoy!"

Whoosh! Up went the fire batons!

The room rocked with applause as Nectarine, looking like a million bucks in a brand new gold silk Jill Sander outfit that probably set Marcel back pretty near that, glided gracefully forward to stand next to Tinker.

I glanced quickly over at Battle and Chessy. They looked like they'd been clubbed in the head, while Parker Bell looked outraged and wounded. A former supermodel right here on the premises, and nobody had even thought to mention it to him, probably.

Nectarine's copper-gold Medusa ringlets (as designed by Marcel) shone in the light as she acknowledged the applause and smiled for flashing cameras.

"Thank you so much, everyone," she purred, and blinked those huge sapphire eyes around the room in exaggerated amazement. "My goodness, this isn't Kansas anymore!"

Warm laughter and applause, then Nectarine went on. "I can truly say, that twelve hours ago, this is the last place I expected to be. But now that I am, I plan on having me a *good* time! How about y'all?"

Wild applause and whistles were her answer. Dan looked back over his shoulder and grinned at me.

Nectarine started to get serious. "Now, I know some of you have concerns and questions about everybody getting a fair chance to win the title of Miss Gulf Coast and—" she winked "—that lux-u-ry au-to-mo-bile plus all that cash, right?"

Laughter and applause.

"Well, I do, too. You notice I say a fair chance? As a woman of color myself, I never wanted anybody to just hand me something, just because I was. I only wanted the chance to strut my stuff. And, once I got it, I surely did!"

Wolf whistles and cheers.

"And that's really what we're after here, isn't it folks? *Whoever* wins will do so, not because of what she was born *as*, but because of what she's got now. Her *stuff*!"

More applause. The Hollywood people looked like they'd died and gone to heaven. Nectarine could wind up getting nominated for political office. Battle and Chessy had disappeared, and Parker was looking around agitatedly.

"In conclusion, just let me set your minds at rest. I'm really glad to step in here, but I don't know who on earth gave y'all the idea it was necessary. I have known this lady—" she indicated Tinker "—for a while, and I am very close to several other people involved with this pageant in one way or another. And I can tell you, a less bigoted bunch of white folks you're not likely to find anywhere!

"So come on, y'all. Get over it! Let the games begin. Or, as they say in my town, *laissez les bontemps roleur*! In other words, parTEE, par*TEE* . . ."

"ParTEE, parTEE, parTEE!" The crowd took up the chant and the cameras went berserk again.

Dan took my hand. "Come on, darlin'," he said, and pulled me along behind him until we'd worked our way to the front. There was no point in trying to get to Nectarine yet, but we reached Marcel, who glowed with such virtue you could practically see his halo. "Somebody's going to put you on the dashboard of their car if you're not careful," I warned him.

Foley bellowed, "What a team, huh, Danbo!"

"Wasn't Nectarine fabulous?" Charlotte demanded rhetorically.

Beaming, Shelby and Tinker rushed over and shook our hands. "Dan, Foley," thundered Shelby. "My boys, how can I ever repay you?"

"Oh, if we think real hard I believe we can figure out something, Shelby," Dan said meaningfully.

Shelby nodded in complete comprehension. "Of course, I know you aren't referring to the permanent supply of cigars I promised."

"Hey!" Foley cut in. "I get cigars too! But Marcel here is the guy that really saved our collective ass. If he hadn't surprised Nectarine with this little trip, we wouldn't have had a rabbit to pull out of a hat."

Marcel silkily amended, "More accurately, you would not even have had a hat."

"Marcel, *honey*!" Tinker gushed. "I can't begin to thank you enough for coming down here in all this old rain to help Claire help my poor little Ricky out. Is there something *special* I can do for you, sugar?"

I laughed. "You might want to give him a generous discount at the boutiques, Tinker. Since he hauled Nectarine down here with just the clothes on her back last night, he's got to buy her a whole new wardrobe!"

Tinker hooted. "Oh, honey! That's my kind of man!

Well, don't you worry about a thing. I'll tell the salesgirls to let Nectarine take anything she wants on approval. When y'all get ready to leave, she can return whatever she doesn't want to keep, and you can have the rest of it at cost. How's that sound?"

Marcel slid me a bewildered look. Was this our tight-fisted Hell's Bell? But not being one to look a gift horse in the mouth he said rapidly, before she could change her mind, "Thank you, Tinker. That is most munificent."

Nectarine had finally extricated herself from the mob and made her way over. "Whew!" she let out her breath. "How'd I do, guys?"

Charlotte hugged her. "Saved the bacon is all, girl-friend!"

Foley put his right hand on his heart, "Sergeant Savoy, we salute you."

Dan said, "Thanks, lady. Above and beyond the call of duty."

Nectarine chuckled, "You got that right, Lawyer Dan. Hey, Claire!" She gave me a squeeze. "Haven't seen you since the wedding!"

She turned away to speak to the Bells, continuing to ignore Marcel, who now resembled a plaster statute of one of the more martyred saints.

Shelby and Tinker, with Nectarine between them, joined us. "I have a great idea!" Shelby proclaimed in a sonic boom. "Tonight, we're going to celebrate with a special dinner in the private dining room. I'm afraid it will have to be early, around seven, shall we say? Because the talent show tonight starts at eight."

Nectarine appeared to notice Marcel for the first time. "In that case, I think Daddy here better go lie down and take a nap. I understand he's working this afternoon."

Oh, shoot. So was I. I'd almost forgotten.

Nectarine began to walk away, then turned. "Well?" she addressed Marcel. "Are you coming, or what?"

Marcel seemed to snap out of a trance. "Oh! But certainly, my dear." He scrambled after her without a backward look.

"Ooh-wee ! Pussy*whip*! " chortled Foley, and the rest of us laughed.

"Oh, isn't it just so nice to be able to laugh and not have to worry about anything!" Tinker exclaimed.

"There's still a hurricane coming," Dan reminded her.

"Oh, pooh!" Tinker dismissed Babe with an airy flutter of her hand. But the disappearance of Brandon Battle could not be taken so lightly.

CHAPTER 23

I headed for the Bella Salon after leaving Dan at Shelby Bell's office to review some things, feeling both hungry and bloated because I was so far off my regular schedule. Now I was sorry I hadn't at least grabbed a piece of that fried chicken at the brunch to bring along, since I was going to be awfully busy for the next few hours.

On the other hand, I didn't want to either use up my calories or spoil my appetite for the special dinner coming up. I had heard talk of lamb and garlic. So, I stopped off at the Bay Lounge for a couple of liters of Evian and a Power Bar.

As I had surmised from our first evening, the porthole windows did provide a fabulous view of the Gulf, only none of the customers hunched over the bar, or sprawled listlessly in the booths deprived of golf, tennis and sunshine, seemed to much like what they saw. I didn't blame them. The portholes gave the illusion of being aboard a pitching vessel on a dark and windy sea, and if you looked out there long enough you could actually start to get seasick. At least I could, though possibly in my case the stimulus was psychological as well as visual, due to what happened to my parents.

At Bella Salon, Marcel was already reviewing the troops with Ricky Gomez when I walked in. They looked like a pretty promising bunch at that.

There was an elfin blond named Jennifer; Casey, a burly, freckled redhead from the Irish Channel; Bette (formerly plain old Betty, but Marcel, spotting traces of the Divine One, enhanced the resemblance with a retro makeover, which included a name bob); and Delacroix, a handsome Haitian whose family had fortunately immigrated to America just before Baby Doc Duvalier went into exile.

Marcel introduced me to everyone, then we went over today's appointments with Ricky, dividing up the chores. Marcel would work with Delacroix on straight color, cuts, African hair and braids; Ricky and Bette to handle all the perms; Jenny was to assist me with all the blonde stuff, including weaves, plus slap on a few manicures in her spare moments; and Casey would rotate among the three of us, in addition to constructing the fluffier hair and up-dos which were developing into his natural milieu. I figured Casey would be the perfect lamb to toss on Tinker's altar should she require service. Let him get his baptism by fire over and done with.

Marcel was still looking slightly discombobulated. Maybe it had finally dawned on him that, for the first time in his life, he had actually lost his head over a woman to the extent of taking action which crossed the boundaries of romantic impetuousness into unchartered territory. And now that he had gotten Nectarine here, what on earth was he going to do with her?

But Marcel, who was nothing if not the consummate professional, pulled himself together quickly. "What lines do you carry?" he asked Ricky.

"For color, mainly Redken and Goldwell. The rest is a mix of Phyto, Aveda, Futura, some others. And Marcelixir, of course," Ricky added archly, referring to Marcel's own hair products, which were not simply one of the many generics available to stylists to stick their own label on; he actually oversaw their manufacture himself, no animal testing.

"But of course, you would have this," Marcel replied austerely, while at the same time allowing Ricky to see he was pleased.

"But how are we fixed for quantity?" I asked. The last thing we needed was to get in the middle of a toning job and run out of a certain shade. It has happened.

"Follow me," directed Ricky, and led us to the storeroom, which appeared to be as well stocked as a small beauty supply outlet.

"There!" He waved smugly at the crowded shelves. "The result of five years' experience in the pageant business. I now order based on the number of contestants times two, plus two extras of everything in case of screwups."

"Excellent, Ricky!" Marcel praised. "I am most impressed!"

Ricky glowed with pleasure. "*Verdad*, I learned from the best," he returned, elegantly.

By the time Ricky finished showing everybody where

to find the countless impedimenta required *pour le cheveaux*—towels, timers, smocks, capes, clips, combs, plastic caps, gloves—and we did some practice runs to familiarize ourselves with the route from sinks to stations to dryers to color and perm alcove, so that we wouldn't crash into each other, the stampede was almost due to begin.

Ricky, deferring to seniority, graciously offered Marcel his own elevated station in the center of the room, and Marcel graciously accepted. We'd just gotten a stack of Brazilian jazz CDs going when Marlowe Goodkidd breezed in, puffing on a cigarette in defiance of the NO SMOKING sign.

"Oh, Ricky!" she gushed. "I can't tell you how glad I am that everything got worked out about the pageant! Plus, I just had to tell you how much I adored that new style you gave Franny Franks.

"But," she patted her own blonde hair coquettishly, "I think it'd look even better on me!" She plopped into what she assumed to be Ricky's chair without even waiting for an invitation, continuing to talk.

"Oh, I recognize you from last night," Marlowe informed me. "You've got that great big delicious southern fried husband! Come on, be generous. There's enough of him to share and have plenty left over."

Ricky simply could not resist that opening. "Oh, I'm afraid he's way too rich for *your* blood, honey!" he sniped, bitchily. "At your age, you've got to watch that cholesterol!"

Marcel's four students broke into snickers, which they tried to hide behind their hands like a row of geishas. This was living! The actress was at first incredulous, then angry at the putdown, but just as she opened her mouth for a comeback, Marcel stepped forward.

"Surely you are not one of the contestants?" he stated, rhetorically.

She closed her mouth and looked Marcel over, exhaling what she supposed to be a sultry gust of smoke at him. Apparently she liked what she saw. The woman certainly was flexible. "Surely I am not," she mimicked lazily, watching him.

"Then," Marcel glanced pointedly at the wall clock. "may I inquire why you are sitting in my chair?"

"Who's been sitting in my chair?" Marlowe teased, thinking she was the cutest thing in the whole wide world. "Well, I thought it was Little Ricky's chair, but now that Papa Bear's here, I like it even better."

Marcel became his haughtiest, which is haute indeed. "It is my great pleasure to inform you that the remainder of the day is reserved for pageant contestants exclusively, who will begin arriving at any moment. Should you desire to arrange an appointment for some future time, you are at perfect liberty to do so."

"How dare you?" Marlowe sputtered furiously. "Do you know who I am?"

He lifted one shoulder in a dismissive shrug. "But of course. One wonders, however, if you do not perhaps think more highly of yourself than you ought. Many far more famous people than you have visited my salons in New Orleans, but none has been so rude or presumptuous as yourself!"

Actors not only need a chameleon skin but a thick hide

as well. She dealt with Marcel's comments by completely ignoring them, and turned to Ricky. "Then Ricky, if you can't make time for me—which really isn't too smart of you—would Trini be able to do my hair like Franny's?"

Ricky grinned viciously. "He might, if he was here. But he is not."

The actress looked around. "Well where is Trini? And Julian and Viola? I need my polish changed, too. Who are all these other people?"

"It was just the strangest thing, wasn't it, Ricky? "I remarked ingenuously, beckoning for little Jennifer to wheel over a tin tray and start laying out weaving foils. "How all three of those naive children got it into their tiny heads that if they were to boycott their jobs, and leave you stuck with nobody to help you with the pageant girls, some big Hollywood star was going to fly them to L.A. to work on a sitcom!"

The four geishas giggled behind their hands again. Even they knew better than to believe something like that.

I slipped a big mauve Bella Salon chef-style apron over my head and tied the sash around my waist. Hmmm. Large handy kangaroo pocket in front. I'd have to consider the idea for Eclaire. I stole a covert glance at the sitcom actress's face and saw comprehension begin to dawn.

"You see," I chattered on, bringing her into it as if completely oblivious to her involvement, "I own a little salon in New Orleans, and Marcel Barrineau, of course, owns several big salons in New Orleans, and when our friends the Bells called us to help, miraculously we were able to answer the call.

"And," I smiled sweetly at her, "my great big southern fried husband just also happens to be a great big attorney? And he said it was too bad, but those three poor kids had to be fired. But you know what else? He thinks that Julian and Trini and Viola may have very good grounds to bring a suit against whoever it was that talked them into doing something so dumb they lost their jobs, but who also promised them work too.

"Something about breach of verbal contract, or something like that!" I called after the woman's retreating figure. Mention the word "suit" and unless you're talking about Armani, people leave the room in a hurry.

"Thank you, thank you!" I bowed to the applause.

" 'Scuse me, my 'pointment's for 1:30?" Googly blue eyes, dimples and cleavage up to her earlobes. I glanced at the book. Miss Appalachicola Sunfish. Whole head weave. Oh, my Lord, look at those roots!

"Over here, honey," I sighed, patting the chair.

🌿 🌿 🌿

We worked for the next five hours like a team of emergency room surgeons; roll 'em in, cut 'em open, stitch 'em up, roll 'em out. There was only one mishap. Jennifer, somewhat overwhelmed, had begun Miss Appalachicola Sunfish's hair on the right side, while I took the left. But instead of parting it in half-inch segments, she'd done quarter-inches. Fortunately, I saw what she was doing before it went too far, and was able to both correct Jennifer and blend in my corresponding section without Miss A ever suspecting a thing.

More than ever, I was grateful for my incomparable Renee. It was really going to be hard to break somebody else in and let Renee begin to develop on her own, but it was the only fair thing to do. And I would. Eventually.

When we were through, I had exactly half an hour to get ready for dinner. I looked and felt like a droop. I needed a mud mask.

But Dan was in the bathroom shaving at one of the sinks when I barged in. "Try not to watch," I advised him. "It won't be pretty, and there's not time to hide the seams."

He laughed. "Now darlin', I might get a closer shave than I exactly want to if I shut my eyes. You just go on about your girl business, and I promise I'll still respect you."

"Ha-ha, " I said bitterly, getting out of my sweats and knotting a big towel around me. I twisted another around my hair. "Don't say you weren't warned." I bent over the sink and steamed my face until it was red, used a micro-milled pineapple-oatmeal scrub to exfoliate, then slathered on a thick clay mask.

I saw Dan's shoulders quiver slightly. "You looked!" I accused. "Well, I won't stay here and be ridiculed."

I stalked into the bedroom and stretched out across the bed, letting my head hang back over the edge. "Ohhh, I am so sore!" I moaned. "Five minutes, while the mask dries—"

"Come on, honey. It's been five minutes," Dan said, pulling me upright. "Oh, man!" he chuckled. "It's like one of those gangster movies, where they fit the guy for cement shoes, only you got it in the face!"

"You promised," I muttered, as he hauled me off the bed.

"And what did they do when the cement was dry? Why, they threw him in the water. Which is where you're going, lady!"

Dan led me back into the bathroom, and I could hear the shower running. He undid the towel around my body. "Not the one on my hair. I can't let it get wet," I told him. I held my face under the spray until all the mask was gone, feeling like a wilted flower reviving under the water and Dan's gentle touch, as he soaped and rinsed both of us off.

"Is this the stuff you used on me last night?" he asked, holding up the bottle of almond-sesame oil.

"Thanks, baby," I said, reaching for it. "I surely do feel better now."

Dan kept hold of the bottle. "You're about to feel a whole lot better than that." His strong hands stroked the oil into my skin and kneaded my tight muscles until they felt soft as bread dough, particularly when he got down on his knees and worked his way up my legs.

"You monster," I protested half-heartedly." Is this your revenge?"

"Only the beginning baby." He stood and squeezed me tight against him, digging his fingers into the aching spots on my shoulders, and down either side of my spine. I just melted into him like a puddle of ice cream.

"Taste of your own medicine," he said, pushing me gently away.

"I didn't get a taste," I pointed out.

He grinned. "I want to know you're wanting it the whole evening."

He walked out of the bathroom, taking that heap big medicine with him.

CHAPTER 24

"So everything is really squared away with the pageant and Chessy, et al?" I inquired, as he buttoned the neckband of the dress he wanted me to wear, a long black cotton knit halter with a modest slit up the right calf.

Dan frowned. "Far as any immediate legal action is concerned, we shoved a rag in Battle's rifle. Of course, it would be downright unnatural if that old buzzard didn't have something else up his sleeve. Fact is, when Foley and I were down with Shelby in his office this afternoon, Battle called and said he wanted to meet with all of us at three o'clock. That must have been close to 2:30.

"Shelby, who spoke directly to him, said B.B. hadn't quite sounded like himself. Anyway, came three o'clock, and no Battle. About quarter to four, Shelby started phoning around trying to track him down. No answer in his room or any of the bars. Nobody at the desk saw him leave, and where would he go in this weather anyhow?"

Dan surveyed his wardrobe, which had been seriously depleted by Foley. "Nice of Mr. Callant to leave me a few pitiful scraps to wear. Ah, here's one the bastard didn't see, or he'd of stolen it."

He pounced on the dark persimmon linen jacket, pants and shirt. Very few men could pull off an outfit like that. Chuck Woolery is one. Dan's the other. Actually, Foley could too, with a little practice. This style of dressing was new to him, and he'd ransacked Dan's closet with gusto.

"Well, did Brandon Battle ever get in touch?" I asked, as we made our way to the Silver Room, where the victory dinner was to be served.

Dan shook his head. "Not a peep. Obviously, he's up to something. Only I can't think what just now."

"Did anyone check with Chessy or LaWanda?" I asked. "Last time I saw him was with Chessy during the press brunch. I thought you probably noticed how stunned he looked when he realized you'd waved a wand and produced Nectarine like that."

"No, I didn't," Dan said. "Now that you mention it though, I guess I was subconsciously expecting him to crawl up and hiss out a few more threats then and there. But, he didn't seem to be around at all."

"He wasn't," I confirmed. "One minute, he and Chessy were standing there gloating when they thought Tinker was throwing in the towel. The next, they were just gone. Even Parker Bell, who sticks to Chessy like a big old wad of chewing gum, was looking around like he couldn't figure out what happened. I'm guessing, but I'm pretty sure it was about a quarter to one."

Dan said, "Then Battle calls Shelby to arrange a meeting, for which he does not show up. Curious. Ah, here's the Silver Room."

"Mmm, I smell garlic!" I said hungrily. "Let's hurry. I'm starving."

Dan scraped his fingernails lightly down my exposed spine as I preceded him into the room. "I'm counting on that," he murmured.

The Silver Room was lovely; deep rose grosgrain walls, silver art deco sconces with pink glass shades, and a thick silver carpet patterned with billowing pink peonies.

Everybody else was already gathered around a large oval table. Charlotte, in the green shantung dinner suit she'd had made in Hong Kong, spotted us first.

"Hey, it's about time you guys got here!" she called. "Shelby's been making us drool with his description of the menu."

"You shoulda heard him!" Foley, elegant in Dan's black duds said. "It was quite a masterpiece of food foreplay."

Shelby beamed. "I'll be happy to go over it again."

"*Honey*," Tinker intervened firmly. "Why don't you just tell us about it *while* they're bringing it in. You know, like at a fashion show?"

"Like, now?" I whimpered.

Shelby nodded agreeably. "I just wanted to make sure everybody's appetite was thoroughly whetted first."

"My sentiments exactly," Dan remarked, sending me a sizzling look.

Marcel, wearing an uncharacteristically bemused expression, was splendidly suited in Italian silk pinstripes. At his side, Nectarine Savoy, in a green sequined gown that made her look like an exotic African mermaid, maintained her distant attitude toward him.

A waiter appeared, and a warm, fragrant basket of bread began its way around the table.

"Our 'Haute Southern Dinner' begins with hot sticks of cracklin-studded cornbread, accompanied by a spread of sweet butter and Virginia ham bits," Shelby intoned over a chorus of oohs and aahs, mine being the loudest. Those things melted in your mouth and I'd already eaten two before I realized it.

". . . baked souffles of creamed turnips spiced with horseradish, surrounded by puree of turnip greens," crooned Shelby as another waiter set large, hot plates before us. He was quickly followed by another waiter who added racks of juicy, pale pink lamb, lightly charred on the outside, to the plates. Another ladled a thick, creamy sauce next to the meat.

"Rack of lamb marinated in apricot liqueur, roasted in raisin paste, with a cream sauce of mashed roast garlic, whole green peppercorns, and dry vermouth," Shelby concluded rapidly, eagerly plunging in with knife and fork.

Everybody exclaimed in amazement over the food. I doubt any of us had ever eaten a better meal, even in New Orleans. But what should have been a festive occasion remained strangely subdued.

That could be attributed partly to the armed truce between Marcel and Nectarine, and also to the general wave of emotional exhaustion that hits when a particularly wearisome problem has been solved.

Unstable weather, such as we were experiencing, is also known to have a dampening effect upon the spirits, despite the note of comparative levity that had been injected into the latest report of Babe's doings.

Making an unscheduled detour up a two hundred mile stretch of Florida Gulf coastline, Babe, after wreaking some miscellaneous minor damage, had paused just long enough to pitch an uprooted coconut palm through the glass doors of a well-known fast food outlet, before rushing back out to sea and resuming her original route to Mobile.

Fortunately, the establishment had been closed at the time, so no one was injured. But now they were calling her "Babe, the Gourmet Hurricane," because of her apparent aversion to fast food.

"When Babe hears how good the eats are here, Shelby," chuckled Foley, "maybe she'll leave your place alone."

Tinker and Shelby toasted Dan and Foley for diffusing what could have been a terrible and costly ordeal for them. This afternoon, they'd even come up with a contingency plan in case the worst happened and the pageant had to be completely canceled before a winner had been picked, due to evacuation of the Bell Sands.

The Bells hadn't even thought of that and had been extremely grateful—and not a little impressed—with Dan's and Foley's foresight.

In the event—very simply—the prize money would be divided equally among all thirty contestants, and there would be a random drawing for that luxury car.

Tinker glowed as she raised her glass. "You sweet boys really proved you understand how precious my little pageant is to me. This way, with your plan, even if we do wind up having to call the whole thing off, everybody'll have a good taste in their mouths about Miss Gulf Coast."

Shelby stood. "And now, I am delighted to report that via conference call to New Orleans a short while ago, the executive board of the Bell Group has unanimously voted to award the entire S'no Bull account to Blanchard, Smithson, Callant and Claiborne!"

"YESSS!" Dan and Foley shouted in unison, and jumped up from the table to pound each other on the back.

"Leighton's gonna have a fit!" Foley roared with glee.

They shook hands with the Bells, while the rest of us applauded.

Marcel and Nectarine looked bewildered. "This, evidently, is a good thing," Marcel acknowledged. "But what, exactly?"

Charlo and I sneaked peeks at each other and started giggling.

"It's really a cu-cute name for the . . . p-product," I began, then gave up.

Charlotte tried, "As I understand it, Shelby's developed this beef that's humanely raised and hormone free and virtually fat free and all? And so other cattle guys want to try it out, but there's only a limited supply of these special bulls, of course. Well, Shelby can't exactly be sending his prize bulls jetting all over the place to provide their services in person, see?"

I took over. "So, there's some incredibly hi-tech way they can freeze the bull sperm and ship it anywhere in the world. And because not only is it frozen, but the claims are pretty extravagant, Shelby named it, 'S'no Bull'!"

Nectarine smiled evilly. "Extravagant claims, but all frozen up when it gets right down to it, huh? Sounds like every big-talking stud I ever met!"

Marcel snapped his head around at her so fast I was sure he'd given himself whiplash. "I *assure* you," he began, with barely suppressed violence, but was fortunately interrupted when Foley and Dan and the Bells sat down again.

The conversation grew general, but I was aware of Marcel as he cast brooding glances over at Savoy and toyed with his wineglass. A serene little smile twitched upon Nectarine's gorgeous lips from time to time. I knew Marcel wasn't used to being pushed around like this, but I figured Savoy knew what she was doing and how far she could go.

Poor Marcel! I almost laughed when I remembered his story about Dolly, the apprentice from hell. Between those two women, Marcel was finding the going pretty rough.

"And the best part of the whole thing is," Tinker concluded, over the tangy lemon/lime mousse, "you fixed it so that *nasty* old Brandon Battle won't be bothering us any more."

"Now, wait a minute Tinker," Dan warned. "Don't count on that. He's a cat with nine lives if there ever was one, and I don't know what he's up to right now."

Foley added, "He's sure gone to ground all of a sudden. I don't suppose he ever contacted you, Shelby?"

"No," Shelby replied, looking uneasy. "After we tried paging him, I gave up and went to oversee things in the kitchen for our dinner. But I told my secretary to forward all my calls there, which she did. His wasn't one of them."

"I don't much care for these games," Dan said, scraping up the last of his mousse. "But, I expect we'll see him soon enough at the show."

"Ah, yes!" Nectarine observed. "It's almost time for my big debut."

With a flash of green sequins she started to rise from the table like Venus from the sea, but Marcel quickly popped up first, and stood behind her chair. "Allow me, please," he said, formally.

Savoy glanced at him briefly over her shoulder as he pulled out her chair. "Allow you please to what?" she inquired disinterestedly, and model-glided away, Marcel right behind her.

"Uh-oh!" Foley chuckled. "There's another babe getting ready to let loose if I ever saw one. Come on, sugar," he said to Charlotte. "Let's catch up and see if we can eavesdrop."

CHAPTER 25

Dan and I boarded the escalator down to the Liberty Grand Ballroom level, which was packed with passengers, definitely in a party mood.

Rowdiest of all were the hotel guests, possibly because they were suffering from massive cabin fever, and this was an outlet for some of that pent-up energy.

The instant those stairs touched bottom, we were propelled forward by an eager crowd, who rushed, waving fistfuls of dollars toward concession booths purveying all manner of Miss Gulf Coast merchandise.

There were sultry posters of the contestants, campaign-style buttons to boost a favorite, coffee mugs, keychains with tiny tiaras, T-shirts and sweatshirts. The latter were variously emblazoned with the pageant logo, a dolphin standing on her tail atop a wave, wearing the Miss Gulf Coast tiara; or printed with slogans like, "I BRAKE FOR BEAUTY PAGEANTS," and "DANGER. I'M A TIARAIST!"

There was an entire booth selling nothing but baseball

caps, and I fell in love with one of black quilted satin that had an actual rhinestone tiara attached to the front.

When I tried it on in the mirror, Dan laughed. "Oh, you've positively got to have that, Claire! Only, you can't wear it until you're officially crowned."

He lifted it from my head and passed it, along with his credit card, to the vendor to ring up.

I glanced up at him. "You mean, I've got to win this tiara?"

"No, you already did that, darlin'. Far as the judge is concerned," Dan assured me. "But I do think a little formal ceremony might prove interesting."

He signed the charge slip, requesting the purchase be delivered to our suite.

We were surprised to find a bottleneck at the ballroom entrance. Overnight, Miss Gulf Coast had become a sizzling hot ticket, with at least half-again as many people trying to squeeze in for this show as the first.

Dan was approached by two separate scalpers, who stared lustfully at the VIP pass he flashed at a harried usher.

Once inside, we jostled into a small group of the Crestview Cove residents we'd met last night. I recognized them as the Bells' boating friends.

"I've been trying and trying to reach Shel or Tink all afternoon and now there's so many people around I can't get a word in edgewise," one woman complained as we inched down the aisle.

"Would it be too much trouble for y'all to tell them whoever cleared the deck sure didn't do a very good job of securing *Blue*? If anything, she's slipping worse. Shelby better get down there and see to it himself first thing in the morning."

"Will do," Dan promised, as we moved on.

Charlotte and Foley were already settled in when we got to our section. Chief Hepkins arrived, and Dan introduced him to his seatmate for the evening, an uncharacteristically subdued Marcel Barrineau.

Hepkins clearly hadn't understood Marcel was previously known to us. Acknowledging the introduction with a cool nod, the chief appraised the other man's expensive luster with suspicion.

"Well, Mr. Barrineau, you finding the action around these parts up to your usual standards?" Hepkins accompanied his obscure remark with a truly horrible, suggestive little locker room wink.

Marcel emerged from his dark cocoon of self-pity. "I fail to take your meaning, sir," he said, with icy politeness. "If, by 'action' you refer to 'girlie' as in, 'I can't get no,' it is hardly any concern of yours.

"Unless, of course, you suspect me of attempting to purchase it.

"On the other hand, should you be defining 'action' as that of the roulette wheel, slot machine or crap table—with all due respect, were I the most incorrigible addict—which I am not—I would certainly not drive miles in blinding rain for the express purpose of partaking of the dubious amenities offered by Mississippi gaming establishments, when, without leaving New Orleans, I might—should I choose—gamble in complete comfort and comparative luxury."

Hepkins shook his head, as if that would cause Marcel'

s barrage of words to arrange itself into some semblance of order.

With a sympathetic chuckle, Foley said, "Uh-huh. Marcel does tend to have that effect on a person at first, Troy. But in this particular case, I guess that was just his little way of expressing offense at your approach."

Dan, with a quizzical glance at Chief Hepkins, briefly explained Marcel's involvement with the pageant, as well as with the rest of us.

Chief Hepkins looked chagrined. "I apologize," he told Marcel. "I didn't know you were among friends." He extended his hand, and Marcel shook it.

Hepkins continued. "Since Mr. Barrineau plainly is of a rarer cut than we usually get around here, I'm afraid I jumped to some wrong conclusions," He cleared his throat, and looked furtively around before going on.

"See, without getting specific, there's a pretty flammable proposition about to come up for a vote in our state legislature, and we've been getting tips certain dangerous elements are already showing up in town, trying to get their ducks in a row. And maybe even encouraging some of 'em to jump the gun."

"Would that be the dry land gaming act, Chief?" Dan asked, bluntly.

Hepkins seemed both dismayed and impressed. "It would, indeed, but—" he glanced over his shoulder apprehensively "—this ain't exactly what I'd call the right place to discuss it, know what I mean?"

Marcel, who'd begun to sit up and take notice of his surroundings, addressed Hepkins. "Am I to infer, from your previous remarks, that you, solely on the basis of my appearance, immediately suspected me of perhaps falling into the category of, 'a certain dangerous element?' "

"Uh—" Chief Hepkins struggled to interpret. Then, with a rueful grimace, admitted, "I'm afraid that's about the size of it."

But Marcel looked rather pleased to be mistaken for a high rolling gangster, as opposed to some pitiful slave to the dice. "A most natural mistake," he purred, making a big show of adjusting weighty silver cufflinks, shaped, by odd coincidence, like horseshoes.

Spectators continued to pour in like flounders at Jubilee Tide. The wedged-shaped aisles were distinctly narrower, due to the extra added chair at the end of each row.

Parker Bell's usual swagger of wide-legged machismo was severely curtailed by the tighter corridor, but he was hailed on all sides by his celebrity pals, who obviously took full advantage of his concierge-without-portfolio status.

As Tinker had mentioned, he really was at his best with these unpredictable beings, murmuring confidentially into certain ears, assuring someone else that special bottle would arrive at its destination, and so on, accepting their condescending chumminess as genuine tribute.

In other words, Parker Bell was a born flunky, the perfect toady.

The only discomfort he evidenced was at the approach of Marlowe Goodkidd. The sitcom actress, having been unable to achieve a new hairstyle, had compensated by donning a slinky gold gown with a neckline that didn't so much plunge, as bungee jump.

Marlowe threw her arms around his neck and stabbed truly life-threatening breasts (Charlotte giggled they looked like machetes) into Parker's beefy chest.

"Ums big old man going to be baby's good luck charm again, tonight?" she cooed.

Parker turned puce and tried to extricate himself, but the actress had fastened herself to him like kudzu on a fence and seemed to be spreading twice as fast.

I exchanged mystified glances with Dan. Our Parker was certainly turning out to be a dark horse! Here we assumed he just sat around waiting for Chessy to ring her bell when, meanwhile, he was out ringing a few of his own.

Maybe he simply considered it all part of Parker Bell's special Celebrity Service.

But if he expected discretion, he'd picked the wrong woman. "Same time, same place?" she breathed huskily, gnawing his earlobe.

I thought the poor boy would faint right on the spot when Chessy suddenly showed up. She was wearing her costume—which consisted of about five or six yellow feathers and a handful of sequins—as one of the backup dancers for the Latino rock band's version of "Yellow Bird."

"I see I should've brought a hose," Chessy snapped. "But if you can manage to tear yourself away, Parker, my mother's upset because somebody took her seat."

Parker, visibly relieved at the interruption, started to attempt an explanation, but thought better of it. "Oh, sure, Chessy!" he mumbled, "right away!" and hurried off.

That left Marlowe and Chessy, face to face.

"Watch out!" the actress exclaimed, in mock horror.

"Ru-Paul got out of his cage. And he's molting!" Ostentatiously, she brushed wisps of yellow marabou from her cleavage.

Chessy gasped and pointed to the scrap of fabric covering Marlowe's left mammary. "Uh-oh! Is that a silicone leak? Or a big old oil spill?"

Marlowe took a threatening step toward Chessy, long acrylic nails curled into lethal red talons. "You're dead!" she snarled.

Chessy looked slightly alarmed, but stood her ground. "As in, your career?"

Chief Hepkins made as if to intervene, but was spared this degrading necessity by the return of Parker Bell. Parker's arrival coincided with the dimming of the houselights, signaling the show was about to start.

"Yeah, I found her," he informed his sputtering walkie-talkie. "Chessy," he ordered brusquely, "come on! You're supposed to be backstage getting pictures taken with those other two birds!"

Unceremoniously, Parker grabbed one of her feathered wrists and hauled her away. Well! He could be masterful enough when necessary.

Marlowe gazed after them, then turned to take her place at the judge's panel. For the first time, she became aware a reluctant audience of six had been present for the whole performance.

Recognizing Marcel and me, she tossed her head and glared, but at the sight of Dan and Foley, her collagened lips curved in an inviting smile. Her big eyes rhumbaed sensuously between the two men.

It appeared this west coast man-eater had acquired quite a taste for southern-fried.

Mercifully, the houselights went completely out, the orchestra struck up the comedian's theme song, and Marlowe was forced to take her seat.

Following a hilarious opening monologue of what to expect when you order a bagel in Biloxi, the comedian introduced a spotlighted Nectarine Savoy to a footstomping, wolf-whistling audience.

I stole a glance at Marcel. Today, he'd witnessed his ladylove functioning as a celebrity for the very first time, and I had a notion he was having to rethink a few things.

The first contestant to perform tonight was Miss Santa Rosa Island Surfer Girl, a Gidget-sized, adorable Asian-American who came on stage dressed like a four-year-old tomboy going to a birthday party. In short, starched pink organza, with puff sleeves and wide sash tied with a bow in back, black cowboy boots, black cowboy hat, and two cap pistols in a black holster belt, she sang a song about a Chinese girl who could yodel.

Sang it in *Chinese.*

Yodeled in Chinese.

Fired the cap pistols into the air at the end.

In my opinion, she was the evening's winner, but then hers was the only act I saw. Because when she had fired off the last of her caps, leaving traces of acrid blue smoke drifting upward into the lights, Dan looked at his watch.

Under the storm of applause, he said in my ear, "Come on, darlin'. It's time for your medicine."

CHAPTER 26

The next morning, LaWanda and Chessy Scarborough reported Brandon Battle missing.

Shelby Bell's office, while spacious and well-appointed, was not adequate to contain a crowd consisting of both Bells, Chessy and LaWanda, Foley and Charlotte plus Dan and me, and Chief Hepkins. Not to mention the surging emotions.

Tinker was getting right down to basics. "LaWanda Jones, I have just about *had* it with you!" she yelled. "First you come waltzing into my hotel making threats, and now you're accusing us of what? Kidnapping your shyster lawyer? And in between, you've been trying to sue us for everything from being racists to my *precious* Shelby lusting after that nymphomaniac Dracula's daughter of yours."

Chessy merely looked amused, but LaWanda aimed her glassy green gaze at Tinker and gasped, "How dare you!"

"I just do dare, never mind how!" Tinker snarled back. "Listen here, LaWanda. I've been sorry every day of my life for that Miss Palmetto thing. But what you never knew and

I'm just mad enough to tell you now, is that I actually saw you doing what he made you do to get that title in the first place. And I never told a soul.

"You *hear* me?"

The blood seemed to drain from LaWanda's face and she pressed her hand to her heart.

"Why, mother!" Chessy drawled with great interest. "Just what on earth did he, whoever he was, make you do?"

Tinker whirled around. "None of your business, you slut! That's one thing your mother never was."

Chessy did not seem unduly disturbed by Tinker's choice of descriptive nouns. Undoubtedly she'd heard that one before.

"Chief Hepkins," she said, "here is the situation. Yesterday afternoon, Uncle B.B. and I attended the so-called press brunch, at which it became clear that Mr. and Mrs. Bell had used their power and influence to weasel out of some very serious charges we intended to bring against them.

"I then returned with Uncle B.B. to his room to . . . discuss the situation in private. That was the last anyone has seen or heard of him."

Chessy walked over to the sofa where Hepkins sat and bent over until her face was close to his. "Don't you think, Chief Hepkins, it is very odd that an attorney of Mr. Battle's national prominence should simply vanish like this, without a word to Mother or me, his longtime friends and business associates?"

Chief Hepkins studied her impassively, seeming unmoved by the proximity of the bodice of Chessy's lowcut printed silk fairytale dress. She had no way of knowing she was dallying with Biloxi's Most Eligible Bachelor, that jaded fellow.

"In fact, I do agree we should try to locate Mr. Battle," Hepkins stated. "But you are way out of line when you start insinuating that your hosts are responsible for his absence."

"Oh, am I?" Chessy retorted. "Well I think they're responsible for more than that. Uncle B.B. isn't the only one who's gone missing around here."

"Izzat right?" Chief Hepkins remarked, cozily. "And who else might the Bells have disappeared?"

"Freddy Franks, that's who!" Chessy declared. "Nobody's seen him for going on three days now and I have every reason to believe he was going to make a statement to the press against the Bells."

Hepkins smiled grimly. "Well, I just happen to know that Mr. and *Mrs.* Franks have returned to Los Angeles. I drove them to the airport myself."

That was the literal truth.

Chessy looked stunned. "Why, but—that 's impossible!" she stammered. "Freddy would never leave without telling me first!"

"Personal friend of yours, is he?" Hepkins inquired blandly.

Chessy grew haughty. "We made a picture together in Los Angeles and became . . . quite close. I am merely surprised he left so suddenly, that's all."

I was starting to get an idea. Chessy and LaWanda's apparent distress about Battle's disappearance might well signal the beginning of his own cleverly orchestrated charade. I wouldn't put it past him to suddenly reappear at a strategic moment and claim the Bells had abducted him because of the legal threat he posed to them, thereby forcing them to prove they hadn't.

But whatever Chessy's role in Battle's scheme—if that's what was going on here—her astonishment at Hepkins' news about Freddy was genuine.

Also, her assertion that Freddy was fixing to make his own unique brand of noise against Shelby and Tinker pretty much paralleled what Dan and I had been tossing around earlier. Only now, Chessy was added to the equation.

Dan, also thinking along the lines of a possible Battle agenda, spoke up. "Chief Hepkins, I do believe we ought to go up and inspect Mr. Battle's room as soon as possible."

Chessy swept over to him, full silk skirts billowing picturesquely. "Oh, Dan," she breathed soulfully, "Thank you for caring how deeply I feel about this."

"Your feelings don't enter into it at all," Dan informed her curtly.

Just then, the door flew open and Marlowe Goodkidd stalked in. Her heavy perfume vied with what little oxygen remained.

"Shelby, you've got to do something!" she demanded wildly, so intent on her own needs she was oblivious to our presence. "I just rang Bella Salon, and somebody said there were no appointments available until after the pageant!"

Shelby knew Marlowe had been the root of all evil in that department, and rightly concluded Ricky Gomez had decided it was payback time. He said, benignly, "It's quite true the Miss Gulf Coast contestants have priority, Ms. Goodkidd."

Marlowe flicked a wicked eye at Chessy. "Well, they're not all taking advantage of the privilege. Obviously."

Chessy laughed. "I wouldn't dream of letting anybody here touch my hair. I do it myself."

"Oh, really?" Marlowe replied, with acid sweetness. "You mean you got that totally *Petticoat Junction/Beverly Hillbillies* thing going with your very own hands?

"Billy Jo, Bobby Jo, Betty Jo and Ellie Mae! They're all *in* there!" she chortled.

Before Chessy could retaliate, Shelby said hastily, "Ms. Goodkidd, you are interrupting a very important meeting. Since there's nothing I can do—"

"Oh, but there is!" Marlowe snapped. "Since Miss Heehaw here doesn't intend to use her appointment, I'll take it. Or else, I refuse to judge tonight."

Which would put the pageant right back in violation of the number of judges.

I could tell the same thought occurred to Chessy, but without Battle handy to direct her, she hesitated.

Dan didn't. "I believe Ms. Goodkidd has a point," he conceded, with a meaningful look at Shelby. "Claire, why don't you call over and arrange something with Ricky?"

Marlowe deigned to notice me. "Well, what about her?" she demanded. "She could do my hair right now."

"No, Ms. Goodkidd," Dan contradicted, pleasantly. "My wife is assisting me at the moment."

When I buzzed Bella Salon, Ricky answered. He immediately deciphered my coded message and agreed that Casey could squeeze her in, provided she came right then.

Marlowe hurried toward the door, then stopped and

looked back over her shoulder at Chessy. "Winner takes all!" she caroled, and flipped her fingers under her chin.

Moments later, Parker Bell entered, futilely attempting to swab a smear of lipstick from his cheek. If, as we suspected, he had been burning the candle at both ends, it was certainly not agreeing with him.

His eyes were puffy and bloodshot, and he looked pretty seedy in general.

Shelby, who'd been rooting through his large middle desk drawer, glanced up when Parker came in.

"Oh, good. There you are, Parker. Listen, we're going to have to enter Brandon Battle's room."

Parker frowned, looking at Chessy and LaWanda. "You mean, he never did get in touch last night?"

Mother and daughter shook their heads in unison, and LaWanda said, "Like I was explaining to Chief Hepkins earlier, he not only didn't join me at the talent show—but I knocked on his door and rang him on the phone a number of times, with no response."

Tinker elaborated. "This morning, the maid reported there was a DO NOT DISTURB sign on the knob, so she didn't. But now, Chief Hepkins believes we should try to find him. Just in case."

"As if you didn't know," Chessy muttered.

Hepkins asked LaWanda, "And you're absolutely certain there was no sign on his doorknob as late as midnight?" LaWanda nodded. "Then," Hepkins said, "he obviously returned sometime after midnight, hung out the sign, and left again without bothering to take it off."

What the chief didn't say was that Battle could've hung

out that sign, but the reason it was still there was because he was physically unable to remove it.

"Anyway," Shelby said, "since we don't want to involve the housekeeping staff, we'll use my passkey. Except—" he jiggled the drawer agitatedly, "—I can't find the damn thing!"

In frustration, Shelby plowed a trench through the contents of the drawer, causing things to spill out onto the carpet.

Dan retrieved what looked like a set of architectural drawings from where they'd landed near his feet, and Shelby all but snatched them away.

"Here, let me look, Uncle Shelby," Parker offered, and Shelby wheeled his chair back to give him room, still clutching the rolled-up plans.

Methodically, Parker began pawing through the miscellaneous papers, trinkets, gadgets, and all the other dribs and drabs that seem to accumulate entirely of their own accord in any desk drawer. After a minute, his big hand emerged, dangling a key attached to a maroon plastic fob with the Bell Sands logo. He passed it over to his uncle.

Chief Hepkins rose from the sofa and nodded. "Okay, folks. Let's go."

Chessy said, "First, I want to see Mother to her room." She took LaWanda's arm, but LaWanda shook herself loose from her daughter's grasp.

"Let go, Chessy!" she said, irritably. "I'm quite able to walk unassisted, thank you. I propose to accompany this expedition."

With a shrug, Chessy sighed, "Suit yourself."

In the end, all of us went, though we had to travel to the third floor in two elevators—Chief Hepkins, the Scarboroughs, Shelby and Parker in one; Tinker, Foley, Charlotte, Dan and myself in the other.

Shelby's group took off first.

While we waited for the next car, Charlotte observed, "Well, since Dan and Foley diffused the pageant crisis, so far the only hard news story left to report on is Freddy Franks' death. Which I've taken a solemn oath not to do until Chief Hepkins gives me the green light.

"It's just too bad I don't have connections with one of those TV tabloid shows, though," she lamented. "Particularly since I've had a front row seat to all this bad blood splattering between Marlowe Goodkidd and Chessy Scarborough. What's that about, I wonder?"

"Oh, that!" Tinker remarked, as the elevator bell dinged and we piled inside, "Believe it or not, I happen to know. See, they were both in this movie, *Trading Down*—"

"The one with Freddy Franks?" Foley put in.

Tinker nodded. "Uh-huh. Franny told me about it. Seems like Freddy was sort of dividing his down time between Marlowe and Chessy? And when they found out about each other, there was one almighty hairpulling catfight! Even Janet Charlton decided it rated a mention in *Star*."

"While Freddy just stood back and enjoyed the spectacle?" Dan suggested.

"According to Franny," said Tinker, "he was bragging all over Hollywood about how he had two luscious babes scratching and biting for his party favors."

Charlotte gave her a sour nod. "I expect they hadn't counted on all three of them running into each other again in someplace like Biloxi. So, Marlowe and Chessy just picked up where they left off."

"No, Charlotte." Tinker shook her head. "All the judges and contestants were kept completely up to date with pageant newsletters. As of the last mailing, everybody involved knew who the contestants, the judges, and the entertainers were going to be.

"Although you're right about their feud. They started up first thing, at the welcome cocktail party."

Dan said, "Now, that's very interesting. Why didn't Chessy target Marlowe as the culprit judge on grounds of personal bias when she got disqualified? But instead, she tried to create a big, ugly racial crisis—which could've easily spread like wildfire—with terrible consequences for all concerned."

"And," Foley pointed out, "when that didn't work, she tried to paint Shelby as the bad guy."

"But what's really weird," I reminded them, "is that Marlowe Goodkidd is the one who made the biggest noise in support of Chessy's claim of discrimination! It's thanks to her that Trini, Jerome and Viola walked out of the beauty shop."

"Well," Foley mused, as the elevator doors whooshed open, "there is plainly even more going on around here than we thought."

"Yeah, and I got a real bad feeling we better hurry and find out exactly what," Dan said, as we debarked into the corridor.

I trailed along behind the rest, trying to order my thoughts.

So, Chessy, Marlowe and Freddy, who had a history together, knew ahead of time they were all going to be at the pageant.

Chessy and LaWanda Scarborough had brought along Brandon Battle to activate their agenda to wreak vengeance upon Tinker Bell for sins of the past.

Marlowe Goodkidd, Chessy's rival for Freddy Franks, had come out the most publicly in support of Chessy's position.

Meanwhile, Marlowe and Chessy had suddenly started having open confrontations over Parker Bell.

Chessy claimed Freddy was also about to make a statement in her support against the Bells.

Freddy was dead.

Brandon Battle was missing.

There. That was about as orderly as it got, but it made no more sense than before, I concluded.

Our procession halted at Brandon Battle's door, and Chief Hepkins admitted us to the room.

Once inside, it was obvious that, wherever Battle had gone, he hadn't planned on leaving. Or at least, he'd masterfully set the stage to make it look that way.

On top of the dresser, loose change nuzzled against a thick green wad of bills in a gold money clip, along with the key to his room.

An open briefcase occupied a chair, and in the bathroom those cold black contact lenses stared up at us nastily from their sonic bath gizmo.

LaWanda stood rigidly in the center of the room, while Chessy paced back and forth like a panther. For the first time, at least in my opinion, she really did seem worried. Though it could just be part of the act.

"It's going to be okay, Chessy," Parker said, attempting to soothe her. "You don't have to be afraid ever again. I'm here now."

Chessy roughly knocked his restraining hands from her shoulders. "Oh, wonderful!" she sneered. "Just what the doctor ordered. A boy to do a man's job."

Parker looked wounded and confused, as well he might. Was this the same woman he'd practically had to drag away from Marlowe before they came to blows over him? And was he really such a moron as to suppose he could replace Brandon Battle's role as confidante and advisor in Chessy life? Assuming Battle was even gone.

Chief Hepkins wagged his big head dolefully. "Well, it don't look too good, folks." He pointed to the twisted rope of sheets hanging from the bed and dragging the floor. "Signs of a struggle and all. I'm gonna have to bring in some investigators, Shelby. Shorthanded as we are."

"I can certainly understand that, Troy," Shelby sighed. "Is there anything we can do to help meanwhile?"

Hepkins mulled over the situation. "Well in fact there is, Shelby. If you can spare of a few of your security boys to check out the empty rooms. You know, divide 'em up into teams? We can get the place scoped in no time. That way, everything'll stay nice and quiet."

"Can do. I'll call security now!" Shelby declared, reaching for the phone.

Hepkins barked out, "Don't touch that, Shelby! People think fingerprints don't mean nothing no more, but a good few folks have been mighty damn surprised when we showed up at their door."

Shelby snatched his hand back. "Sorry," he mumbled.

Parker suggested, "Hey, Chief. Why don't I just go on down there myself and get the ball rolling?"

"Good thinking, son," Hepkins approved. "Six or eight guys, plus yourself, should do the job. How's that sound, Shelby?"

"Fine," Shelby agreed, "except four men is all we can spare, and they'll need another passkey besides Walter's— that's our head of security—because I still don't want the front office people to know anything about this until absolutely necessary. I guess Parker had better take mine, too.

"Here, Parker!" he called, tossing the key across the room to his nephew, who reached out automatically and caught it. Once a wide receiver, always a wide receiver.

Parker, who'd been moping at Chessy like a whipped dog since she'd put him down in front of everybody, threw her one final imploring look before he left us.

Dan roamed thoughtfully around the room, stuck his head in the open closet where a row of Battle's trademark western-tailored suits hung, then stepped into the bathroom for a moment. When he came out, his blue eyes were snapping with the light of an idea.

"What's shaking, bubba?" Foley demanded.

Dan, instead of answering Foley, addressed Tinker. "This is a real nice room, Tinker. But how does it rate price-wise?"

Tinker looked at him questioningly. "Well, it's certainly not as expensive as a suite. Like y'all have," she added, pointedly. "But it is one of our more deluxe accommodations where we furnish a few extra-special little 'guest amenities' as we call them in the hotel trade."

"Would those amenities include one of those wonderful maroon bathrobes of yours?" Dan asked.

"Yes," Tinker replied. "Why?"

"Because it's not here," Dan stated flatly.

"No shit!" exclaimed the chief. "Pardon me, ladies."

CHAPTER 27

"Ohhhh! Ohhhh!" wailed Chessy. "Uncle B.B. was wearing that robe when I left him yesterday. Oh, my God!"

LaWanda, seeming untouched by her daughter's histrionics, stared out the window.

Battle's room commanded a full view of the Crestview Cove marina, and a dismal one it was in weather like this. The powerful and colorful luxury vessels looked dull and helpless as they hunched miserably in the lashing rain. Here and there, scrambling figures in yellow slickers were hauling some of the smaller craft ashore, staking them down under heavy tarpaulins. I was just getting ready to tell Shelby what the woman had said regarding his boat, but what happened next made me forget all about it.

Chessy was explaining to a noncommittal Chief Hepkins just how it was that "Uncle B.B." had been fully clothed when they'd entered his room at a little before one o'clock, and down to his bathrobe by the time she'd left at nearly 2:30.

"I fail to see what is so hard to understand, Chief

Hepkins." Chessy hid a yawn behind a slender hand. "I guess he just wanted to get comfortable, and no reason why not. After all, Uncle B.B. and I have been very close for years and years."

"You also said you were 'very close' with Mr. Franks," Hepkins observed. "Are we talking about the same definition of 'close' here? And are you 'very close' with anybody else we should know about."

Chessy looked demure. "I like to be friendly, Chief Hepkins," she purred, flashing big dark eyes at Dan, then drew a bead on Foley.

"Yes, I surely do," she said, still studying Foley.

The steam shooting out of Charlotte's ears like a cartoon character was almost visible. I wouldn't have been surprised to hear Popeye's voice saying, "That's all I can stands, I can't stands no more!"

But when she spoke, it was in her usual voice, which she kept under tight, professional control. "You need help real bad, Chessy," Charlotte said, quietly.

Chessy giggled. "Aww, are you feeling threatened? You and your toy blonde pal? Serve you right! Naughty little girls oughtn't to play with great big men."

Now I felt my own ears start to boil. I didn't dare look at Dan. Her remark struck too close to that ugly fear he'd expressed to me. I prayed he was over it.

Charlotte went on calmly, "But naughty little Chessy did, didn't she? When did 'Uncle B.B.' start playing with you, Chessy?"

Momentarily unable to speak, Chessy stared at her with hatred.

The room fell dead quiet. The only noises came from outside, the dull roar of the sea and rain, the rattle of windows in a sudden gust.

Before Chessy could respond, LaWanda interposed. "Actually, it was the other way around," she remarked dispassionately, still staring out at the dreary seascape. "Chessy went after Brandon.

"Of course, her daddy started the whole thing when she was about five. That's why I was real happy when they told me Eddie had to go. After that, I tried to get help for Chessy, but the psychiatrist said Chessy knew exactly what was going on and refused to cooperate.

"Instead, she went after Brandon as a replacement, and she got him. She was ten years old at the time. Ever hear of a man leaving his wife for a ten-year-old girl? The great Brandon Battle was her hopeless love slave!

"I was furious, but there was nothing I could do. You wouldn't believe the payoff they gave Polly Battle to keep a lid on the scandal! They said he was too important—"

"Mother!" Chessy snarled warningly, and LaWanda seemed to emerge from a stupor. She fell silent.

Chessy smiled. "I have been officially diagnosed as a sexual addict. Which does not mean I'm unhappy or," she aimed twin looks at Dan and Foley, "not particular."

"There must be a lot of us in Florida," she mused. "Remember that big trial that made the TV news, where the woman pleaded sexual addiction as her defense? She was from Florida, too. A cop's wife."

Chessy surveyed Chief Hepkins thoughtfully. "What's *your* wife like, Chief?"

Troy Hepkins rose heavily to his feet from the chair matching the one holding Battle's briefcase. "That'll be enough, Miss Scarborough," he said stonily. "You and your mother can go back to your rooms now. Pending further investigation, you are for all intents and purposes being detained on these premises as material witnesses in the disappearance of Brandon Battle. You will not be permitted to leave town."

"Like we could actually *leave*," Chessy jeered, gesturing at the elements outside the window. "Ready, Mother?"

But Tinker was already at LaWanda's side. "Come on, LaWanda. I'll walk you to your room. I think we've got us a few matters to discuss."

Chessy sashayed out behind them, and Chief Hepkins closed the door practically on her heels. "Whew!" he sighed.

"You think one of them did Battle in, Chief?" Foley questioned, gripping a wrung-out Charlotte hard against his side.

Hepkins took his time before replying. "Ordinarily, I'd say either or both. They got motives up the kazoo that we know about and probably lots more we don't. Only, my strong feeling is, this ain't ordinary.

"For instance, I'd be mighty interested to know who is that 'they' Mrs. Scarborough kept mentioning."

"Would it help if I told you LaWanda's late, unlamented husband's name was Eddie?" Dan asked.

Comprehension dawned upon Chief Hepkins's broad face. "It would. So, that's Eddie Scarborough's widow, huh? And Battle's their lawyer. Of course. Remember I said I've been expecting that crowd, plus a lot more to start showing up around here? Except I wasn't looking for suspicious women. Which just goes to show you."

Shelby jerked nervously. "I don't get it, Troy. What's legalized casinos got to do with the Redneck Mafia? They've already got their own operation all over the South."

"Them little old crap games is peanuts, compared to the gold mine this stretch of coast is gonna be if that bill passes, Shelby. It'll be legal, then. Nothing to hide from the cops. No more dredging, no more hauling in some old bucket decked out to look like a fancy dice club.

"See, then the only problem will be who controls the games. Which is whoever owns the most casinos. Like in Monopoly. I wouldn't be a-tall surprised if our friend Mr. Battle isn't just the first of many soldiers yet to fall. In the battle, so to speak."

Shelby had his hanky out again. "What battle?" he asked in a faint voice.

Chief Troy Hepkins waved a big arm. "Why, Shelby! Same one it always is. For *territory*!"

CHAPTER 28

Using his own handkerchief, Hepkins carefully lifted
Battle's telephone receiver and called his office, ordering
whoever was on the other end to drop everything else and
get some investigators to the Bell Sands in ten minutes, tops.

That done, he addressed us. "Okay. Now, long as I got
y'all here, I need a favor."

He explained that, at the airport, Franny had given him
the key to hers and Freddy's adjoining rooms to return to the
hotel, and pleaded with him to dispose of her husband's
belongings; donate them to charity or something.

So, when the investigators got here, would we please
come along as witnesses? And, oh, yes. Help pack up the
stuff.

Investigators Blalock and Snellgrove duly reported,
taking notes as Hepkins brought them up to speed.

A sudden violent pounding on the door startled everybody. Snellgrove, having already donned plastic gloves,
yanked it open.

Parker Bell stumbled inside, half-carrying a large,

dazed-looking young man wearing the maroon and green uniform of the Bell Sands Security staff. His name tag read, CARR.

"Ray!" Shelby cried. "What happened to you?"

"Dunno, Mr. Bell," Carr slurred, groggily. "My head sure hurts, though." He rubbed at a spot behind his right ear. "Ow!"

Parker was even more flushed than usual and perspiring in his efforts to keep Ray, who was no lightweight, aloft. "I just found him lying in the hallway on the sixth floor," he panted.

He said that he, along with four security people, had covered all the empty rooms on floors 1-5, finding no trace of Brandon Battle, alive or dead. Since there were only three or four vacant suites on the two remaining floors, Walter, seeing no reason to send everybody up, gave Ray his pass-key and put him on six, then told Parker to take seven.

Parker, finding nothing suspicious on the seventh floor, rode down to six to see if Ray was still there.

"Good thing he did," Ray said, gratefully. "I was bending down to unlock a door, when—wham!"

Shelby was thinking rapidly. "There's only two vacant rooms on six. Was it 624 or 608?"

Ray looked sheepish. "I dunno, Mr. Bell. I'm sorry. See, they're in opposite directions, and for some reason, those arrows on six always confuse me. I kinda wandered around for a bit, then went for the first room I spotted. Whichever it was.

"Then I got clobbered."

Parker said, "It was 608, all right. But after I made sure

Ray was okay, I checked both rooms, just in case. Nothing. Nada."

"Nada, my ass! Excuse me, ladies!" Hepkins exploded. "Looks like our so-called missing person is alive and well and hanging out somewhere on the sixth floor!"

"Maybe." Dan frowned, "Or maybe somebody just wants you to think so, Chief. If I may offer my completely unprofessional opinion? I'd just go ahead and proceed as you intended."

Hepkins' breathing slowed to normal, as he considered Dan's suggestion. "May as well, I guess. Long as my men are here, anyway."

Nodding to Blalock and Snellgrove, he said, "Get snapping, boys!"

While the investigators opened up their satchels and prepared to do as ordered, Hepkins asked Shelby, "Anybody interesting currently residing on the sixth floor?"

Shelby shrugged. "To be perfectly honest, that is not our best floor—to put it mildly. I can understand Ray's confusion. There's lots of twists and turns, because it's basically built to accommodate the configuration of our climate control and plumbing systems.

"Right now, almost every room is occupied by a senior's package golf vacation from Defuniak Springs in Florida, and they can't leave because of Hurricane Babe.

"The only people connected with the pageant are Marlowe Goodkidd, who specifically asked to be switched from the fourth floor to Room 613, since, according to her, those are her lucky numbers; and our emcee. He's in 617 because, paradoxically, that's the best and biggest ocean view suite in the entire hotel.

"Of the two empty rooms, 624 was occupied by a couple from Mobile, who checked out at the first sign of the storm because they wanted to secure their property.

"But 608 is rarely, if ever, used. Unless someone is totally desperate. Even then, we make them look at it, first."

Ray had recovered enough to stand on his own, and Parker sagged with relief. With a grunt, he remarked, "608 is a dog. Dark. One little window, which opens smack into a pine tree. The elevator cables run behind one wall, so it's noisy. You can't even hear the ocean. Nobody's been in there since the big tennis tournament."

Foley said, "Sounds like a perfect hideout."

"Yeah," Parker agreed. "But I'm sure if somebody had been using that room, I'da been able to tell. Besides, whoever belted Ray wasn't in there."

"Speaking of Ray!" Shelby exclaimed. "Troy, can Parker take him down to the infirmary? We've got a nurse on duty. She may want to call the house doctor."

"Aw, I'll be all right, Mr. Bell!" Ray protested.

"No, you better get that head seen to," Hepkins said. "Take him on down, son," he added to Parker.

"Oh, Parker! When you get done, you might want to bring up one of them luggage carts to Mr. Franks' room!" he called, as the two big men departed.

Dan looked at Hepkins. "Well, what do you think?"

Hepkins scratched his chin. "On one hand, I'm relieved to hear Mr. Battle may still be on the premises. Alive, that is."

"And on the other?" Foley prompted.

"On the other hand, I think Parker's right when he said he didn't believe Battle had been camping out in that hell-hole.

"Can you think of one reason a man like Battle would leave this perfectly fine room, along with every stitch of clothes he brought, to go skulking around up there in his bathrobe?"

"I can think of *two*!" Charlotte responded. "One. He sneaked up to six jaybird nekkid because he wasn't planning on needing clothes for what he had in mind. Remember, Marlowe Goodkidd lives up there in lucky 613!

"Ten to one—if I may continue the gambling meta-phor—she caught on to the pseudo-incest thing Chessy had going with Battle, and decided to try a sample."

"It's just what she would do, given how they've been carrying on," I agreed. "Those twisted sheets could be signs of another kind of struggle, entirely. And they simply moved upstairs to, um, resume relations."

Chief Hepkins looked from Charlotte to me, seeming shocked at us nice girls thinking such thoughts.

Tell the truth, I was a little shocked, myself.

Charlotte went on. "Number two. He could also have gotten caught with his britches down because he found out at the very last split-second somebody was about to come after him, and he didn't have time to get dressed!"

Dan said, "So, if Marlowe Goodkidd doesn't have him tied to her bedposts, and he hasn't been holed up in an empty room, and if he'd had a sudden fit of amnesia and was wandering around here in his bathrobe, we'd've heard about it before now—who knocked Ray Carr in the head? And why? And where is Brandon Battle?"

Hepkins grimaced. "At the moment, it beats me, son. But I sure as hell—forgive me ladies—aim to find out!"

CHAPTER 29

Whatever her other faults, Marlowe Goodkidd was not guilty of holding Brandon Battle as her sexual prisoner.

When Parker Bell met us outside Freddy Franks' room with the required luggage cart, Chief Hepkins commandeered both Shelby's passkey, and Parker himself, for a quiet little excursion to the actress's room.

Parker's function in this possibly illegal entry was to serve as witness on behalf of the Bell Sands that Hepkins didn't steal any of Marlowe's jewelry.

There wasn't the slightest need for him to also do lookout duty, considering my own contribution to the scheme entailed a phone call to Ricky Gomez, ascertaining Marlowe was still in the salon. And hinting he should ensure she stayed put for the next fifteen minutes or so.

Meanwhile, the rest of us began packing Freddy's innumerable pieces of black leather Gucci luggage, which had all evidently been full upon arrival.

No wonder Franny needed her own room! Even if they were getting along, she'd've been crowded out.

The huge, walk-in closet rack was jammed one end to the other, and he seemed to have utilized every dresser drawer as well. Not to mention chairs and sofas, where even more garments were flung haphazardly.

It was going to be a daunting task. Some vacation! I'd never worked so hard at a stretch in my life.

A glance out the window at the dark, swollen sky reminded Dan to tell Shelby about those loose moorings on *Wedding Bell's Blue*.

Shelby made an exasperated noise. "Parker told me he'd already taken care of that! Well, he's just going to have to do it soon as he gets back, before the rain starts up again.

"Last thing I need is to get sued because some insurance company can blame damage to their client's boat on *Blue*, instead of *Babe*."

When Hepkins and Parker returned with their verdict of Marlowe's innocence concerning Brandon Battle, Shelby took Parker to task for his faulty mooring job.

Parker looked aggrieved. "I'm sorry, Uncle Shelby. I guess I got so busy clearing the decks, maybe I did miss a line or two."

"One line could cost several other people their boats, Parker. Say nothing of us losing *Blue*," Shelby rebuked him sternly. "I want you to get down there right now. Haul her tight into the berth, and tie her six ways from Sunday, if that's what it takes.

"Got that?"

"Yessir." Parker nodded dolefully and left.

Poor Parker. So far, this was not his day.

After he'd gone, Chief Hepkins pitched in to help with the packing.

"Nice threads," Foley commented judiciously, holding a new-looking tuxedo beneath his chin in the mirror,

"Yeah. Too bad none of us can get our big toe inside them," Hepkins lamented. "I could use me a suit or two."

It was when I was turning out the pockets of a really fine navy cashmere blazer that I found the answer. Or rather, remembered the question that had been teasing at me ever since Foley and Charlotte had celebrated their engagement with Harvey Wallbangers.

Stuffed inside the right-hand pocket was a pair of filmy white silk and lace bikini panties, with a little tag stitched to the back of the expensive label that read, "Property of C.S."

"Um, Shelby?" I held up the blazer. "Do you remember if this is what Freddy was wearing the day Chessy displayed her charms to you?"

Shelby adjusted his thick glasses. "Yes. I can see him now, standing there like he was posing for a painting with his hand stuck in his pocket while he was yelling at Franny."

"Then these explain not only what he was groping in his pocket, but who he was wallbanging, and why she was able to 'Stone' you so spontaneously," I said, waving the panties, then dropping them hastily onto the bed.

Shelby blanched. "Good heavens!" he yelped, and explained the incident to Hepkins, who drawled, "Right nice company y'all keep around here. High class."

"Real good detective work, Claire!" Dan congratulated.

"Thank you," I said. "I know it actually doesn't get us anywhere, but at least it clears up something."

"Most of the time," Chief Hepkins informed me, "that's all detective work is. Don't get you no further, but it gets stuff out of the way."

Another vague question I'd had about one of Freddy's actions stirred briefly, but settled out of sight again.

About a half-hour later, there was a knock on the door, and Hepkins admitted a windblown Parker Bell.

Parker removed his Bell Sands blazer, shook it out, then carefully hung it over the back of a recently cleared chair. "It started sprinkling again, just as I came inside," he reported.

Shelby looked up. "You're sure you've got everything battened down solid, *this* time?"

"We're cool," Parker assured him. "Like I thought, it was just one or two lines."

His uncle tossed him a grudging thank-you, and I couldn't help but feel a little bit sorry for Parker. If ever there was a jack-of-all-trades, master-of-none, it was him.

He did seem to take a chewing-out pretty well, though, appearing more hurt than resentful at criticism. And what did he have to resent anyhow?

After all, Parker would never be fired from this cushy, glorified errand-boy job at a luxury hotel, no matter how badly he screwed up, because Shelby Bell, who wasn't even his blood kin, had promised Parker's stepfather he'd take care of him.

Surveying the partially filled suitcases, Parker commented, "Boy, that's a big job, Uncle Shelby. Looks like the guy brought along enough clothes for a year!"

"Yes, but the chief promised Mrs. Franks we'd see to it

personally," his uncle told him. "If you want to help, I'd sure appreciate you packing up that stuff in his bathroom. The bag's already in there."

"You bet," Parker responded amiably.

The rest of us continued to work silently. As Parker observed, Freddy had come prepared for every contingency. Except one.

When Parker came out of the bathroom, he was shouldering a bulging leather duffle crammed with expensive masculine toiletries, a pharmacopeia of holistic vitamins and herbal formulas, and a pile of paperback bestsellers. He carried it over to the bed and shook the bag around to redistribute the contents in order to zip it up. His eye fell on the panties where I'd dropped them, and he blushed. "Mrs. Franks accidently left some of her own stuff, huh?"

Intent on tracking down a shirt stud that had fallen into the carpet and sunk without a bubble, Shelby muttered distractedly, "No, those seem to be the property of Miss Chessy Scarborough. Claire found them in Freddy's pocket."

Parker swallowed hard, and clenched his fists. "No. They can't be Chessy's!" he protested, but his voice carried more plea than conviction.

Hepkins clapped Parker's back consolingly. "In fact, they are, son. Got the initials to prove it."

"Remember when Freddy and Franny had that blowup the other day, Parker?" Shelby asked, rhetorically. "Well, there's your explanation. I'm just thankful Franny isn't here to see this."

"What do you want to do with these, Shelby?" Hepkins inquired, gesturing at the offending lingerie.

Shelby lifted a dismissive shoulder. "My feeling is, toss 'em," he said unfeelingly. "Miss Scarborough's hardly likely to want the things back, at this point."

Parker made a strangled sound, and Shelby rounded on him angrily.

"Oh, get over it, Parker!" he ordered, brusquely. "It's time you woke up to the fact that Chessy Scarborough is not the helpless damsel in distress you insist on taking her for!"

Getting right up in Parker's face, he continued, "Just take my word for it, boy. She is bad to the bone, I'll spare you any further details. And those," he jerked his thumb contemptuously at the panties, "should be sufficiently hard evidence, even for you!"

Parker, who'd been standing there like a brick wall while Shelby ranted, was now the color of one.

"I understand, Uncle Shelby," he said, in a low voice. "But I'd like to leave now. If that's okay."

Shelby took a deep breath, and waved Parker toward the door. "It's okay. Go ahead on."

Without looking at the rest of us, Parker exited from Freddy's chamber, shoulders slumped.

Definitely not his day.

When the door had closed behind him, Shelby gave an embarrassed little laugh. "Sorry about that scene," he apologized. "But, I'm so fed up with Parker's attitude about women.

"He thinks he's just all softhearted and old-fashioned and romantic, when he is actually dangerously deluded. His expectations of the female of our species are totally unrealistic.

"What's more, he invariably falls for women who, to put it mildly, are neither old-fashioned nor romantic, yet somehow convince him they are. For their own obvious reasons. Consequently, he winds up crushed like an old beer can, every damn time.

"Tinker and I have had to nurse him through the aftermath of quite a few of these episodes now, and frankly, it's a bloody bore."

Heaving a philosophic sigh, he added, "But—you can't pick your relatives, can you?"

"Waddya gonna do?" Foley grinned. "I imagine I got some humdingers to meet in Georgia!"

Charlotte laughed. "You have no idea!"

"Well, I'm off duty," I announced, checking my watch. "I've got to go down and start my day job."

"Wait, Claire," Charlotte said. "I'm coming with you."

Dan moved close and said softly, "Now don't go working too hard, darlin'. I got something real special in mind."

I lowered my voice. "We can skip the talent show?"

"Not necessarily," Dan smiled mischievously down at me. He has this way of looking at my lips that makes them quiver like Jell-O. "I'm expecting to see some real talent in action."

CHAPTER 30

Charlotte left me at the entrance to Bella Salon, after exchanging a quick wave with Marcel.

Inside, rock music was thumping and the joint was jumping.

Everywhere was hair, being shampooed, blown, cut, colored, rolled, teased, relaxed and otherwise coerced into crowns of glory. Hairspray hung over the styling area like smog.

Marcel's four acolytes (Ricky nicknamed them the "Marcelves") dashed hither and yon with Pavlovian fervor at every ding of a timer bell.

For some reason, rock and roll brings out Ricky's *flambeau*, and he was in full swing—shimmying his shoulders, wagging his hips, and tossing his long brown ponytail, thrusting a pair of scissors into the air with a disco kind of gesture reminiscent of Travolta in *Saturday Night Fever*. Any minute he'd start shrieking, "*Andale!*"

I wondered how long Marcel would put up with it.

The great man himself was being the aloof maestro,

moving around his client's chair with slow, exaggerated elegance, his long aristocratic nose twitching as if he smelled something unpleasant. Though a few permed heads were processing nearby, I figured it was something more than that.

When I took my station next to his, waiting for Miss Pecan to show up, I found out what.

"Claire!" he called over the whine of the blowdryer he was wielding. "Dominica telephoned me this morning with a most disturbing revelation. She has learned that Dolly has a roommate—though as to the nature of their domestic arrangement Dominica would not presume to speculate—who is a feminist attorney! I tell you, Claire. They are out to get me!"

I bit my lip to keep from smiling. "You poor thing," I sympathized. "You are having a bad time of it, aren't you?"

"Yes," Marcel brooded. "I have sown the wind and I am reaping the whirlwind, as Dr. Billy Graham mentioned in his somewhat ominous Inaugural prayer a few years back. One cannot escape the feeling he was referring to the results of the election.

"I have been thinking that perhaps the solution to everything would be for me to become religious. Possibly, I shall enter a monastery on extended retreat. I fail to understand why you find this such an occasion for hilarity, Claire."

I couldn't help laughing. The vision of Marcel in cowl and habit, tending a humble plot of earth or, more likely, inflicting the latest in tonsures upon his fellow monks, was too funny to contemplate with a straight face. Certainly a vow of silence was out of the question.

Just then Miss Pecan (honey blonde touchup and trim) arrived, and there was no more time for Marcel's woes. I stayed pretty busy from then on.

Things went smoothly until Miss Perdido Sweet Potato arrived. She was a lovely Asian-American with glossy black hair that only needed a blunt cut, usually my forte. But I had little experience with Asian hair and hers, in particular, was like trying to cut into a thick, slippery, silk waterfall.

Marcel used the situation to deliver a classroom lecture, demonstrating the proper techniques, and we all learned something.

I was taking a break with my feet propped up on the reception desk, when Parker Bell came in and plunked a big vase of roses on the counter by my ankles.

"They're for you. This time," he said, with the ghost of a smile.

I exclaimed over the flowers, which were of a red so deep as to appear iridescent black. The rich perfection of each bloom could have been sculptured from velvet.

Smiling at Parker, I said, "Thanks a bunch. Now, just maybe I can get through the next couple of hours without keeling over."

"No problem," he muttered, not meeting my eyes.

He left quickly, and I surmised he hadn't yet forgiven me for being the one to discover Chessy's undies where they had no business to be. But surely it couldn't have come as *that* much of a shock.

He'd seen for himself how she behaved around all men. Besides, Shelby said Parker kept putting the same kind of deceptive, unsentimental and promiscuous woman on a pedestal, then going to pieces when she inevitably toppled off.

The major difference between Marlowe Goodkidd and Chessy Scarborough was that Marlowe made no pretense of being sentimental or monogamous.

Maybe that was how Parker was able to take advantage of her freely-bestowed favors—thinking of her as half-floozy, half-celebrity—and still rationalize he was really being true to pure, pristine Chessy. Who, of course, was neither.

How had she managed to convince him otherwise? Or did she just dish out enough to whet his appetite, making him think he was special?

Probably the latter. Which was even more mystifying. Why bother to get him dangling after her like that? Just to keep her seduction skills honed? Or was she playing some deep, dark game, with Parker as the witless pawn?

And, for that matter, wasn't it odd, strange and curious how Parker had become the latest bone of contention, so to speak, between Marlowe and Chessy?

Bizarre, too, was how each fit his sense of stereotype so perfectly; loose city woman and chaste country girl.

Parker's schizo sexual identity could go all the way back to Shelby's dead brother's second wife, Parker's mother Alva.

Whatever the case, he was just one big old lonely co-dependent, looking for his partner in misery. Which was a tough cycle to break.

Charlotte knew. Before Foley came along, she had also ridden that self-destructive merry-go-round with the exact same man, over and over again. Only, he came wrapped in a new and enticing envelope each time.

Maybe Parker would be willing to listen to her at some point. Though I doubted it.

I forgot all about Parker's problems when I extricated the card from its little prong thing and read:

Hey, Beautiful! This is to let you know I want you desperately. Bring your tiara, and wait for me in the whirlpool. I'll be there at seven to crown you my Queen of Love. I left your key under the mat.

Dan.

In spite of everything else, he was seeing to it that we got some quality honeymoon time! And what a tactful way of telling me I'd forgotten my room key.

I smelled the roses, but could barely make out their scent because of all the chemicals floating around the salon. Probably if I let them sit here, they'd be dead in an hour.

Inserting the card back into its trident, I quickly ran the flowers up to our suite, finding my key under the mat just as he promised. After placing them prominently on the coffee table, next to my tiara baseball cap—my crown—I decided to put the key back where Dan had left it. I'll never know what would've happened if I hadn't done that. It did occur to me later, though, I have a history of not being very good with keys. Unfortunately, somebody else always winds up paying the price.

Back at the salon, they'd turned on the television. The weatherman, now a frail shadow of his former self, droned that Babe had made no more deviations to wipe out fast food joints, but was holding her course. No further delays were anticipated. She was expected to reach Mobile around noon tomorrow, and slam into the Mississippi Gulf Coast within an hour after that.

"Shoot!" fumed one girl with a headful of foils. "I really wanted to do some gambling out on one of those big riverboats while I was here."

"Oh, now honey! Those floating casinos can be real dangerous," cautioned her friend, whose head was wrapped in plastic through which could be glimpsed a virulent orange foam. "See, they've got these professional gambling men who ride around every night, just like old-time riverboat gamblers."

"Ooh, sounds sexy!" squealed the first girl.

"It is!" her friend giggled. "But listen. Somebody invited me to a private little club the other night. Only, they can't start playing until real, real late, because—"

Catching sight of me, the girl lowered her voice and I never heard the rest, not that I would've understood its significance.

Things got so busy from then on, it was 6:30 before I was able to break away. As I hurried to catch an elevator, I glanced into the Bay Lounge, and there sat Shelby, Foley and Dan, wreathed in cigar smoke, going over some papers in one of the booths.

Dan happened to look up just then. When he saw me, he smiled and pointed to the ceiling. I moved on, knowing he'd be along, soon as he could.

But when I retrieved my key again and unlocked our door, I discovered he'd apparently already been up here, setting the mood for our night of love, because the radio was playing, and I could hear the whirlpool bath gurgling seductively.

Lusty rhythm and blues saxophone music brayed an invitation to disrobe, which I accepted.

I smiled at that hilarious tiara baseball cap lying on the coffee table. So Dan wanted to play beauty pageant, did he? He really was the sexiest man in the world. I thought about putting it on, but no. He could bring it when he crowned me Queen of Love.

Ignoring the slight impression that there was something missing, I left an eager trail of shed clothing behind me—just in case he got lost—and stepped into the bathroom.

I wasn't really shocked when I saw Chessy Scarborough had beat me to the punch and was already lying in our bathtub, wearing nothing but her Miss Tampa Tangerine tiara. After all, it was just the kind of thing she *would* do.

She wouldn't be doing it anymore though, because she was dead. Strangled, apparently, with something white knotted around her throat. Oh, Lord. I bet I knew what it was, too.

I had to call Dan right away. So much for our night of love, I thought selfishly, reaching for one of the Bell Sands robes hanging on the back of the bathroom door.

I barely had time to wonder why the door was jammed so tight against the wall I couldn't pull it toward me, when whoever was hiding behind it suddenly shoved it into me with such force that the knob dug into my diaphragm, and the wind went out of me like a punctured tire.

I remember hearing the thunk of wood connecting with my forehead, immediately followed by the pain of a million firecrackers exploding behind my eyes, and I was going down, down, down, down, like in the old Otis Reading song, "Your Feelings and Mine."

Funny, I thought I cold hear Otis singing it now, I hoped it was the radio, because dear Otis had long since departed for that Dock of the Bay over in glory.

Then something heavy and soft was thrown over me, and everything went black.

CHAPTER 31

". . . and when I got here, Claire was lying on the floor between the bathroom and the bedroom, with one of those robes covering her," Dan concluded, tenderly applying a towel filled with crushed ice to my throbbing brow. He tried to smile at me, but he was too upset.

Foley, Charlotte and Tinker hovered anxiously, while Shelby paced at the foot of the bed. He looked at me, a little furtively, I thought, but maybe my vision was still impaired from that clonk.

Chief Troy Hepkins stared down at me grimly, arms folded across his khaki chest. This was the first time I'd seen him in uniform, and he looked like a forbidding stranger. Especially with that .357 Magnum in his holster. "Appears you interrupted somebody setting up a frame for your husband, Mrs. Claiborne."

"What?" I tried to sit upright in bed, but slid back down against the pillows when I realized I didn't have any clothes on.

The chief displayed a plastic bag, inside which reposed

the card Dan had written and sent along with the roses. "We found this lying next to a vase of roses in Miss Scarborough's room."

"But, that's mine!" I protested.

"So Mr. Claiborne has given us to understand. Be that as it may, somehow the message ended up in Room 308."

"Along with your flowers, Claire," Tinker put in. "Like I told you, Troy. I was helping out down in the Blooming Belle when Dan came in and ordered them for Claire. There was only one girl working today because some people couldn't get here on account of the storm and all the traffic on Highway 90.

"So I got Parker to bring them straight over to Claire in the beauty salon so she could enjoy them right away, since everybody else was busy draining the swimming pool and bringing in outdoor furniture and piling up sandbags and all."

"What time was that?" Chief Hepkins asked.

"About four o'clock," I responded, promptly. "I know because I was taking a break between appointments and I was afraid the chemicals would spoil them. So I dashed up here and set them on the coffee table, card and all. I didn't come back up until 6:30."

Hepkins looked alert. "Were the flowers here then?"

I began to shake my head, but quit because it felt like an enormous blister about to pop. "I didn't notice—no, wait." Closing my eyes I tried to recall the scene. Music playing, water gurgling, silly baseball cap lying on the coffee table . . . that was it! Nothing else had been on the table.

"No, they were not," I said, positively. "I remember having the vaguest notion something was missing, but I had . . . other things on my mind just then and I didn't pay much attention."

Dan stroked my hair gently. "So between when Claire brought the flowers up and went off, and the time she got back, somebody came in here, stole them and—"

"—and used them to lure Chessy here," Charlotte broke in. "That means it was somebody who knew Chessy'd been hitting on Dan so hard she would have come running without a second thought, after getting a note with a bunch of gorgeous flowers like that."

Foley's lips twitched humorously despite the gravity of the situation. "And the little touch about the tiara was just enough to make it seem personalized to her." He raised a quizzical eyebrow at Dan, who glowered back.

Chief Hepkins cleared his throat in embarrassment. "An unfortunate convenience for the killer that it was addressed to 'Beautiful' and not 'Claire'."

"And just to make things even handier for the bastard, I wrote down exactly where he could find Claire's key," Dan grunted, angry at himself.

I touched his arm. "It's not your fault, Dan. If I hadn't forgotten my key in the first place . . ." suddenly, a terrible thought hit me, with about the same force as that doorknob in the gut.

"Oh, Dan! It's just like what happened with Angie. Oh, my God!"

Dan tried to calm me down as I sobbed I was a jinx who just left keys around for people to get killed, while Foley and Charlotte explained to a bewildered Chief Hepkins about the angel doorknocker where I'd kept a key to my beauty shop, which a murderer had used to enter and kill my manicurist.

"Listen, anybody who came in to the flower shop and happened to see the flowers waiting on the counter to be delivered could've read that card," Tinker pointed out. "We don't use envelopes. They're a waste of time and money. We just keep a numbered list of orders and put little round stickers with the corresponding number on the bottom of an arrangement."

"Lot of customers come in today?" Hepkins inquired.

"I'd say so," Tinker agreed. "I guess more people were buying flowers than usual, because it's so gloomy outside."

"I purchased a few petals myself," Foley revealed, with a smile at Charlotte, which faded abruptly. "Hell, I hope nobody else got ahold of that card!"

"Not a chance, my big old lovecake," Charlotte assured him, and Foley grinned sheepishly. Now we all knew how he'd signed it.

The murder weapon was, as I feared, Chessy's own panties. Shelby, Foley and Dan, all loath to touch them where they lay on Freddy's bedspread, had watched Hepkins scoop them up onto a maroon plastic Bell Sands guest amenity shoe horn, and drop the lot into the wastebasket.

Doctor Dumas, the little grey coroner, (Hepkins called him Dr. Doom), came out of the bathroom. He had examined me and dished out a few pills before he'd gone in to see to Chessy. "You'll live," he assured me briefly. If it wasn't dead, Dr. Doom wasn't interested.

Now he said, "Okay, Chief. All through here. They're going to bring her out now, so we can get back to the morgue before the road up to Beach Boulevard gets any worse. Nothing much less amusing than getting stuck in red clay mud indefinitely with a dead body."

"Hey, Blalock! You through fingerprinting in there?" Hepkins called tiredly.

The investigator appeared in the bathroom doorway. "Just finished, Chief," Blalock replied, standing aside as the white-suited morgue attendant wheeled a sheeted Chessy out on a stretcher.

The rest of us looked away as she went by.

"Okay, Shelby. You want to show them how to get her out of here without being seen? Last thing we want is to start a panic."

Shelby said, "If we can make it to the elevator, we'll be fine. I can just lock the box and we'll ride express all the way down to the garage." He followed the stretcher out.

Hepkins rubbed his face. "Okay, Blalock," he addressed the officer. "Go see if Snellgrove needs any help down in 308. When y'all finish up, better get on back to the station."

"Yessir, Chief." Blalock left.

"Shit, this is all I need!" Hepkins complained, for once neglecting to beg the ladies' pardon for his language. "This ain't New Orleans where they've got all them special units and teams. Hell, you're basically looking at the unit! We got to wear all the hats around here.

"And now, because of this hurricane, the Harrison County Sheriff's Department and the State Troopers, who are ordinarily more than delighted to horn in even when they're not wanted, got their hands full with trying to keep Highway 90 from turning into one big old stretch of roadkill.

"You wouldn't believe the folks who suddenly decided to evacuate. Only now, after they jumped into their cars, they can't make up their minds which way to go. So they're driving around all over the place like chickens with their heads cut off."

"Baby, you feel up to moving now?" Dan asked me.

Tinker elaborated. "Obviously, you can't stay here. We're evacuating *you* to Suite 420, honey. It's just down the hall, and nice as this one, only it's got a better view. Or it will, until they board up the windows tomorrow."

"The Box Brothers here have already packed everything up," Charlotte said. "Except I kept some clean jammies and slippers, and your big leather bag out for you."

"You'll just be going a few steps down the hall so don't bother to bring that bathrobe," Tinker told me. "There's two fresh ones waiting in 420."

"And now, if you don't need me for anything, I'd better get back and see how LaWanda's doing."

"I'll come along too," Hepkins said, following her out. "Maybe she can answer a few questions now."

"Troy Hepkins, I won't have her badgered!" Tinker warned.

Charlotte waved Dan and Foley out, too. "You boys go on ahead to the new room while I help Claire get dressed," she commanded. "Order us something to eat while you're at it. We'll be along in a minute or two."

All at once, I was ravenous. I crawled into the relatively

modest lilac lace pyjamas with a silk lining Charlo had waiting for me, then she gingerly brushed out my hair.

"This is a switch, huh? Me doing your hair!" She smiled at our reflections. "Oops, sorry," she apologized as I winced when she hit a tangle.

I studied my bruise in the mirror. Actually, it felt worse than it looked, and was higher on my forehead than I thought. Between my bangs and some concealer, maybe nobody would notice.

Charlotte told me news of Freddy Franks' death had broken this afternoon in L.A., and her producer was both amazed and impressed she was the only reporter east of the Mississippi who had a taped report all ready to roll. Naturally, she didn't tell him she'd shot it two days before, or that Chief Hepkins had given her a running start after a telephone conversation with Franny Franks.

But Charlotte was more interested in the big picture.

"Claire!" she announced, excitedly. "I think I've solved the murders!"

"Murder, singular," I corrected. "Remember, Freddy's death is still officially an accident, and we still don't know if Battle's dead."

"Yes, my queen," Charlotte teased. "You'll have to explain that tiara business to me sometime. Anyway, name one person among us who really thinks Freddy wasn't murdered, or that Brandon Battle isn't dead."

"Brandon Battle is capable of anything, including faking his own death," I retorted. "And as to Freddy, well, it could be those two things aren't even related."

"Exactly!" Charlotte exclaimed, as if I'd agreed with

her. "And Chessy's the common—very common—denominator here.

"Now, we know she's been carrying on with Freddy ever since they did that movie out in Hollywood together. We definitely know they were bopping away here.

"*Zzzzt!* Exit Freddy.

"Then there was this weird pseudo-incest between Chessy and her Uncle B.B. Ugh!" she made a face. "Anyway. Exit Uncle B.B."

"But who and why?" I asked, checking drawers to make sure Dan and Foley hadn't overlooked anything.

"Shelby Bell!" Charlotte said, nodding positively.

"What!" I exclaimed. "You're outta your mind!" I neglected to mention my own suspicion that Shelby might have a private agenda.

"No, Claire. Listen." Charlotte spoke persuasively. "He's been like a cat on hot bricks ever since I got here."

"Because that Battle-Scarborough consortium was getting ready to sock it to him good," I interrupted.

"Uh-uh," she argued. "There's more to it than that. You notice how freaky he gets when anybody brings up the subject of the Redneck Mafia? Well, I think Shelby's in the thing himself.

"Like Chief Hepkins said, it's a battle for territory, and the Bell Sands will be to Biloxi what Caesar's Palace is to Las Vegas, if that casino bill goes through. Didn't you see the look on Shelby's face when Hepkins started talking about that?

"I believe here's what happened. Brandon Battle and LaWanda and Chessy's branch (obviously they're all in it) have got a fix in to a few key state senators and they know for a solid gold fact that the gambling act's going to pass.

"Now. What is the biggest, finest, most famous resort hotel on the Mississippi Gulf Strip, where all they'd have to do is haul away a little furniture to make room for those crap tables and roulette wheels and whatever? The Bell Sands, of course! How could this place not be a target for every legal and illegal gambling interest there is?

"Plus, just to sweeten the pot, LaWanda's got a major grudge match to settle with Tinker. The Miss Gulf Coast Pageant was the perfect opportunity, because even if Chessy hadn't won Miss Tampa Tangerine, they could still have paid the entrance fee for her.

"But meanwhile, they're coming up against one of their own Redneck Mafia factions, in which Shelby Bell is a big player. He's not about to let the opposition snatch his hotel away. But if he smokes all three of them, he knows somebody else will show up and there would be a bloodbath. Just like they did in Vegas in *The Godfather*, remember?

"Shelby decides to meet Battle on his own turf with a legal fight. Notice he didn't call in his regular law firm, but gets Dan involved through you. And by association, Foley. He dangles a taste of the Bell Group business for bait.

"Well, Dan and Foley come through with flying colors, beating Battle at every turn. Meanwhile though, Freddy Franks has been getting hints about what's going on from Chessy. He wants to cut himself in. Battle won't give him the time of day. So, he tries to get heavy with Shelby, and goes *adios*."

"Wait! Stop!" I begged. "You're making my head hurt

worse. Look, I have no problem believing in either a Redneck Mafia or that they might even kill each other for a chance to get control of the Bell Sands and casino gambling in general.

"I don't even have a problem believing Freddy Franks would try to muscle in on the deal. Maybe he saw himself as a main room headliner at a Vegas-type oceanfront hotel for the rest of his life.

"But there could be any number of hillbilly gangsters staying here who belong to either the Gillises or the Scarboroughs. If you're going to accuse Shelby, you may as well go ahead and include Chief Troy Hepkins."

Charlotte's eyes widened. "Claire, you just might have something there. I'm serious."

"And *I'm* a pitiful invalid and I can't take any more of this," I told her. "Shelby had already whipped Battle, thanks to our legal beagles. Why would he kill him?"

Charlotte pondered. "I haven't figured that out yet," she admitted. "Maybe Battle had another ace in the hole nobody knew about. Remember, Shelby was the only one who spoke directly to him yesterday. We have only his word for what was said on the phone."

I conceded the point. "Okay. But what about Chessy?"

"Oh, there could be any number of reasons for that," Charlotte shrugged. "Maybe Chessy got Shelby in bed after all and threatened to tell Tinker.

"Or maybe she knew he killed Freddy and was trying to blackmail him."

"Maybe I don't want to think about this anymore right

now," I snapped. Because convoluted as it sounded, Charlotte's scenario made a frightening kind of sense.

Unbidden, there came to my mind a vision of that roll of what looked like plans Shelby had knocked out of his drawer that morning. And, when Dan picked it up, as good as yanked it way.

Could those be plans for a fabulous new casino at the Bell Sands? Was Shelby simply getting prepared, just in case, or—did he already know the bill was going to pass?

Charlotte was right. Shelby Bell wasn't about to just roll over and let somebody walk off with his hotel.

Yes, Shelby was very fond of Franny, though I doubted it was more than that. He'd even admitted he'd been ripe to tear into Freddy because of how he'd treated her. Freddy was also potential trouble on a stick for the pageant. He'd already threatened to pull the act from the show, and now we knew that he'd promised Chessy to take a loud Hollywood liberal position against the Bells to the media.

However, I couldn't see Shelby killing the comedian for any of those reasons. But, if Freddy had started monkeying around with Shelby's hotel—that was something else.

Shelby could've heard about the treadmill problems from Parker and arranged for the execution.

Shelby could've slipped away from the kitchen long enough to, for reasons unknown, bump off Battle. Still and always with the provision Battle wasn't strolling around the hotel in drag, sans mustache and sneering at us all.

Shelby could've had a reason to kill Chessy we knew nothing about.

Shelby had known about the panties.

Shelby could've heard about the roses from Tinker and immediately realized how they could be used to frame Dan.

Shelby had his own passkey, he wouldn't have needed mine under the mat.

I felt a cold chill in my stomach. Shelby *had* been looking at me funny just now, maybe wondering if I'd recognized who whacked me.

But Charlotte hadn't carried her hypothesis the next inevitable step further. There was no way Shelby Bell could have done all—or any—of that without Tinker's full and complete knowledge. And assistance.

Because on my way up to the room, just before I'd found Chessy in our bathtub, I'd looked into the Bay Lounge and seen Shelby sitting with Dan and Foley.

Shelby had an alibi for the time of death; he couldn't have been the one who attacked me.

But what about Tinker?

CHAPTER 32

Our new suite, done in restful Santa Fe tones, featured a massive lodgepole bed, covered with an Indian blanket. All the furniture was pine and rawhide, and the smell was homey and comforting.

There was a sunken whirlpool tub in this bathroom too, but for various reasons, I opted to take a shower.

Afterward, I snuggled in my fresh Bell Sands robe, half-watching a *Mission Impossible* rerun, starring that creamy-smooth, ladylike, and oh-so-lethal, Cinnamon.

As a young girl, I'd wanted to grow up to be Cinnamon, and seeing this particular episode again—where she performs a Marlene Dietrich-type cabaret act—merely confirmed my long-held opinion that no other woman on television has ever come close to achieving the ultimate cool of Barbara Bain.

The food, however, was hot.

Dan and Foley's idea of dinner consisted of the Beach Club's Five Alarm Chili, topped with shredded jack cheese; something called a "Mexican Survival Kit," which included guacamole, fresh tortilla chips, salsa and whole pickled jalapeños; and a mountain of Black Pepper french fries.

There was Dixie beer for everybody else and a couple of Classic Cokes for me. The only way I like beer is to taste it on Dan's lips when he's through drinking it.

Dan, who's got a castiron stomach, chewed on a whole jalapeno, while joining Foley to methodically refute Charlotte's entire case against Shelby Bell.

True, they had only heard Shelby's end of that conversation when Battle requested the meeting. However, they themselves were Shelby's alibi, waiting with him until well after Battle failed to show up, hearing Shelby order the hotel operator to page him, and being present when he'd sent Parker up to knock on the lawyer's door.

Then, they'd left Shelby at the kitchen to supervise our victory dinner. And there he'd stayed, surrounded by witnesses, until he went up to his and Tinker's suite to change clothes.

Today, all of us, plus Chief Hepkins and Parker Bell, could vouch for Shelby's whereabouts at the time of Chessy's death, which Dr. Dumas unofficially estimated at between 6:00 and 6:30 p.m.

"Okay, okay!" Charlotte laughed. "As long as you're not being blinded by S'no Bull."

"Although," Foley conceded, finishing his chili and washing it down with a slug of Dixie, "you could have a point about Tinker. I wonder how she's fixed for alibis."

Dan mused, "Well, she knew about the roses and the note, because she personally took my order. But she couldn't have known about the . . . murder weapon. At least not then.

Because she wasn't with us when Claire found it—them—in Freddy's blazer pocket."

Charlotte looked doubtful. "Obviously, Shelby told her soon as possible, since it explained the peep show. But somehow, I can't see Tinker laying such a convoluted trap. She strikes me as direct and to the point. Besides, Dan, what possible reason would she have to frame you?"

"Only if it were a question of sacrificing Dan to distract attention from Shelby," I said. "Anyway, she knew they were together at the critical times."

"Claire's right," Foley agreed. "Hell, she couldn't frame Dan without wrecking Shelby's alibi."

Charlotte ruminated. "Not Tinker, then. But the web-spinning aspects of the whole setup do hint there's a superior female mind at work, here."

"You must mean Marlowe Goodkidd," I said. "Because the only other female involved is me. That is, if you're not factoring in some disgruntled Miss Gulf Coast hopeful."

Until that instant, I hadn't even thought of how good a case could be made against me as a suspect. Chessy had hit on my man in the presence of witnesses. People have been killed for much less. And, been indicted for less, come to think of it.

"Claire! Of course, Marlowe Goodkidd!" Charlotte chided. "That woman's got an ego big as her implants, and we've seen for ourselves how she and Chessy were always at each other's throats, figuratively.

"Except this time, it was Chessy's throat, literally."

"But how did she know about the roses and Dan's

note?" Foley demanded. "And what would even make her think of framing Dan?"

Charlotte shrugged. "Like Tinker said, anybody could've walked into the flower shop. It'll be easy to find out if Marlowe dropped by to order flowers before Parker delivered Dan's roses to Claire.

"As to why Dan? Don't forget, Chessy and Marlowe always went after the same man." Charlotte looked at Foley with affectionate pity. "Of course, you wouldn't understand this, but your friend Dan Claiborne would be one tempting hunk of cheese with which to bait a trap for some hungry girl mouse."

Dan looked embarrassed. "I guess I should take that as a compliment."

Foley said, "It sure didn't sound like an insult, Danbo!"

"Well," laughed Charlotte, "I'm only stating a fact. And I wouldn't be surprised if Parker hadn't run straight to good old Marlowe for a little touch of comfort, when he realized what Chessy's panties in Freddy's pocket meant. He would've needed to talk to somebody, and I bet Marlowe managed to suck that news item right off his tongue!"

Foley looked at her. "Hmmm. Your language is getting mighty visceral—or is it visual?—lately."

"Must be verbal compensation," Charlotte murmured, returning his look.

Foley squeezed her to his side. "You sure know how to make out . . . a case, lady!" He accompanied the double entendre praise with a greasy kiss. "Maybe I better enroll you in law school, and we'll go into practice together."

Charlotte drew little circles with her forefinger on

Foley's thigh and looked up at him from beneath her lashes. "Maybe we should practice practicing?" she suggested.

Foley's eyes grew hot. "Maybe we should," he said, in a husky voice.

Dan cleared his throat. "Excuse me! Before court convenes! You've created opportunity for Marlowe, and suggested how she could've accessed the murder weapon. But what about motive?"

Charlotte started to speak but the phone rang.

Dan answered. "Yeah, we're still up, Shelby," he said, and listened, a frown gathering between his strong brows.

Finally he said, "Under the circumstances, we will undertake to act on behalf of the pageant. Just tell the chief we'll be there in a few minutes."

He put down the phone and said, "Chief Hepkins has informed Shelby he discovered $47,000 worth of IOUs in Chessy's room. All of them dated within the past three days, and all signed by Ms. Marlowe Goodkidd."

Chief Hepkins had agreed to wait until the talent show intermission to question Marlowe.

After all that had happened, I was amazed to see it was only 10:30, and to remember the pageant was still going on. In fact, tonight the winner would be announced on the live television broadcast, when all the girls would appear in bathing suits and evening gowns.

Minus one. How had Chessy's absence been explained to the others, I wondered.

And if Chief Hepkins arrested Marlowe Goodkidd for murdering her before the votes were in, the pageant would also be minus one judge.

"If the Bells are so determined to have eight judges for Miss Gulf Coast, maybe next year they should consider installing a viewer's phone-in, like Miss America. Lord knows, it's got to be less trouble!"

Charlotte made this observation after Dan and Foley had gone to meet Chief Hepkins, Shelby and Marlowe in Shelby's office.

Foley agreed with Dan, that they should make themselves available counsel for Marlowe Goodkidd on behalf of the pageant, though technically, they weren't representing either.

"Just think of this inconvenience as adding another big, juicy diamond to your wedding band," I consoled Charlotte.

"A diamond is not exactly the noun I'd pick out to go with those particular adjectives, Claire!" she groaned, laughingly. "And, please! Don't let's get started on *that* subject. December 24 is a long way off."

"Poor you," I sympathized. "Meanwhile, how come Chessy Scarborough lent nearly fifty thou to a woman she hated?"

Charlotte started walking around the room. "Do we really know they hated each other, Claire? Buddy has been hanging out with some of the paparazzi, tanking up on Hollywood gossip.

"Evidently, it's not uncommon for stars who prefer their own sex to stage all kinds of scenarios to make it look otherwise."

I sat up, heedless of my throbbing head. "Wait a minute! Are you saying Marlowe and Chessy were only pretending to fight over guys because they were really . . . involved with each other?"

Charlotte held up a hand. "I'm only mentioning it as a possibility, Claire. Buddy said one of the photographers told him there'd been 'bi' rumors about Marlowe for years.

"If so, jealousy could be a motive for Marlowe to kill her. It might also explain why Chessy never pointed a finger at Marlowe when she, LaWanda and Battle were trying to wreck the pageant."

I said, "Be that as it may, it still doesn't explain why Chessy gave Marlowe so much money, or where she got it in the first place."

Charlotte stabbed at the carpet with her toes. "That's true. You know, when Dan mentioned the amount, my first thought was blackmail. Only, since when does a blackmailer accept IOUs?"

She'd no sooner asked the question than I knew the answer.

When the blackmailer is a celebrity who's made a big deal about being a recovered gambler, of course.

"That's it, Claire! That's it!" Excitedly, Charlotte began to jog in place. "Marlowe was gambling, and lost. For some reason, she had to go to Chessy for money. Chessy kept covering her, until—" she stopped, uncertain as to what came next.

"Yes. That's where it gets fuzzy," I said. "Until what? Did Chessy give her an ultimatum and Marlowe couldn't— or wouldn't—pay up?"

Charlotte sat down. "What if those labia-locking scenes were supposed to climax into something really nasty tonight, during the broadcast?" She was thinking aloud. "Something that would make Miss Gulf Coast and the Bell Sands look so smutty-tacky-trailer-bubba nobody who mattered would ever want to be involved with either again?"

"That makes the most sense of anything we've come up with, yet," I told her. And it did. What could hurt the pageant worse than for an ugly catfight—or worse—to break out on live TV? Oh, the ratings would soar for the rest of the night, but after that, Miss Gulf Coast and the Bell Sands Hotel would be just one more redneck riviera joke. Forever.

Yes, Marlowe was about to start yet another new sitcom. Although, as one critic observed, with her crash record, if she were an airline, the FAA would've canceled her license to fly years ago.

But even so, she'd still be able to count on a chunk of pay or play money, and that might be how she intended to honor her gambling debts.

If, indeed, we were right about Marlowe colluding with Chessy on a pageant ruination scheme. Perhaps Marlowe had simply thought of it as a contingency plan. Then discovered it was the only payment Chessy would accept.

"There's one small detail we're overlooking, here," Charlotte said. "All of the seagoing gambling boats are docked and dark, and have been for several days. And most of the legal floating barge casinos have closed down because of Hurricane Babe."

"So?" Dr. Doom's pills were starting to kick in and I suddenly felt tired and irritable.

"So where did Marlowe Goodkidd manage to lose

$47,000 in the last seventy-two hours?" Charlotte demanded.

CHAPTER 33

"She won't tell," Dan said, when he and Foley returned, bearing four huge Mississippi Mud milkshakes, courtesy of the Beach Club.

"Clams are talkative compared to that one," Foley elaborated, eagerly plunging a striped straw into the plastic lid of his shake.

Basically, what it came down to was that if Marlowe had been faking her shock at the news of Chessy's murder, she was a far, far better actress than anyone ever knew.

According to Dan, she'd turned white as a sheet, and if Chief Hepkins hadn't caught her in time, she'd've crashed to the floor.

When Marlowe recovered sufficiently to answer questions, she'd readily acknowledged the IOUs as gambling debts, and pleaded hysterically for Chief Hepkins not to release that information to the press.

She even confessed to staging those vignettes with Chessy but, as Charlotte and I guessed, only did that to cover her until FedEx—undaunted by Babe—had delivered a sizeable check that very morning.

However, when she'd attempted to make a payment Chessy had told her, in effect, no dice.

"She said Chessy had something double-dirty planned for tonight, but didn't know what," Dan said.

Marlowe swore the last time she'd seen Chessy was when she'd tried to pay her. Chessy had shown up at Marlowe's door shortly after she returned from Bella Salon.

Not only would Chessy not take the money, she threatened Marlowe she'd better go along with tonight's plan. Or else.

Marlowe was really frightened by that because, while actually kind of enjoying the improv bits with Chessy, she'd never had the slightest intention of pitching a fit on national television. It would've ruined her.

But then, so would exposure of her phony gambling rehab.

Marlowe apologized to Shelby for all the trouble she'd caused, but her contrition had not extended to revealing where she'd lost so much money.

The most she would say was that it was a private, high stakes, illegal casino.

Foley added, "Maybe she just went actressy and dramatic on us, but she said she'd be dead if she told."

"Well, but where is the threat coming from?" I wondered, feeling drowsier by the minute. "Certainly not from her major creditor. She's already dead herself."

"Seems to me, it gets down to who's left," Charlotte suggested. "The two people most closely connected with

Chessy—namely Freddy Franks and Brandon Battle—are, respectively, dead and missing. So that leaves LaWanda."

"At least it appears that way," Dan said. "However, after Chessy's murder, I have a hard time seeing LaWanda as even capable of sustaining her grudge match against Tinker, much less being hazardous to Marlowe Goodkidd's health."

Foley set his empty milkshake container on the table. "What it *really* gets down to, in lawyer talk, is *cui bono*? Who's been bankrolling this thing from day one? And how do they expect to make a profit? Because you can't convince me it's all been about sweet revenge."

Dan nodded. "You're absolutely right, Foley. Which brings us back to our Redneck Mafia friends. That's the only source of financing this venture on such a grand scale I know of."

Goggling exaggeratedly, Charlotte squawked, like Jim Nabors, "Well, gah-ah-ah-lee, Andy! I am mighty glad to have me some company on this here lonely two-lane black-top!"

In her normal voice she added, "What was I just saying a while ago? I'm telling you, Shelby Bell is—"

Foley butted in. "Sorry, baby, I can't let you say it again. It's just not true."

Dan said, "Charlotte, listen. We haven't exactly been blind ourselves as to how Shelby acts whenever somebody mentions the dry land bill or the Redneck Mafia. So, after Marlowe resumed pageant duty, and Hepkins left, we confronted him."

Between Dan and Foley, they explained that Shelby had

practically sobbed with relief at the opportunity to unburden himself.

Because Shelby was indeed approached by the Redneck Mafia, who were definitely expecting that bill to pass, and fully intended to buy up every luxury hotel on the Gulf Strip.

Why should they go to all the trouble, not to mention waste valuable gambling time, building things when they could just take them over?

Yes, he'd received threats, but stuck to his guns. After all, Shelby Bell was a man of great wealth and power in his own right. And that's where his guilty behavior came in.

Because Shelby maintained his very own private pipeline to the state legislature, through which he'd received information that the dry land casino bill was good as passed.

So Shelby, acting on that insider tip, had secretly hired a famous architect to design a fabulous, Monte Carlo-style casino addition to the Bell Sands, plus some minor remodeling to the existing structure for a game room during the interim.

Shelby Bell could thumb his nose at the Redneck Mafia because he was prepared to beat everybody on the Gulf Strip to the punch and cash in first.

The threats had become more frequent and more vicious. Until about two months ago, when they'd stopped completely.

"And then, they literally came at him through Miss Gulf Coast," Charlotte concluded, mollified now that she knew she'd been taken seriously. Then she frowned. "Wait a minute!

"That means there's an unidentified grits-eating gangster still at large because Marlowe's so scared. But would it be a Gillis, or a Scarborough?"

Dan shook his head. "The problem is, it could be either. I'm not all that well-versed on the subject, but I do recall reading an article that said, back when they split, some Gillises sided with the Scarboroughs, and vice-versa."

"Plus," Foley reminded him, "all the other families, like the Rayburns and Huttos, for instance. They were divided over it, too."

Charlotte wanted to know, "Are there any Gillises, Scarboroughs, Rayburns or Huttos employed at the Bell Sands?"

"Excellent thinking!" Foley beamed at her. "Especially since Danbo and I have already volunteered you to go down and help Shelby with a computer search of employee records first thing tomorrow morning."

"Always provided the storm hasn't knocked the terminals out completely by then," Charlotte cautioned.

By now I could hardly keep my eyes open. "Maybe you don't even have to bother," I mumbled. "Maybe Tinker's mother or father was a Gillis-Scarborough, or a Scarborough-Gillis, or whatever. Maybe she's the one gunning for Shelby. Maybe she's running that private game herself down in their big old blue boat."

The last thing I remember, the three of them were staring at me as if my hazy maunderings had actually made sense.

CHAPTER 34

I was sitting at a child's desk in a classroom, while Tinker, wearing her blue tea-drinking suit and veiled hat, busily drew yellow chalk diagrams on a green blackboard.

"Well, you plainly *don't* understand the theory of relativity, Claire," she said, in an exasperated voice, waving a long, wooden pointer at me. "It's really very simple, because it's so close to home.

"You pay careful attention now, honey," she commanded, and turned back to the board. Tinker clicked the pointer beneath each group of drawings, sighing as if she despaired of me ever comprehending the message.

I really wanted to please her, so I tried and tried to make sense out of the fuzzy squiggles, until suddenly, they fell into place.

"By George! I think she's got it!" crowed an unseen Alistair Cooke.

The first group of outlines was a mother, father and daughter.

The second showed a mother, father and son.

Next came a group of masculine figures, with one tall distinct figure in the center.

Then the two fathers were together, until one was erased by the other.

But the remaining father was immediately erased by the tall man.

One mother and son were together, then somebody from the group erased the mother.

One mother and daughter were together, until somebody erased the daughter. But I couldn't tell who.

I was thrilled when Tinker exclaimed, "Very good, Claire!"

Then she drew a big boat with blue chalk, and tapped it with the pointer. "Claire," Tinker said gravely, "it is vital that you know where and how to park her for the battle."

BANG! BANG! BANG!

"What's that noise?" Tinker demanded, and vanished in a flash of pique.

BANG! BANG!

I struggled awake to find our windows in the process of being boarded up against Babe. We'd just have to take Tinker's word about the view being so much better.

After that weird dream, Tinker was on my brain. Did it really mean something, or was it simply the aftershock from a blow on the head, combined with spicy food on an empty stomach late at night?

I felt across the bed for Dan but he wasn't there.

Although I sensed he was gone, I called out anyway. Silence.

The clock on my nightstand read 7:00 a.m. Why was he

out so early? How long had he been gone? I sank back into the pillows, but the constant hammering made sleep impossible.

Feeling jumpy and nervous, I got up and went through the suite, turning on every lamp and overhead light.

Then I freshened up with what *Tante* Jeanette used to call a "French bath," and threw on some jeans and a denim work shirt.

All that effort exhausted me. I flopped onto the sofa and closed my eyes, allowing my mind to drift, since it obviously wasn't capable of doing much else.

The theory of relativity, the dream Tinker had lectured me, was really very simple because it was so close to home.

Not home.

Close to home.

I thought I'd understood and so had Tinker because just before the hammering woke me, she was going to show me how to park her precious blue boat for a war or something.

No, not a war. The battle.

How to park her boat for the battle. How to park her . . oh, my dear God.

I went over to the desk, shuffling through the astonishing pile of papers that we'd somehow accumulated in less than a week. At last, I found what I wanted: the article about Eddie Scarborough's deer-hunting accident.

The man who allegedly felt so bad about shooting his friend he'd committed suicide was named Jerry Hutto.

I knew where Dan was.

Disregarding fatigue, I laced up my sneakers and stuffed my hair under the tiara baseball cap. It would be ruined but it was all I had. I could always get another cap. I couldn't get another Dan.

The only rain gear we'd brought along were our light tan waterproof jackets, and as I got mine off the hanger, I saw Dan's was missing. It didn't offer much protection, but it would have to do.

The hotel was totally quiet, except for that distant hammering. The calm before the storm. I was the only human being in sight. Everybody else was hiding from Babe, due in a few hours now. But I had a feeling she was closer than that.

When an elevator actually responded to my push of the button, I was startled; the building seemed so still.

The lobby was deserted.

I struggled out through a side door, first against the wind, then into it. Squinting through the rain, I got my bearings and slogged down what was left of the beach, through the wet sand toward the marina. I tried to hurry but that sand, so white and silky and squeaky-hot in the sun, now dragged like molasses, and the waves rushed up and tried to tackle me around the knees. Once I did fall but managed to scramble up again, and the wind propelled me forward.

At last I saw the boats. Water was already sloshing over the piers, which were laid out in a maze of blind alleys. I didn't know I was looking for a sixty-foot, custom-built Bertram Sedan Cruiser, and it wouldn't have helped me if I had. I just rushed up and down, searching for a big blue boat.

After an eternity, there it was. Two golden wedding bells joined with a bow adorned the prow. Tinker and Shelby, till death did them part.

My hands slipped as I grappled up the ladder. A huge flume of spray nearly knocked me off into the angry water.

Finally, I stumbled onto the deck trying to find things to grab to keep my balance, but there was only the slippery metal railing. Every portable on deck must have been stowed away in the cabin, which in turn was secured with a steel bar and huge padlock.

I peered through the smallish portholes into darkness that seemed empty.

Clinging to the rail, I crept hand-over-hand to the bow and there was Dan, slowly being forced to back away, closer and closer to the edge until he would soon go overboard, by the man stalking him with a huge hunting knife.

Rolling around near Dan's feet I recognized our long heavy flashlight. Obviously he had stopped in the garage to take it out of the trunk on his way over.

"DAN!" I howled desperately into the wind with every ounce of lung power I possessed, and Parker Bell whirled around and came after me.

"Watch out, Claire!" Dan yelled, hurtling after Parker with a flying tackle. But Parker Bell, wide receiver, Ole Miss 1984, had played football, too, and he eluded Dan, who fell and skidded face down like a huge hockey puck across the wet deck.

But my hero had bought me enough time to scramble up the metal rungs to the top of the cabin.

Parker hesitated, spotted me on the roof and started up after me.

"Parker Hutto!" I screamed. "It was you! You killed them all!"

Parker halted midway. His face contorted, "It was her own fault!" he cried. "Chessy Scarborough took everything away from me. Everything!"

Over his shoulder, I could see Dan groggily raising his head from the deck.

"They made your daddy kill Chessy's daddy, didn't they?" I asked.

Parker nodded. He was bawling hard as a sick calf. "They told him Eddie wasn't fit to live, 'cause of how he did little girls. Said a thing like that might bring them all down, someday."

Dan was up on all fours now.

"And then they killed Jerry, made it look like suicide to cover up?" I asked, willing Parker to focus completely on me, to keep talking. And he did. Unfortunately, the story was short as it was sordid.

Whatever Gillis/Scarborough alliance had eliminated both men, they'd paid off LaWanda and Alva, Parker's mother.

A few years later, Alva remarried to Shelby's brother Ken, a man with no gang connections. But Alva wasn't satisfied. She missed the excitement of being the wife of a gangster, and her payoff money was running out.

Unwisely, she started poking around on her own into Redneck Mafia business and discovered what Brandon was getting up to with Chessy.

She demanded more money to keep quiet, so it was bye-bye Alva.

But before she died, she told her son the whole story.

The only thing Parker had to cling to all these years was

that the little curly-haired playmate he'd fallen in love with as a child was, like himself, an innocent pawn in a grownup game of greed, lust and power.

How else could he have reconciled losing both his parents because of her?

And then, just a few months ago, Chessy had come to him, pleading for his help in Battle's scheme to get control of the Bell Sands, telling him her life was in danger, Battle would do disgusting things to her, Parker was the only one who could save her, he'd be a millionaire, he was the only one she'd ever really loved, they'd do what Battle said, then get rid of him and be together forever, and isn't this good, Parker, don't you want lots more of this, Parker, you'll be my only boy.

Parker wagged his head sadly. "But she lied!" he yelled, "She was a lying, no-good, filthy slut, just like the rest of you!"

He reached for the next rung, but froze when Dan shouted, "Parker! You touch her and you're dead meat!"

Parker looked over his shoulder to see Dan back on his feet again and bearing down on him like a crazed locomotive. He had managed to retrieve the flashlight and was getting ready to swing it with all his considerable might into Parker's skull.

Parker jumped off the rungs, then he was over the edge and swarming down the ladder, onto the dock.

We didn't dare go after him yet. Parker knew those piers like the back of his hand and it would be our sorry flashlight against his big knife. One wrong turn by us and we'd be kabobs.

After maybe five minutes, Dan said, "Well, I hope we're all prayed up, as my Granny Blaine in Kentucky used to say. Because I think we better make a run for it, baby."

He grinned, then kissed me. "Ready, darlin'?"

I smiled back. "I am now."

But it was too late.

Parker had used that knife to sever the spring lines mooring *Blue* to her berth, and we were already at least twenty feet from the pier.

Dan and I were up the creek without a paddle, and moving fast.

For true, *cher*.

CHAPTER 35

What I feared has come upon me.

That was Job's famous lament and I knew exactly how he felt. Had I always secretly feared I was destined to meet the same fate as my parents? Remembering that eerie moment back at Captain Ezra's, when I'd realized they'd loved each other as deeply as Dan and I did, when I'd breathed that heartfelt little prayer that whenever we went, we'd be together like my mother and father had been, I almost laughed. I hadn't expected an answer quite so soon; certainly not quite so literally.

But I also remembered the strange sense of peace I'd felt at the time.

Okay, I'd go with the peace.

All the while I was thinking these things I had been helping Dan, as best I could, to lift the heavy sea anchor lying in the bow. We strained and struggled until we were finally able to heave it over the port side. I heard it thud against the hull as it went over. So much for that nice blue paint job.

Both of us were such landlubbers, we didn't know we hadn't done it correctly. But that was about as relevant then as what make of boat we were trapped on.

Dropping anchor seemed like the only sensible thing to do, and if it didn't help, we figured at least it couldn't hurt.

My baseball cap had been snatched away by the wind. Somewhere, perhaps a proud dolphin was wearing my tiara. Long strands of drenched hair whipped into my face, stinging like wet ropes. If we got out of this alive, I'd probably need cosmetic surgery.

Dan, unshaven and bristly, was wearing brown sweats under his jacket. He looked like a soaked bear.

The cabin was completely inaccessible to us.

If Dan managed to break the thick double glass of a porthole with the flashlight, even I wasn't small enough to squeeze through the opening. And even if I could, the door was bolted and padlocked from the outside.

Hypothetically, if I made it into the cabin, there would probably be some kind of tool I could pass out to Dan so he could wrench open the door. Not to mention call for help on the radio, if it was still working.

Two things stopped us from attempting what would probably be a futile exercise anyway.

If Dan used the flashlight as a hammer, not only might it not be sufficient to break the glass, but it would surely demolish the flashlight. While we still had the light, we could use it to signal. As long as the batteries held out.

The second reason was that the cabin was occupied by Brandon Battle, his maroon bathrobed corpse traveling snug

and dry in first class, while we struggled just to keep from
getting washed overboard.

There was only one place that offered any shelter at all,
a built-in bench across the stern. If we could just get back
there, we could at least crawl underneath and . . . wait.

Dan gripped me from behind, squashing me tightly
against him as he took my arms. Then slowly, hand-over-
hand, we inched our way along the slippery railing like
dancers in a nightmare ballet. It occurred to me that I was
indeed standing on his shoes, as Chessy had jeered.

To take our minds off our immediate surroundings, Dan
filled me in on the rest of what happened before I showed
up.

After my garbled signoff last night, Dan had put me to
bed. Then, he, Foley and Charlotte discussed the possibility,
however farfetched, of Tinker being a villainess.

The idea of running a private game on her boat was
hypothetically appealing, but logistically impractical,
mainly because of the weather.

But also because "Shel and Tink's" nosy boating neigh-
bors would surely comment if *Wedding Bells' Blue* was
suddenly starting to light up from after midnight into the
wee small hours.

However, when they' d begun thinking about the elec-
trical requirements of running gambling machines, Dan all
at once had known just where to look.

It was after 2:30 a.m. when he'd summoned Shelby to
inspect Tinker's family tree for any Gillis, Hutto or Rayburn
roots.

Shelby had been astounded, then offended, then profoundly disturbed. Because he remembered the honkytonking Alva's first husband was named Jerry Hutto.

And Shelby had already come to the same conclusion as Dan about the illegal games people were playing.

About an hour before, he'd quietly slipped down to 608, which might've been a dog of a room, but it made for one bitching casino.

That big old Reddy Killowat, Parker Bell, had rigged up a pint-sized playpen, including slot machines, roulette wheels, off-track betting and on-line Caribbean Lotto access.

Of course, that's why he'd slugged Ray that afternoon they were supposedly looking for Brandon Battle, to keep his secret safe.

Shelby himself had told the maids on six not to bother with that room unless it was needed, so there was no danger of them disobeying his orders.

Parker, who'd been sneaking Shelby's passkey, realized his uncle was going to be more aware of its whereabouts. Given his ubiquitous position at the Bell Sands, who would've suspected him of evil intent when he brought that key in for duplication?

Nobody noticed when Shelby peeked into Room 608. The crowd of high rollers consisted of most of the celebrities, Marlowe included, plus the new Miss Gulf Coast. Who turned out to be Miss ("Tramp") Captiva Island.

At least I'd been right about something. Too bad I didn't put money on her.

What disturbed Shelby more than anything, even

Parker's betrayal, was that he realized the Redneck Mafia had to be behind it.

In fact, he'd been dithering about what to do when Dan called. Tinker already knew what she wanted to do, which was to have Parker arrested that exact minute.

And that was before Dan had broken the news Parker was not only a traitor and thief, but most likely a murderer as well.

Of course if Brandon Battle wasn't in the hotel, dead or alive, he was somewhere else. And what better place than *Wedding Bells' Blue*, where nobody would look for days?

Shelby had mentioned to Dan in passing he always ran the boat himself with only a few hired hands, unless it was for a long distance. So there was no regular crew hanging around.

Naturally, Parker had been charged with stormproofing the vessel. Nobody would even think to question his carrying a heavy bundle aboard.

Was the lawyer already dead by the time Parker got him into the cabin? I guess it meant either six or one-half-dozen to Brandon Battle now. Dead is dead, and he sure was.

Dan had seen him lying on a sofa in the cabin when he aimed the flashlight into a porthole. He'd then looked all over the deck for something to break open the door, and that was when Parker caught him.

At this point in his narrative, we realized with amazement we had made it to the stern! Cautiously, we let go of the railing and crawled under the bench.

It was so wonderful not to have the rain pelting us in

the face, that we almost forgot how bad things really were for a moment. Nothing is more relative than comfort.

Or more simple than the theory of relativity, as the dream Tinker pointed out. Parker was, in theory, a relative.

And we hadn't looked close enough to home for a motive or a murderer.

CHAPTER 36

After we caught our breath, Dan picked up his tale again. "I don't care to speculate why Parker was down here with that knife so early, but I suspect it had something to do with turning Battle into easily digestible portions for the fish.

"Or maybe he saw me leave the hotel. Anyway, I sure wasn't expecting him, and he caught me with my pants down. I don't know what would've happened if you hadn't shown up just then, baby. All of a sudden, there you were in your tiara, screaming your head off!

"You saved my life, darlin'." He paused, and added with irrepressible humor, "So far."

"But why did you leave without letting me know?" I demanded. "Did you tell Shelby or Foley or anybody?"

Dan shook his head regretfully. "Honey, I thought I'd just be gone a few minutes. I wanted to check it out myself first. After all, even when I figured out it had to be Parker, I wouldn't have any proof unless I found Battle's body.

"You've seen how funny Shelby gets about Parker, and

I knew I needed some hard evidence. And if Battle wasn't aboard, dead or alive, I couldn't let Parker find out I suspected him before coming up with some other plan."

In the end, as my dream had revealed, it could have only been Parker.

Who else but someone with a history of sexually motivated violence, mixed with excessive prudery, would attack me with such force, then modestly cover up my naked body, even though he was planning to frame my husband for murder?

He hadn't covered up Chessy's nakedness, though. Maybe the time element prevented it. Or, possibly, he was making a statement. Because Parker had read the card, he knew I'd be bound to show up soon. Why, after planning so carefully, had he cut it so close? Had he given Chessy one last chance to repent? Promise to be faithful to him?

Maybe she'd laughed.

Whatever she'd done, it had been the wrong thing. It had pushed him over the edge.

Because Freddy Franks' death by treadmill, and Brandon Battle's removal had nothing to do with Mississippi's potential legalization of gambling casinos. That had been a complete red herring. Red*neck* herring.

As Charlotte had correctly pointed out, it was Chessy Scarborough who was the very common denominator here, and Parker couldn't take it anymore.

Now, when it was too late, I finally understood the clue of the cold champagne, which sounded like a *Perry Mason* episode.

Shelby had told us Freddy interrupted their phone conversation to answer his door, then came back on the line and demanded cold champagne sent up immediately.

Fitness fanatic Freddy would never have partaken of alcohol so close to his six-thirty workout. Unless it had been a very special occasion indeed. And from the way he looked at her in the gym, Chessy showing up for a post-British Club Tea romp, was an occasion that called for champagne.

And who was the Bell Sands' semi-official bearer of champagne? Undoubtedly, Parker had seen Chessy when he'd delivered the bubbly to Freddy's room. This less than two hours after he'd delivered Chessy's floral tribute to Dan.

But afternoon delight or not, Freddy was at the gym right on the button. Even if Parker had actually attached that warning sign to the deadly treadmill, Freddy Franks was just the kind of guy to arrogantly insist on trying to use it anyway.

That was *his* treadmill.

Rarely did anyone but Freddy use the gym after six-thirty. But what if someone had come in and witnessed the terrible event? Parker could still pass it off as an accident.

We simply overlooked that vital piece of trivia Shelby mentioned, about Parker's extended employment in electronics manufacturing.

As to Brandon Battle, Parker apparently never suspected that Chessy had been lying to him about her feelings for Battle, until the other day at the press brunch.

I remembered the stunned look on his face.

He might have seen Chessy touch Battle in a way that left no doubt as to who was really in charge of their relationship. But he still didn't want to believe it.

All he had to do was follow them upstairs, lurk around until Chessy left.

And then . . .

He'd eliminated the two men he could blame for her sexual behavior, only to watch her blatantly keep going after others, including Dan, without missing a beat.

You don't have to be afraid ever again, Chessy.

Probably, she'd figured right then he'd murdered Battle and she had rejected his affection in front of everybody.

Chessy had destroyed his delusions about her victimization, so she had to be destroyed.

Parker knew about the panties, and he'd had access to Shelby's passkey or a duplicate.

I knew he was in the habit of reading the cards accompanying the flowers he delivered. I'd practically caught him in the act, doing that very thing with the bouquet Chessy sent Dan. And when Tinker had Parker bring Dan's roses to me, she'd unwittingly put what he'd immediately recognized would be an irresistible lure to Chessy, right into his hands.

And now, here we were, on our way to the Yucatan or Heaven, whichever came first.

"Well, this ain't exactly the luxury cruise I had in mind to take you on one day, Claire," Dan said, ruefully.

That got me. "Dan, what's going to happen?" I wailed. "I don't want the sharks to eat off our faces and toes. I'm scared!"

Dan cradled me in his arms like a child. "Hush, now," he scolded, gently. "Like Granny Blaine used to say, 'If the devil's lips are moving he's a-lying!'

"Soon as it gets a little darker, I'll start signaling with the flashlight. And then, we'll see."

He tilted my chin to look up at him, tears mingled on his cheeks with the rain. "Claire, I've got to tell you. You've brought more joy to my life than I ever expected to have. I just love you so much, darlin'. And *whatever* comes, we're together."

We were both crying now, saying things there might never be another chance to say.

Finally, I was all cried out. I lay back exhaustedly in Dan's arms, and he began to sing softly.

I recognized the famous old hymn, "It Is Well With My Soul." Dan has a wonderful voice, and the melody was rich and beautiful. But when he got to the part about sorrows rolling like seabillows, I thought dully those lyrics were entirely too pertinent.

Later, I discovered Horatio Spafford penned that song after his two daughters were lost at sea.

"My Granny Blaine taught me hymns when I'd go visit her in Kentucky," he revealed. "She would bang away on that organ she kept in the parlor, and we'd sing harmony on songs like, 'Nothing But the Blood of Jesus,' 'On Christ the Solid Rock I Stand,' 'Oh, Happy Day.'

"We had a great time," he chuckled. "Granny Blaine was some character. She used to belt out, 'Tis So Sweet To Trust In Jesus', then tell me, 'because Lord knows, Dan Louis, I can't trust that husband of mine'!"

Dan shifted us a little. "Yeah, Grandpa Blaine was a real horse-training hellraiser. But he'd always come back feeling so bad, he'd run down to the church and get baptized.

I think last count, he'd been baptized about fourteen times! I remember him telling me he'd nearly drowned himself trying to get saved!"

"I think we've broken Grandpa's record today!" I laughed. "If we're not baptized by now, we never will be!"

Dan smiled reminiscently, "Granny Blaine never held with Mamma turning Episcopalian when she married Daddy. She always called them, 'Whiskeypalians'

"One of the last things she ever said to me before she died was, 'Dan Louis, I don't know if them Whiskeypalians will ever tell you this, so I better tell you. You ever get in trouble, boy, you call on Jesus.' "

I considered being trapped aboard a runaway boat, somewhere on the Gulf of Mexico, with a dead body below and a hurricane above, counted as trouble.

It's certainly enough to make you get very serious in a big hurry as to how you really feel about Jesus. As Granny Blaine might've expressed it, there are no atheists on sinking ships. At least, not the *Wedding Bells' Blue*.

We lay there in nearly two inches of water, clinging tightly together and yelling at the top of our lungs for Jesus to come save us, not overly concerned about looking foolish.

Suddenly, there was a mighty rattling sound above the howling wind, and a strong beam of light blasted down onto the deck.

A loud voice called, "Mr. and Miz Claiborne. Y'all down there?"

Dan and I stared at each other for a heartbeat. Then he grinned. "Well, that was fast!"

We rolled out from under the bench. I figured that officially made us holy rollers.

The searchlight swept the deck again, capturing us crouched prayerfully on our hands and knees.

I saw the helicopter hovering, low as it could get, close enough for me to see who was flying it.

It wasn't Jesus.

It was Captain Ezra.

But we shouted hallelujah anyway.

CHAPTER 37

"Darlin', you better let me rub some more sunscreen on you," Dan warned.

"Mmm," I said drowsily. "You're just looking for a good excuse to put your hands all over me."

"This one's good as any." He grinned, coming over to sit on the side of my chaise lounge. Squeezing some high SPF onto my bare tummy, he began to massage gently.

Ordinarily, neither of us lies out in the sun. But it was just so wonderful to see it again, to be *dry* again, we were making an exception.

It was a week after Captain Ezra fished us out of the briny deep, and many things had been cleared up, including the weather.

Babe had stepped briefly into Mobile, headed for Biloxi, then suddenly changed her mind. For some reason, she got all confused and swung back around into the Gulf, fizzling out practically back where she started from.

The mystery of Captain Ezra had also been partially explained. He was involved in a quiet government experiment, running a paramilitary boot camp for non-violent offenders. His program lasted eighteen months, longer than most similar setups. During that time, the inmates worked in the oyster beds, and were taught various skills. Captain Ezra even trained certain boys to fly helicopters.

Shelby Bell and Captain Ezra had been buddies, ever since their Vietnam helicopter days. Shelby occasionally went out to Ezra's place in Bay St. Louis as a flight instructor.

When Shelby called our room that morning and got no answer, he'd alerted Chief Hepkins. Hepkins arrived at the marina shortly after Parker Bell cut us adrift. Fortunately, Officer Blalock was along. They both knew where *Wedding Bells' Blue* was docked and were headed that way, when Parker Bell spotted them and started to run.

Blalock had finally maneuvered Parker to the end of the pier and drawn his gun, ordering him to throw down his weapon. But Parker lunged for Blalock with the knife instead, leaving the officer with no choice but to fire point blank.

Or so he said. We still didn't know who might be doing Gillis or Scarborough work. Maybe Charlotte should check on whether any Blalocks were connected to the Redneck Mafia.

Hepkins had seen us being swept out to sea, and he'd notified Shelby, who in turn called upon fearless Captain Ezra. The Bells' own "whirlybird," as Tinker referred to it, was grounded at the municipal airport.

So far, there had been no sightings of *Blue* and her lone passenger.

As to the Miss Gulf Coast runners-up, in second place was the Chinese yodeler, and the Peggy Fleming-type on Rollerblades finished third.

Though it wasn't his objective, poor Parker had effectively removed all threats to Miss Gulf Coast. Plans were already underway for next year's pageant, which promised to be bigger and better than ever.

An independent restaurateur had made an offer for that damaged Florida fast food joint. He wanted to plant the palm tree right in the middle of the place, and call it Burger Babe.

The Redneck Mafia owned LaWanda, of course. Ever since Miss Palmetto, she'd done whatever they said, including covering up for the man who'd first executed her husband, then taken over her daughter's and her own life. But she hadn't really been all that interested in becoming the Gambling Queen of Mississippi. She'd just wanted to destroy Tinker.

When she realized Tinker had known her real shame all these years and hadn't squealed, the fight just went out of her.

LaWanda promised to tell Charlotte some stories that would make her hair curl, if she kept her source a secret.

Somehow, Marcel had managed to induce Nectarine to take the rest of her vacation on Grand Cayman. At last report, she was in a separate room on a different floor.

As for Dan and myself, we were spending what was left of our time together home and alone.

Our eight-foot wall allowed us to disport ourselves *au naturel*, which is exactly what we were doing now, except for sunglasses.

There was a fresh pitcher of iced tea on the table, and back-to-back Louis Prima and Keely Smith tapes playing. Who could ask for anything more?

Languidly, I sipped tea with fresh mint, and wielded an old-fashioned cardboard fan, the kind stapled to a tongue depressor. Juanita had brought it as a gift from her church, after hearing our rescue story.

On the back was printed, *"Jesus es El Senor."*

The front was a picture of Jesus, standing up in a storm-tossed boat, rebuking the wind and waves while a few apostles cringed in terror. They had no idea.

"Claire." Dan's voice drifted over to me above the strains of Louis and Keely's *Bie Mir Bist du Schoen.* "I don't think that cream's strong enough to do the job."

"Why not? They swear by the stuff in St. Tropez," I said.

"Well, it may be just fine for St. Tropez," he allowed. "But these hot New Orleans rays require something considerably heavier between you and them."

Actually, during the last fifteen minutes or so, I'd noticed that sunkissed sensation had started to feel more like I was getting sun hickeys.

I was about to reluctantly agree he was right, we better go back inside, when a sudden huge shadow loomed above my chaise, totally cutting me off from the burning glare.

And, as everyone knows, when the moon comes between the earth and sun, there's about to be a solar eclipse.

And try these titles by some other terrific mystery writers

The Charlie Parker series by Connie Shelton
Deadly Gamble

Charlie doesn't want to be an investigator. She's a CPA and partner with her brother in his PI firm. But when her former best friend (now married to Charlie's ex-fiance) needs to locate a missing watch, Charlie figures it couldn't hurt to help solve the problem. Little does she know that she's taking her life in her hands!

"This is a dandy. Don't miss it!"—*Book Talk*

Vacations Can Be Murder

Charlie takes a vacation to Hawaii, where she meets a handsome helicopter pilot and learns that all is not as it seems in the tourist business.

"Charlie is slick, appealing, and nobody's fool—just what readers want." —*Booklist*

Partnerships Can Kill

Just back from her Hawaiian vacation, Charlie finds her brother Ron madly in love with a devious younger woman. Before she can worry much about that, though, a friend's business partner is killed—suicide or murder?

"Charlie is a fabulous amateur sleuth." —*Midwest Book Review*

Small Towns Can Be Murder

The fourth Charlie Parker mystery is coming this spring! Charlie and her secretary, Sally, take a drive to Sally's hometown in northern New Mexico. A series of mysterious health problems there leads Charlie to discover heinous crimes in the sleepy little town.

"The action is steady, the characters believable, and the romance satisfying." *Book Talk/Prime Time*